Intrigue and Ecstasy

Dressed in her loveliest outfit, and carrying the gift for Lord Hartcourt, Gardenia did not find it difficult to gain admittance to the embassy, or to the Lord's private rooms.

As soon as she was left alone, she hurried nervously to her task of finding the book that contained the secret code. She was absorbed in the contents of a desk drawer when the door behind her opened and Lord Hartcourt entered. As she turned slowly to face his fury, she thought her heart had stopped beating . . .

How could Gardenia know, at her moment of greatest shame, that the minutes to follow would be those of ecstasy, and dangerous love?

Also in Pyramid Books

by

BARBARA CARTLAND

AN INNOCENT
IN PARIS

(Original Title: A VIRGIN IN PARIS)

Barbara Cartland

 PYRAMID BOOKS • NEW YORK

AN INNOCENT IN PARIS
(Original Title: A VIRGIN IN PARIS)

A PYRAMID BOOK

Pyramid edition published June 1971
Fourth printing January 1975

ISBN 0-515-03564-5

Printed in the United States of America

Pyramid Books are published by Pyramid Communications, Inc.
Its trademarks, consisting of the word "Pyramid" and the por-
trayal of a pyramid, are registered in the United States Patent
Office.

PYRAMID COMMUNICATIONS, INC.
919 Third Avenue, New York, N.Y. 10022

AN INNOCENT
IN PARIS

'Is this the house?' Gardenia asked a little nervously in French, as the ancient *fiacre* slowed down outside the porticoed door of a large mansion standing on a side road which ran parallel with the Champs Elysées.

'*Oui, Ma'm'selle,*' the cabman answered. 'This is the place—it would be hard to mistake it.' He pulled his horse to a stop as he spoke, then spat forcibly on to the other side of his cab.

Gardenia felt herself shiver. There was something frightening both in the man's insolent manner and in the fact that the house was a blaze of light and that there was quite obviously a party in progress.

It was, indeed, difficult to get near to the front door. There were a number of shining automobiles standing on the gravel drive as well as many elegant broughams with silver-bridled horses. In charge of them there seemed to be almost an army of attendant chauffeurs in their smart leggings and double-breasted uniform coats, their goggles lifted on to the peaks of their caps; coachmen with cockades and tiered capes to their driving coats; linkmen wearing a claret uniform which to Gardenia's unsophisticated eyes seemed theatrically flamboyant.

The cabman climbed down from the front of his ancient vehicle, making little effort to hitch up the reins because his horse, whose bones were showing pitifully, was far too tired to move without compulsion.

'This is the place you asked for, *Ma'm'selle,*' he said, 'unless, of course, you've changed your mind.'

Again there was that gleam in his eyes and something in his voice which made Gardenia stiffen instinctively.

'No, I am sure you have brought me to the right address,' she replied stiffly, 'Please tell me what I owe you.'

The cabman named a sum which she knew was exorbitant. She hesitated, but it was too embarrassing to argue with so many people within earshot. Also, she realised that many of the chauffeurs and coachmen were staring at her with undisguised curiosity. She saw thankfully that she actually had enough money in her purse, and though it took practically everything she possessed she added a small *pourboire* more as a gesture than because she felt the man deserved it.

'Kindly bring in my trunk,' she said in a quiet, lady-like voice which made the man obey her without any further comment, and she stepped ahead of him up the wide, stone steps. The front door was ajar, and now she could hear music, gay and exquisite music from a number of violins. It was, however, almost drowned by the chatter of voices and shrill, rather ugly laughter that had something abandoned in it.

There was, however, little time for many impressions. The door was swung wide open by a resplendent footman wearing the same claret-coloured livery as the linkmen, his coat ornamented with innumerable bands of gold lace and what appeared to be an inordinate number of gold buttons. He wore a powdered wig, knee-breeches, and white gloves which seemed a size too big for him. He stood stiffly at attention, his chin up, his eyes looking over Gardenia's head. She found her voice was unexpectedly tremulous as she said:

'I wish to see the Duchesse de Mabillon.'

The footman did not reply. Another individual, even more resplendent, with a staff of office which proclaimed him a Major-Domo or some very superior servant, stepped forward.

'Her Grace is expecting you, *Ma'm'selle?*' he asked, in a tone which showed only too clearly that he would be very surprised if that was the truth.

Gardenia shook her head.

'I am afraid not,' she said, 'but if you will give her Grace my name I know that she will see me.'

'Her Grace is engaged this evening,' the Major-Domo said loftily. 'If you were to return tomorrow . . .' He broke off and turned scandalised eyes to the cabman who was struggling up the steps with a shabby leather portmanteau on his back. He watched as the man put it down with a crash on the marble floor, then stepped foward. 'Imbecile!' he spat in a *patois* which was difficult for Gardenia to understand. 'Do you imagine you can bring that kind of trash in here? Take it out at once! Take it away!'

8

'I have done what I was told,' the cabman replied surlily. 'Bring in the portmanteau, the lady says, and bring it I have.'

'Then take it out again!' the Major-Domo said furiously. 'You're blocking up the doorway, getting in the way of guests! Do you think we countenance *canaille* like you?"

The cabman let out an oath which seemed to reverberate round the hall.

Gardenia stepped forward.

'The man obeyed my instructions,' she said. 'Don't speak to him like that, and kindly take my name immediately to my aunt.'

There was a stupefied silence.

'*Votre tante, Ma'm'selle?*' The Major-Domo's voice was lower now, as he spoke with an air of incredulity mingled with a slight note of respect.

'I am her Grace's niece,' Gardenia said. 'Will you please tell her I have arrived, and send the cabman away? I have no further need of him.'

The cabman needed no further bidding.

'*A votre service, Ma'm'selle,*' he said, touching his battered top-hat. With a grin on his face he shuffled towards his cab.

The Major-Domo hesitated.

'Her Grace has a party, as you see, *Ma'm'selle.*'

'As I can both see and hear,' Gardenia said. 'But I am quite certain when I explain why I am here, her Grace will understand.'

The Major-Domo turned away towards the broad thick-carpeted staircase which led to the first floor from where the music was coming. Several guests in evening dress were moving down the staircase towards a large room at the far end of the hall where there was a glimpse of tables covered with white cloths and laden with silver.

Gardenia felt somewhat embarrassed being left alone in the hall. The Major-Domo had not suggested that she should wait elsewhere, nor had he offered her a chair. For a moment the hall itself was empty save for the one young footman standing stiffly by the now partially opened door. She might have sounded brave in dealing with what promised to be a row between the Major-Domo and the cabman, but the effort had made her heart beat quickly and her lips were dry.

Why, she asked herself hadn't she waited for a letter

9

to reach her aunt before she arrived, or sent a telegram? Even as she posed the question she knew the answer: it was because she could not afford to wait, and she had no money to spare for a telegram.

She had not eaten since she had left Dover very early that morning, and now the music and noise made her feel dizzy. Because she was afraid of disgracing herself in this strange, frightening house, she sat down on the edge of her trunk, conscious as she did so of the shabby, scratched leather and its bare corners. She knew also that she herself, after travelling for over twenty-four hours, was badly in need of a bath. She had done her best to wash on the train; but the toilet facilities were almost non-existent, and she had not liked to wait at the station in case she lost her trunk after it had been disgorged from the guard's van.

She had chosen what had looked the cheapest and most dilapidated *fiacre* simply because she thought that it would be cheaper than a better-equipped hackney-carriage.

There were sudden shrieks of laughter from upstairs and Gardenia was aroused from the contemplation of her own troubles to stare with some astonishment as a woman, elegantly dressed and with diamonds glittering on her bare neck, came running down the stairs lifting her frothy skirts high above her ankles. She was pursued by three young men in stiff white shirts and high collars, the tails of their evening coats seeming to dance behind them as they followed her. They caught her at the bottom of the stairs amid a turmoil of gruff laughter and high, almost hysterical protests.

It was difficult to understand what they were saying, but Gardenia caught the words 'choose' being spoken several times by the gentlemen, then some response which made them laugh even louder. Finally they picked the lady up in their arms and carried her upstairs again.

Gardenia stared after them in perplexity. She was not used to the ways of the sophisticated world. The fact that one gentleman carried the lady's feet and the other two supported her round the shoulders appeared to her very daring and in some ways even scandalous. She was so intent on what was happening on the staircase that she was suddenly startled to hear a man's voice say:

'*Mon Dieu!* And what is this new enchantment that Lily has for us?'

10

She looked up to see two men looking down at her. The one who had spoken was quite obviously a Frenchman, dark, young, handsome, with eyes that appeared to take in every detail of her creased travelling-dress of black bombasine and plain turned-up black hat, below which her hair, owing to the extremities of the journey, had escaped in tiny curls.

'But she is enchanting!' the Frenchman exclaimed again, speaking in English.

Gardenia, feeling the colour rise in her cheeks, looked at the other man. He was English she decided. He also was handsome, but there was a kind of deep reserve about his stern, almost cynical face which made her sure she recognised a fellow-countryman. And strangely there was something in his eyes which made her drop her own. It seemed to her it was a kind of contempt, or had she been mistaken?

'It must be a new entertainment,' the Frenchman said, still speaking to the Englishman. 'We cannot go now, Lord Hartcourt, this will be amusing.'

'I doubt it,' the Englishman said in a slow, almost drawly voice, 'and anyway, my dear Comte, enough is as good as a feast.'

'No no, you are mistaken,' the Comte replied. He put out his hand and to Gardenia's surprise took hers in his. '*Vous êtes charmante,*' he said. '*Quel rôle jouez-vous?*'

'I am afraid, Sir, I do not understand,' Gardenia replied.

'I see you are English,' Lord Hartcourt interposed. 'My friend is anxious to know what is your act. Does that ancient portmanteau on which you are sitting contain conjuring tricks, or do you play a musical instrument?'

Gardenia opened her lips to speak. Before she could say anything, the Frenchman interrupted.

'No, no! Do not tell us! Let me guess! You pretend to be a *jeune fille* from a convent; you go into your trunk dressed as you are now, and when you come out—pouff,' he kissed his fingers to the air, 'there is very, very little, and what there is is all golden glitter, am I right?'

Gardenia pulled her hand from his and rose to her feet.

'I must be very stupid,' she said, 'but I have no conception of what you are trying to say. I am waiting for a message to be taken to my aunt to tell her that I have arrived here ... unexpectedly.' She caught her breath on

11

the last word and looked, not at the Comte, but at Lord Hartcourt, as if appealing to him.

The Comte threw back his head and laughed.

'Wonderful! Magnificent!' he said. 'You will be the talk of Paris! Come, I will visit you tomorrow. Where else do you perform? At the Mayol? Or is it the Moulin Rouge? Whichever it is, you are the prettiest thing I have seen in a long time and I must be the first in this house to salute you.'

He put his hand under her chin and Gardenia realised with a kind of horror that he was about to kiss her. She turned her head away just in time, pushed at him with both her hands and struggled to free herself.

'No, no!' she said. 'You are mistaken! You do not understand.'

'You are enchanting!' the Frenchman said again.

Now, with a feeling of helplessness, Gardenia realised that his arms were going round her, drawing her close to him.

'No, no! Please will you listen to me?' She beat ineffectively against him and knew that, from his hot breath against her cheek, he was drunk and that her resistance was merely inflaming him. 'Please, please!' she cried.

Then suddenly a quiet Englishman's voice said, 'Wait a minute, Comte, I think you are making a mistake,' and, to her surprise, Gardenia found herself free with Lord Hartcourt standing between her and the Frenchman.

'Make him . . . understand,' she murmured, her voice trembling. Then, to her own horror and consternation, she felt her words fading away on her lips and the hall swimming dizzily around her. She knew she was going to fall; she reached out to hold on to something and felt a man's arm go round her. This time it gave her a strange sense of security as she slid into a darkness which seemed to come up from the floor and encompass her utterly. . . .

She came back to consciousness to find herself lying on a sofa in a strange room. Her hat was off, her head was resting against a pile of satin cushions, and a glass was being held to her lips.

'Drink this,' a voice said commandingly.

She took a sip and shuddered.

'I don't drink alcohol,' she tried to say, but the glass was pressed closer.

'Drink a little,' the same voice said. 'It will do you good.'

She obeyed because she did not seem to have any choice. The brandy trickling warmly down her throat cleared away the mist from her eyes, and she looked up to see clearly that it was the Englishman who was holding the glass. She even remembered his name—Lord Hartcourt.

'I am so sorry,' she said, blushing in embarrassment as she realised that he must have carried her on to the sofa.

'You are all right,' he answered. 'I expect you were tired from travelling. When did you last have something to eat?'

'It was a long time ago,' Gardenia said. 'I could not afford the meals on the train and I did not like to get out at any of the stations at which we stopped.'

'I rather thought that might be the case,' Lord Hartcourt said in a dry voice. He put down the glass he had been holding to Gardenia's lips, opened the doors of the room and she heard him speaking to someone outside. She looked round her and guessed that this was the morning-room or the library which opened off the hall.

With an effort she sat up, her hands going instinctively to her dishevelled hair. Lord Hartcourt came back into the room.

'Don't move,' he said. 'I have sent for some food.'

'I can't just lie here,' Gardenia answered a little weakly. 'I must find my aunt and explain why I have arrived.'

'Are you really a niece of the Duchesse?' Lord Hartcourt enquired.

'Yes, I am, really,' Gardenia replied, 'although your friend didn't believe me. Why did he behave in such an extraordinary manner? I think perhaps he had been drinking.'

'I think perhaps he had,' Lord Hartcourt agreed. 'These things happen sometimes at a party.'

'Yes, of course,' Gardenia agreed, realising how very few parties of any sort she had been to, and certainly not ones where gentlemen got drunk and ladies were carried upstairs.

'Did you let your aunt know you were coming?' Lord Hartcourt enquired.

'I couldn't,' Gardenia replied. 'You see . . .' She checked what she had been going to say and added: 'There were

13

reasons which made it imperative for me to come to her at once. There was no time to let her know.'

'I dare say she will be surprised to see you,' Lord Hartcourt said in a quiet voice, which somehow made Gardenia say hotly:

'I am sure Aunt Lily will be pleased to see me!'

Lord Hartcourt seemed about to say something of importance when the door opened and a footman entered carrying a huge silver tray on which reposed a number of different dishes. There were truffles in aspic, ortolans decorated with asparagus tips and *pâté de foie gras*, lobster with a golden mayonnaise, and many other strange and delicious-looking concoctions to which Gardenia could put no name. The footman set the silver tray down on a small table beside her.

'But I couldn't eat all this!' she exclaimed.

'Eat what you can,' Lord Hartcourt advised. 'You will feel better afterwards.'

He walked away, as he spoke, towards the far end of the room and stood by a writing-desk fidgeting with the numerous *objets d'art* which lay upon it.

Gardenia was not certain whether he was being tactful in allowing her to eat hungrily without his staring at her, or whether the sight of anyone indulging in food at this late hour was slightly nauseating to him. Anyway, because she was so hungry, she sat up and started to eat first some lobster, then one of the ortolans. But she could not finish either: there was far too much. As Lord Hartcourt had predicted, however, even after a few mouthfuls she felt stronger. She was thankful to see there was a glass of water on the tray. She drank it, and setting down her knife and fork she turned with what was almost a defiant gesture to the man standing behind her.

'I feel much better,' she said. 'Thank you very much for ordering the food for me.'

He came away from the writing-table to stand on the hearth-rug beside her.

'I wonder if you will allow me to give you some advice?' he said. It was not what Gardenia expected him to say and she raised wondering eyes to his before she asked cautiously:

'What sort of advice?'

'It is,' he replied, 'that you should go away now and come back tomorrow.' He saw the surprise in her face and

14

added: 'Your aunt is busy. She has a large number of guests here. It is not the moment for relatives to arrive, however welcome they may be.'

'I can't do that,' Gardenia said.

'Why not?' he persisted. 'You can go to a respectable hotel, or do you feel that is not proper? I could take you to a convent that I happen to know near here. The nuns are very hospitable to anyone in distress.'

Gardenia felt herself stiffen.

'I am sure your intentions are kind and honourable, Lord Hartcourt,' she said, 'but I have journeyed especially to Paris to see my aunt, and I feel sure that when she knows I am here she will welcome me.'

As soon as she had spoken Gardenia had the uneasy feeling that perhaps she might not be so welcome. She had assured herself not once but many times on the train that Aunt Lily would be delighted to see her; now she felt uncertain, but she was not going to allow Lord Hartcourt to realise her feelings. Besides, apart from anything else, how could she say to a strange man that she had no money? Her purse was empty except perhaps for two or three francs left from the English money she had changed at Calais.

'I will stay here,' she said firmly. 'Now I am feeling better, I could perhaps go upstairs and look for my aunt. I am afraid the butler or whoever he was did not give the message I sent to her.'

'I can only advise you it would be a mistake,' Lord Hartcourt replied.

'Are you a very great friend of my aunt's?' Gardenia asked.

'I am afraid I cannot claim that privilege,' Lord Hartcourt answered. 'I know her, of course; all Paris knows her. She is very,' he hesitated for a word, 'hospitable.'

'Then I am certain she will extend her hospitality to her only niece,' Gardenia said. She rose from the couch and picked up her hat from where she saw it had been flung on the floor.

'I am grateful to you for your kindness in bringing me here and for arranging that I should have some food. I shall ask my aunt tomorrow to express her gratitude to you too,' she said, then, as Lord Hartcourt said nothing, she held out her hand. 'I think before I fainted so very

15

foolishly you wanted to leave. Please, Lord Hartcourt, do not let me keep you.'

He took her hand in his and said abruptly in a voice curiously devoid of any emotion;

'Will you not allow me to tell the servants to take you upstairs and show you your bedroom? In the morning, when your aunt is awake, she will be far more pleased to see you than she will be at this moment.'

'I think you take too much upon yourself,' Gardenia said icily. 'Far from creeping up the back stairs as you seem to suggest, I have every intention of seeing my aunt at once.'

'Very well,' Lord Hartcourt said. 'In that case I will bid you good night. But just reflect, before you do anything stupid, that, seeing you in the clothes you are wearing now, other people at this party may get the same impression as my friend the Comte André de Grenelle.'

He walked out of the door as he spoke and shut it behind him.

Gardenia stood staring after him. Then the implication of his words, and what she felt was the insult in them, hit her. Her hands went up to her flaming cheeks. How dare he mock her? How dare he sneer at her clothes, at her appearance? She felt she hated him, the stuck-up aristocratic Englishman with his cold manner and cynical twist to his mouth. What impertinence to suggest that she would not be welcome in her aunt's house, or that she was not good enough for her smart friends who were making so much noise upstairs.

Then, as suddenly as it had been aroused, Gardenia's anger ebbed away. But of course he was right! It was the way he had said it that annoyed her. She felt it had been a battle of wills between them: Lord Hartcourt had been determined that she should not see her aunt tonight; and she was equally determined that she should. Even so, he had won because he had struck at what was always a vulnerable point where a woman is concerned—her appearance.

The moment of terror and panic that she had felt when the Comte's arms had gone round her, and she had known that his lips were seeking hers, returned to frighten her. How could he have imagined that she was nothing but a play-actress of a music-hall turn to amuse the guests

16

upstairs? What had he said about her getting into the trunk . . . ?

She put her fingers up to her ears as if to shut out the memory of his voice. She wished she could also forget the expression in his eyes. And yet, if she did not go to her aunt, what was she to do? Lord Hartcourt was right! To walk up to the ballroom in her travelling-dress would be to cause a sensation, to be an object of curiosity and speculation.

Gardenia might have been defiant with Lord Hartcourt because she resented his attitude, but she knew, now that he had gone, that she was, after all, too much of a coward to do as she had intended.

'Well, one thing is certain,' she told herself with sound common sense, 'I can't stay in this room all night.'

She thought of going into the hall and asking for the Major-Domo; then she remembered that because of her shabby appearance she had already aroused his surprise and contempt.

'If only I had some money,' she thought despairingly, 'I could tip him. That at least might make him respect me.' But she knew that the few miserable francs left in her purse would mean nothing to the Major-Domo nor to any of the grand, supercilious footmen with their powdered wigs.

She crossed to the mantelshelf and rang the bell. The bell-pull was a beautiful piece of tapestry hanging from the cornice with a gold tassel on it. Gardenia could not help the involuntary thought that even the price of the bell-pull would provide her with a new dress. The bell was not answered for some minutes. In fact Gardenia was wondering if she should pull it again when the door opened.

It was a footman who had come in answer to her summons, the same footman, Gardenia thought, who had brought in the tray of food at Lord Hartcourt's command. For a moment Gardenia hesitated, then she spoke slowly in her excellent, almost classical French.

'Will you please ask the Housekeeper to attend me,' she said. 'I am not well enough to join her Grace's party and I would like a room prepared for me upstairs.'

The footman bowed.

'I will see if I can find the Housekeeper, *Ma'm'selle,*' he replied.

It was a long wait. Afterwards Gardenia wondered if

17

the Housekeeper had retired to bed and had been forced to rise and dress herself again. At length she appeared, a rather blowzy-looking woman, big-bosomed with somewhat untidy greying hair, not at all the austere type of her English counterpart which Gardenia had somehow expected.

'*Bonjour, Ma'm'selle,* I understand you are the niece of *Madame?*' the Housekeeper said.

'That is correct,' Gardenia replied. 'But I am afraid I have arrived at rather an inopportune moment. Of course I am impatient to see my aunt; but as I am rather tired and indisposed after the long journey, I think it would perhaps be wise if I waited until the morning when my aunt will be less occupied.'

It would indeed be much wiser,' the Housekeeper agreed. 'If you will come with me, *Ma'm'selle,* I will show you your bedroom. I have already told the footmen to take your trunk there.'

'Thank you very much,' Gardenia said gratefully.

The Housekeeper turned towards the door and opened it. It seemed to Gardenia as if a sound entered the room like a whirlwind. There were high, shrill voices, men shouting, a woman's shriek, a crash as of some heavy object, followed by a burst of laughter which had almost the impact of a cannon-ball. What was happening outside in the hall Gardenia could not imagine.

The Housekeeper shut the door.

'I think, *Ma'm'selle,* it would be easier if you would condescend to come up the back way. There is a door from this room which leads to the back staircase.'

'Yes, I think that would be wiser!' Gardenia agreed. She would not have liked Lord Hartcourt to think her a coward, but she shrank with every nerve of her body from going out into that noise and turmoil and running the gauntlet of that shrill, insistent laughter.

The Housekeeper crossed the room. She must have touched a secret switch, for a part of the bookcase swung open, and there was a doorway leading into a long, narrow passage. Without any comment she let Gardenia follow her through the opening and pulled the bookcase to again. Then she led the way along the passage and up a narrow, rather dark staircase. She passed the first floor and, climbing still higher, reached the second. Here the Housekeeper seemed to hesitate at the door of the landing, and Gardenia thought she was about to open it. Then, after apparently listening for a few seconds she changed her mind.

'I think a room on the next floor would be best, *Ma'm'-selle.*'

They climbed again and this time the Housekeeper opened the door on the landing at the top of the stairs on to a very well-lit and heavily carpeted passage. Moving along it, they reached the main staircase. Gardenia glanced over the banisters. She could see, it seemed to her, there were men and women bulging out from all floors beneath her. The noise of their voices was deafening and it was even hard to hear the violins above the roar of their laughter.

There was something frightening about the laughter itself. It sounded strange and uncontrolled, as though the people who laughed had drunk too much. Then she dismissed the thought from her mind. It was unpleasant and disloyal. These people were French. It was obvious that being a Latin race they were not so reserved as the English would be in similar circumstances. Nevertheless, she almost ran from the banisters to follow the Housekeeper who had opened the door of a small room.

'Tomorrow, *Ma'm'selle*, I am sure her Grace will want a bigger and better room prepared for you,' the Housekeeper said. 'Tonight this is the best we can do. I made a mistake in the room which I told the men to carry your trunk. I will find them and send them here immediately. Is there anything else you wish?'

'No thank you,' Gardenia said 'and I am very grateful to you for the trouble you have taken.'

'It is no trouble, *Ma'm'selle*,' the Housekeeper said. 'I will get her Grace's personal maid to tell you in the morning when her Grace is awake. She will not wish to be disturbed before midday at earliest.'

'I can quite understand that after a party,' Gardenia said.

The Housekeeper gave a little shrug of her shoulders. 'Here it is always a party,' she said, and went from the room.

Gardenia sat down on the bed. She felt as if her knees were too weak to carry her any further. 'Here it is always a party.' What did that mean? Would she be expected to live at this high pressure, to join the laughing crowds whose noise seemed to increase rather than diminish although it was past two o'clock in the morning? Had she made a mistake? Should she not have come? She felt as though a cold hand clutched her heart. It was almost physical in its intensity. But what else could she have done? Where else could she have gone?

Suddenly there was a knock on the door.

'Who is there?' She did not know why she was frightened. It was just that for a moment the fear of all that laughter downstairs seemed to bring her uncertainly to her feet, her voice trembling, her heart leaping in her breast.

'Votre baggage, Ma'm'selle.'

'Oh yes, of course,' Gardenia breathed to herself. She had forgotten her trunk had been sent to the wrong room. She opened the door. Two footmen carried in her shabby trunk, and, setting it down at the end of the bed, they undid the worn straps and with respectful bows went from the room.

'Bonne nuit, Ma'm'selle,' they said as they went.

'Bonne nuit et merci,' Gardenia replied.

As the door closed behind them she got to her feet. Crossing the room, she turned the key and locked the door. It was something she had never done in her life before. But now she locked herself in and locked out whatever lay outside. Somehow only with the door fastened did she feel safe. Only with the key held tightly in her shaking hands did she know that the laughter and noise downstairs could not encroach on her, not come near her!

Two

'So this is where you have moved to,' Bertram Cunningham said as he entered the large sunny room in the British Embassy where, at the far end, Lord Hartcourt was seated at a desk writing.

'I forgot to tell you I have been promoted,' Lord Hartcourt answered.

The Honourable Bertram Cunningham seated himself on the edge of the desk and tapped his shiny black riding boots with the tip of the leather switch he held in his gloved hands.

'You'll have to be careful, my boy,' he said in a jovial tone.

'You were always a bit of a swot at Eton. If you don't look out they'll be making you an Ambassador or something!'

'There's no fear of that,' Lord Hartcourt replied, 'Charles Lavington went ill and decided to chuck in his hand; so I have taken his place.'

'If you want my opinion,' Bertram Cunningham said, 'his illness was entirely due to too much Maxim's and the expenses of that little ladybird he was always taking to Cartier's the morning after.'

'I shouldn't be surprised,' Lord Hartcourt replied in a rather bored tone. He disliked conversation which veered on gossip. It was something which had never interested him and in which he seldom took part.

'Incidentally,' Bertram Cunningham chatted on, 'while we are talking of ladybirds, what's this story André de Grenelle has been telling me? I met him riding in the *Bois*. He was full of a sensational denouement at Lily de Mabillon's last night.'

'Never listen to anything the Comte has to say,' Lord Hartcourt said coldly. 'It is inevitably inaccurate, if not entirely invented.'

'Oh don't be stuffy, Vane,' Bertram Cunningham said. 'There must be something in the story. Why, de Grenelle

21

told me that the Duchesse had imported a new turn from the Moulin Rouge who looked like a nun or a schoolgirl. But before she could appear upstairs she collapsed into your arms and you carried her away into another room and locked the door!'

Lord Hartcourt laughed briefly. The sound had no humour in it.

'Well, is it true?' Bertram Cunningham persisted. 'I can't credit de Grenelle with having made all that up.'

'It has a slight element of truth somewhere, lavishly ornamented with the Comte's very vivid imagination,' Lord Hartcourt said drily. 'Mind you, I like de Grenelle up to a certain point. He is amusing when a trifle foxed. But, the morning after, he is a dead bore! Personally I avoid him, and I advise you to do the same.'

'Now stop evading the question,' Bertram said slapping his whip down on the polished desk. 'I want to know what happened, and by Jove, Vane, you are going to tell me!'

'And if I don't?' Lord Hartcourt enquired.

'Then I shall go straight round and demand to see her Grace and find out what really happened.'

Lord Hartcourt laughed again.

'You will get pretty short shrift at this hour of the morning. Besides, I can imagine nothing more depressing than to see the débris after one of the more spirited parties *chez* Mabillon!'

'Then who was the charmer? André was extremely flowery in his description of her. Fair hair, grey eyes and heart-shaped face combined with an air of real or assumed innocence! It sounded most intriguing to me.'

'De Grenelle was drunk!' Lord Hartcourt commented.

'I shouldn't imagine any of you were very sober,' Bertram Cunningham chaffed, 'but it's just my luck to have to escort the Ambassadress to a party when all those excitements were going on. Very dull it was too. Would you believe it, we sat on gilt chairs for over two hours listening to some long-haired Pole playing the piano, and afterwards we danced. There was not a woman in the room under fifty!"

This time Lord Hartcourt laughed without reservation. Then he rose from the desk and put his hand on his cousin's shoulder.

'Poor Bertie,' he said. 'You really do earn your salary at times like that!'

'I don't mind telling you,' Bertram said hotly, 'if there are many more of them I'm going to send in my resignation. I'm getting fed-up with the whole thing. If it wasn't for you being here and one or two other chaps, I would go back to London. After all, it will be Ascot in a few weeks.'

Lord Hartcourt sauntered to the window and looked out over the Embassy garden. The lilacs and magnolias were in bloom. Tulips made a glorious patch of red beneath a tree of golden laburnum.

'England is always beautiful at this time of the year,' he said quietly. 'Perhaps we are fools to waste our time and our money in any foreign country—even Paris.'

'Henriette being difficult?' Bertram asked with a sudden sympathy in his voice.

'Oh no!' Lord Hartcourt replied. 'She's just as entrancing as ever. It is only that occasionally, Bertie, I find the whole thing so damned artificial. Too many parties, too much drink, too many people like the Comte making a drama about nothing.'

'You still haven't told me what "nothing" was,' Bertram Cunningham said pointedly.

Lord Hartcourt turned from the window to walk back to his desk.

'It is of little significance,' he said. 'As the Comte and I were leaving we found a girl sitting in the hall. She was English, shabby, travel-stained, obviously very out of her element, and when De Grenelle tried to kiss her she protested. I obviously had to go to her rescue. Then she fainted from lack of food, not from fear of the Comte's Latin attentions.'

'So he was telling the truth!' Bertram Cunningham exclaimed. 'Was she outstandingly pretty? André has gone into eulogies over her.'

'I really didn't notice,' Lord Hartcourt said in a bored voice. 'I told the servants to bring some food, gave her my advice, which she had no intention of taking, and came away.'

'You left her after all that excitement?' Bertram Cunningham asked.

'It really wasn't very exciting,' Lord Hartcourt said with a twist of his lips. 'The girl was exhausted. She had been travelling since early morning, and, I fancy, the wooden coaches of a French train are none too comfortable!'

'But who was she? Did you find out?' Bertram Cunningham enquired.

'She said she was the Duchesse's niece."

'Her niece!' Bertram exclaimed. 'Then in that case André is very likely right. She is a chip off the old block! You undoubtedly spoiled her grand entrance or something of the sort. According to André, she was going to get into her trunk in her travelling-dress and get out with little on save a few spangles.'

'De Grenelle talks the most utter nonsense,' Lord Hartcourt said. 'I don't think for one moment she was anything but a genuine traveller. As for being a niece of the Duchesse, who knows?'

He shrugged his shoulders and started to tidy the papers on his desk.

'What are you doing, Bertie?' he asked. 'Let us go and have lunch at the Traveller's Club. They have got a new chef who can produce the best roast beef I have tasted outside Piccadilly.'

'All right,' Bertram agreed. 'And I tell you what, Vane, we will drop in on the way and see what this new protégée of Lily's is like. She's worth a look over. It will be amusing to get in before André and the other boys. He is swearing that nothing will keep him away from Lily's tonight; but his mama has got a reception to which all the diplomatic corps are going, so I don't know how he is going to get out of it.'

'I never have been able to face the Duchesse or her like in the daytime,' Lord Hartcourt said stiffly.

'Oh, Vane, really! The old girl's not as bad as all that! My father says that thirty-five years ago she was the most beautiful thing he had ever seen. And I can assure you my papa was an experienced judge in his day!'

'Really?' Lord Hartcourt ejaculated, and it seemed for a moment as if he were slightly interested, 'Who was she, by the way? I always thought that her title was entirely bogus.'

'Oh no! You are wrong there,' Bertram Cunningham replied. 'The Duc actually existed. I saw him myself once many years ago when I was only a boy. I remember it well. I came over to Paris in the holidays. My father was First Secretary at the time and he took me to lunch at the Ritz. 'You had better see the élite of the capital, my

24

boy,' he told me. "It will stand you in good stead when you are in the Foreign Office yourself." '

Bertram was silent for a moment, as if his memory had gone back to the first sight of what was always to be to him an enchanted city.

'Well, go on,' Lord Hartcourt said. 'You were telling me about the Duc.'

'Oh yes, of course!' Bertram said. 'He was sitting by a table at the door and looked exactly like a tortoise: his neck choked by his collar, his face deeply lined, and he had hardly any hair on his head. My father pointed him out to me. "That's the Duc de Mabillon," he said, and as I stared a woman came into the restaurant and all heads turned round to look at her. It must have been Lily, of course, but I was too young to appreciate women in those days. I was looking at the Duc and thinking that he was not in the least my idea of what a French Duc ought to look like.'

'So he really existed!' Lord Hartcourt said in quiet surprise.

'Oh, very much so!' Bertram answered. 'Years later when I came back to Paris I heard the whole story from my father. It appears that Lily was married to another Frenchman, a rather unsavoury chap, a hanger-on of nobility, who had just enough decent blood in him to be accepted on the outer fringe of their stuffy and stuck-up society. Anyway, he married Lily in England, brought her over to live here, and somehow or other they met the Duc. The old man, twice widowed, had one look at *Madame* Reinbard and took them both under his wing, so to speak.'

'A dirty old man, in fact!' Lord Hartcourt exclaimed.

'But, as my father used to say, a great connoisseur where beautiful things were concerned, and Lily was undoubtedly the most beautiful thing he had ever seen. The three of them became inseparable. Of course, the Duc paid Reinbard's debts, set him up in a better apartment than he could afford and altogether made life very easy for him—and, naturally, particularly easy where his wife was concerned.'

'You tell the story well, Bertie,' Lord Hartcourt smiled. 'If you aren't careful you will find yourself writing a novel about the redoubtable Lily.'

Bertram laughed.

25

'I got it all from my father and, I assure you, if anyone ever knew the truth about Lily de Mabillon it was he. Apparently he was rather besotted himself at one time.'

'So I understand it could be said of half the men in Paris,' Lord Hartcourt remarked drily. 'The 'nineties must have been very gay!'

'By Jove they were!' Bertram agreed, 'and apparently Lily had rather a soft spot for my old boy. Anyway, she used to tell him about herself: that she came from a decent English family and that she would never have married Reinbard if she had not been so terribly poor. And, of course, the idea of living in Paris had seemed so attractive.'

'It certainly paid a dividend where she was concerned,' Lord Hartcourt said cynically.

'It did when Reinbard died,' Bertram agreed. 'He was drinking far too much and got pneumonia one cold winter. Lily's enemies, of course, always say that she was too busy entertaining the Duc to send for the doctor. Whatever the reason, he died, and the bets were a hundred to one against the Duc ever marrying her.'

'But he did,' Lord Hartcourt said, sitting back in his writing-chair, a twinkle in his eyes as he listened to his friend's story. There was, however, a cynical twist to his mouth, as though he was not prepared to believe the whole story, even while he was ready to give it his attention.

'Oh, Lily saw that he married her all right,' Bertram said. 'One of the Russian Grand Dukes came along at that time—I have forgotten which one it was—but, just like Boris and that other chap who are here now, he was splashing his money about, snaffling all the best women for himself, and giving parties and presents with which no ordinary fellow could compete. My father always said that Lily gave the Duc exactly twenty-four hours in which to make up his mind.'

'As to whether he was going to marry her?' Lord Hartcourt asked.

'Exactly!' Bertram agreed. 'It was a gold ring or the Russian roubles. The Grand Duke had offered her a château on the outskirts of Paris. She already had a rope of pearls from him, which she had the impudence to wear with her wedding-dress.'

'So that was how Lily became a Duchesse,' Lord Hartcourt said. He got to his feet again and walked to the door. 'A very salutary lesson for all young ladies who aspire to succeed in life. Come on, Bertie, I'm hungry.'

'Damn you, if you aren't ungrateful!' Bertram Cunningham said, getting down from the desk. 'I kill myself entertaining you with one of the most intriguing *histoires* that Paris has ever produced and all you can think about is your stomach.'

'I am really thinking about my head,' Lord Hartcourt replied. 'The champagne last night was a good vintage, but there was too much of it.'

'It sounds a tip-top party,' Bertram Cunningham said wistfully. 'I just can't understand why you left so early.'

'I will tell you why,' Lord Hartcourt said as they walked down the broad marble staircase into the hall of the Embassy. 'They were starting their usual wild horse-play. Terence was squirting the girls with soda-syphons and Madelaine—what's her name—was screaming so loudly that it got on my nerves.'

'The Archduke Boris seems rather interested in her.'

'As far as I am concerned, he can have her!'

'Well, actually none of them measure up to Henriette,' Bertram said convivially. 'I must say one thing about you, Vane: your taste in horses and women is impeccable.'

'It is exactly what I have always thought myself,' Lord Hartcourt said, 'but I am gratified that you agree with me.'

'Damn it all, I always agree with you, don't I?' Bertram asked. 'That's the whole trouble. If I had seen Henriette before you I should certainly have offered her my protection.'

Lord Hartcourt smiled.

'Poor Bertie, I pipped you at the post, did I? To console you, let me say that you are not rich enough—you are just not rich enough for Henriette.'

'I'm prepared to agree over that too,' Bertram said in a resigned tone. 'But I can tell you, if I don't find a ladybird soon, I shall be getting myself a very odd reputation in Paris. All the toffs like you seem to have got themselves fixed up. I'm just unlucky. Do you remember that blasted German Prince who enticed Lulu away from me? I just couldn't compete with a villa at Monte Carlo and a yacht. As it was, it nearly broke me buying her an automobile. A rotten machine it was too! It was always breaking down.

27

They all do. Give me a decent piece of horseflesh every time.'

They passed through the Embassy door into the courtyard.

'That reminds me,' Bertram continued. 'I'm thinking of buying a new racehorse. I would like your opinion on it. It is from the Labrisé stables.'

'Don't say any more,' Lord Hartcourt replied. 'The answer is no. Labrisé is one of the biggest crooks on the French turf. I wouldn't touch anything he offered me, even if it were a donkey.'

Bertram's face fell. 'Damn it all, Vane, you do damp a fellow down,' he grumbled.

'Where you are concerned,' Lord Hartcourt said. 'You can lose your money much more easily and more pleasantly on women.'

'Perhaps you are right,' Bertram said brightening. 'Let's go and look at André's little nun. She might suit me, who knows?'

Lord Hartcourt did not answer, and it appeared to his friend as though he had lost interest in the subject.

Gardenia all the morning had been waiting a little apprehensively for her first meeting with her aunt. She had slept late—far later than she had intended—and when she awoke it was to find the sun struggling through the heavy curtains which covered the window. Getting out of bed, she threw them back and had her first glimpse of the grey hotch-potch of French roofs which seemed to stretch almost interminably away into the distance. There were pigeons flying across the blue sky and a kind of magic in the air which made Gardenia throw the window wider open and lean out, breathing in with ecstasy the fragrance and freshness of the Paris spring.

The doubts and apprehensions and fears that she had known the night before had gone. It was morning, it was sunny, and already she was falling in love with Paris! She turned from the window, not knowing what to do. Should she ring and ask for breakfast? Should she go in search of it? While she was still hesitating there came a tentative knock on the door. Quickly, Gardenia wrapped her old flannel dressing-gown around her before she turned the key to see who was outside.

'*Votre déjeuner, Ma'm'selle*,' a young voice told her as

she peeped into the passage, and she opened the door wider to admit a rather saucy-looking French maid with a white cap awry and dark eyes which seemed to hint at mischief. She set down the tray on a table by the bed.

'The Housekeeper said I was to unpack for you, *Ma'm'-selle*,' she announced. "She also said that you were to move your room this morning, so it doesn't really seem worth starting, does it?'

'No, indeed, it does not,' Gardenia answered in her slow, rather careful French. She found the swiftness of the maid's words a little difficult to follow. It was one thing to speak almost perfect French in England, but quite another to follow the *patois* of a French girl speaking at double the pace of anyone she had ever listened to before.

'No,' she said after a moment. 'You are quite right. I will get dressed; then perhaps my trunk can be taken to the other room, after which I will be most grateful if you would unpack for me.'

'Very good, *Ma'm'selle*.'

The maid went from the room with a sidelong glance of her eyes which Gardenia found somewhat disconcerting. What was there about servants in this house, she wondered, which made them seem so strange? Then the aroma of fresh coffee and the sight of crisp, warm croissants told her that despite what she had eaten the night before, she was extremely hungry.

The croissants were delicious, although the butter had a strange taste. It was very unlike the Jersey butter she had enjoyed in the village where she had lived since a child. But the coffee was better than anything she had tasted before. She poured herself out a second cupful, and then eagerly started to wash and dress.

Whatever else she did, she must make a good impression on her aunt. 'First impressions are always very important,' she could hear her mother saying, and just for a moment her tears gathered in her eyes before she hastily wiped them away.

The dress she had worn the night before was hanging in the wardrobe. She looked at it and realised in the spring sunshine how desperately shabby it was. It had belonged to her mother. It was the only black dress there was in the house, and everything else in her trunk was coloured, though hardly less shabby or less worn. Gardenia found a clothes-brush and brushed the skirt. The mud which had

29

attached itself to the hem when she walked from the train was now dry and came off easily. But nothing could hide the shabbiness of the cloth where the veneer had been worn away, or the fraying of the cuffs, even though she had mended them before she had started on her journey. All her endeavours did nothing to improve the coat or the skirt; and finally, in despair, she dressed and busied herself with making her hair as neat and tidy as possible.

She looked very young and, if she had known, very lovely as she turned away dejectedly from the contemplation of her own reflection in the mirror and walked tentatively towards the door. She was not very tall and was too thin to be fashionable; but she held her head proudly. Her fair hair which persisted in curling, however hard she brushed it, clustered on her white oval forehead and made a frame for her tiny, pointed face with its dark grey eyes and full, sensitive mouth.

Gardenia felt her heart give a little leap as she walked from the room, which had seemed like a sanctuary the previous night, down the deep-carpeted passage towards the main staircase. Now the house was still after the turmoil and noise when she had arrived. There was, however, a left-over smell from the night before which she could not help recognising. As she got to the end of the stairs it grew stronger—the fragrance of cigar smoke, of the flowers which had begun to die, of exotic perfume and, though at first she hadn't recognised it, of alcohol.

The floor beneath that on which Gardenia had spent the night was in darkness: the lights in the passage had been extinguished and the curtains over the windows had not yet been drawn. Gardenia guessed that this was where her aunt slept and she continued on down the stairs.

She came to the first floor and after a few steps across the broad, beautifully furnished landing she stood looking through big double-doors which opened into what she imagined must be the main Salon. She stared in astonishment!

It was an enormous room running the whole length of the house and, as Gardenia realised, decorated in the most extravagant manner. The curtains surmounted by carved, gilt pelmets were of pink brocade interspersed with gold thread and matched the silk panels let into the white and gold walls. There were exquisitely carved gilt mirrors and inlaid marble-topped furniture. But what held Gardenia's attention after the first, quick glance were the tables dotted around the Salon—green-baize tables which, though she had never seen them before, she recognised instantly. So it had been a gaming party last night, she thought to herself! But why, then, so much noise?

Amid the débris on the floor were broken champagne glasses, a great vase of hot-house flowers which had been turned over, and a Dresden china ornament with broken cupids. At the far end of the room there was a large serving table, covered with a stained linen cloth, empty bottles and dirty glasses.

It was the sort of party that Gardenia could not envisage or even imagine. She could see the platform in the ante-room where the musicians had sat and played so exquisitely. But why had there been music if people wanted to sit on these gilt tapestry-covered chairs and lose their money at the tables? Then she remembered that she was in France. She had heard people talk of the gambling at Monte Carlo, and at Ostend where people crossed the Channel especially for a flutter. She had not imagined that she would find it in Paris and least of all in her aunt's home!

What would her mother have thought, she wondered, knowing that her mother disapproved of gambling in any form and protested vehemently when her father had wanted to bet on a horse.

Despite these beautiful furnishings and the ceiling exquisitely painted by what Gardenia recognised as a master hand, the room had somehow an unpleasant atmosphere. It was not the smell or the débris; it was something deeper and more fundamental. Embarrassed by her own impressions, Gardenia walked swiftly down the stairs to the hall and into the room off it into which Lord Hartcourt had carried her the night before. The room was just as she had left it. Someone had indeed pulled back the curtains, but the food on the big silver tray stood beside the sofa, and the sofa cushions against which she had lain still bore the imprint of her head.

The room was, as Gardenia saw now, expensively and artistically furnished. Yet there were no homely touches, nothing cosy, comforting or even welcoming. She felt herself shiver. She didn't know why, except that she knew, without even expressing the words to herself, that this was

31

not the sort of house that she could ever think of as home. And that was what she had come to find!

She looked at the clock on the mantelpiece which had stopped, and she wondered why there was no one to see to such matters in such a luxurious house. Ink in the inkwell, pens ready for those who wished to write, clocks which were wound up, drinking-water by the beds—these were the sort of small details in which her mother had so often instructed her. 'That is a woman's job, dear, to see to the little things,' she used to say. 'For it's the little things that make comfort, and comfort is something that every man wants, whether he is rich or poor, old or young.'

'Perhaps I can help Aunt Lily with the little things!' Gardenia told herself, and then as an excuse she remembered that her aunt was a widow.

'*Bonjour, Ma'm'selle!*' a voice behind her made her jump.

Gardenia turned to see a very elegant, sharp-featured young female in a black dress with a tiny, ridiculously small lace apron.

'Oh, good morning,' Gardenia said, somehow flustered by the woman's sharp eyes which seemed to take in every detail of her shabby appearance.

'I am her Grace's personal maid,' the woman said. 'Her Grace is now awake and I have informed her of your arrival. She wishes to see you.'

There was something in the sharp words which made Gardenia feel apprehensive. Perhaps she was unduly sensitive, but she had the impression that her aunt was not particularly pleased with the information she had received of her presence. However, there was no time for introspective thoughts.

'I am very eager to see my aunt,' she said.

The personal maid's expression of aloof disdain did not alter.

'Kindly follow me, *Ma'm'selle*,' she said sharply and led the way through the hall and up the stairs.

With a sinking heart Gardenia followed her. Perhaps this would not be the pleasant reunion that she had expected. In the back of her mind she could not help feeling Lord Hartcourt had been right: it would have been far worse if she had climbed these stairs last night to confront her aunt amid a welter of green tables in the ornate Salon.

The maid led the way to the second floor, knocked perfunctorily at the mahogany door of a room, opened it and ushered Gardenia inside. For a moment it was difficult for her to see, for the windows were shaded by sunblinds, and though the curtains had been drawn very little light seemed to illuminate either the room itself or the big bed set in an alcove and surmounted by a huge shell carved out of mother of pearl.

Then a voice from the bed, hoarse and rather weak, said:

'Who is it? Can it possibly be you, Gardenia?'

Gardenia's embarrassment and apprehensiveness fell away at the sound of the voice.

'Oh, Aunt Lily, dear Aunt Lily! It is I, Gardenia. I arrived last night. I do hope you aren't angry. There was nothing else I could do, absolutely nothing, except come to you.'

There was a movement amongst the pillows; then a hand came out towards Gardenia, which she clasped thankfully.

'Gardenia, my dear child, I have never been so surprised in my life. I thought Yvonne must have got it wrong when she told me that my niece was here. I tried to think who else it could possibly be, but you are my only niece. But why didn't you write?'

'I couldn't, Aunt Lily. I had to come at once. You see, Mama is dead.'

'Dead?' The Duchesse sat up, and even in the dim dusk of the shrouded room Gardenia could see the expression on her face.

'But it cannot be true! Your mother dead! Poor darling Emily. The last time she wrote to me, after your father's accident, she sounded so brave, so full of fortitude, determined to look after you and to keep her home going.'

'She did try to do all those things,' Gardenia said. 'But it was too much for her!'

'Wait a minute, wait a minute, child!' the Duchesse exclaimed. 'I have got to hear all this. Oh, my poor head! It feels as if it is going to crack open. Yvonne, bring me my *cachet faivre*, and pull back the curtains a little, I want to see what my niece looks like. It is years, yes years, since I have seen her.'

'Seven years at least, Aunt Lily,' Gardenia said. 'But I have never forgotten how beautiful you looked when you

33

came down to see us and brought us all those wonderful hampers: the boxes of little plums, and the *pâté de foie gras* for Papa and that lovely lace négligée for my mother. You seemed to me like a fairy godmother!'

'Dear child! Fancy your remembering all that,' the Duchesse said. She put out her hand as if to pat Gardenia's shoulder and groaned again. 'My head, it's agony to move. Be quick, Yvonne.'

She spoke to her maid in French and to Gardenia in English, and the latter could not help being impressed with the ease with which her aunt switched from one language to another. But when Yvonne raised the sunblind a little, so that more light came flooding into the room, Gardenia could hardly restrain a start of astonishment as she saw her aunt's face!

She remembered her as being breathtakingly lovely, a blonde junoesque figure of a woman, with an exquisite pink and white complexion, golden fair hair and blue eyes, which had made everyone describe her as a perfect English rose.

'You were wrongly christened,' Gardenia could remember her father saying gallantly. 'Lily is a pale, reserved, rather cold flower. You are warm and glowing, and as beautiful as my *Gloire de Dijon* on the porch outside.'

'Henri, you are a poet,' her aunt had answered, flashing her eyes at him and curling her lips in a manner which, young though she was, Gardenia had recognised as being almost irresistibly attractive. The woman she saw now against the pillows was a very pale shadow of the English rose that had burst upon them unexpectedly one day in their tiny village, causing a sensation among the inhabitants by arriving in something most of them had never seen before, a horseless carriage, the much discussed and much feared automobile.

'I have persuaded my husband to come to England to buy a Rolls-Royce,' Lily had told them. 'French cars are not nearly as smart or as distinguished. I was determined to see you while I was here; so I drove all this way just to have a glimpse of you.'

'Darling Lily! Isn't it like you not to let us know, but to drop out of the skies unexpectedly?' Gardenia's mother had laughed.

The two sisters had kissed again, clinging to each other for a moment as if they would somehow bridge the great gulf which lay between them—a gulf of money, position and, though Gardenia was too young to realise it at the time, an entirely different way of life.

She had often dreamt of Aunt Lily's beauty, her exquisite face, framed by the long chiffon motor-veil which fell from her flat white motoring-hat and flowed over the pale dustcoat which protected her elegant dress. It was difficult to recognise that radiant loveliness in the tired-eyed, heavily lined face, with puffy eyes half closed against the light, which she saw now.

Aunt Lily's hair was still golden, but it had a tinny, almost garish look, instead of being the pale yellow of ripening corn. Her skin seemed grey and listless, and, even while she was covered in the bedclothes, Gardenia could see that she had grown much fatter than she had been in the past, only her neck seemed to have lost its ivory roundness, the column on which she had held her head so proudly that sculptors had fought for the privilege of portraying her in marble.

'Gardenia, you are grown up!' Aunt Lily exclaimed.

'I am afraid so,' Gardenia said. 'You see, I am twenty.'

'Twenty!' Aunt Lily seemed to gasp the words, and closing her eyes for a moment she said: 'Where is it, Yvonne? Where is my *cachet faivre?* The pain in my head is intolerable.'

'They are here, your Grace.' Yvonne was standing beside the bed with a small silver salver in her hand. On it rested a glass filled with water, and a small black and white cardboard box on which reposed a row of white *cachets.*

'Give me two,' the Duchesse said, putting out her hand for the water.

'You know, your Grace, that the doctor said . . .' Yvonne began, but she was silenced sharply by the Duchesse.

'Never mind what the doctor said! When I have had a night such as I had last night and my only niece comes to tell me that my sister is dead, I need something. Bring me a brandy and soda. I don't want any coffee. The mere idea of it makes me feel sick.'

'Very good, your Grace,' Yvonne said in a resigned manner which expressed far better than words her disapproval.

35

'And be quick about it,' the Duchesse said. 'I don't want to wait all day. I want a drink now.'

'Immediately, your Grace,' Yvonne said, seeming to flounce across the room.

'Twenty!' the Duchesse repeated, looking at Gardenia. 'It cannot be true. It cannot be possible.'

'One grows older, Aunt Lily,' Gardenia said.

Her aunt put her hand up to her forehead. 'Alas, that is indisputable,' she said. 'God! How old I feel!'

'I didn't like to disturb you last night,' Gardenia said apologetically, 'but I felt it was rather rude to creep up to bed without telling you I was here.'

'You did entirely the right thing,' the Duchesse approved. 'I should not have been able to attend to you. Besides, I don't suppose you had the right clothes for a party.'

Gardenia could almost see the cynical smile on Lord Hartcourt's lips.

'No,' she said humbly. 'I am afraid my clothes would not have been right at the party.'

'You are in mourning, of course,' her aunt said, 'but the dress you are wearing, dear, is very old-fashioned if you will forgive my saying so.'

'It was Mama's,' Gardenia explained, 'and I am afraid it is all I have got.'

'Well, I don't suppose it matters,' the Duchesse said limply, 'because you will not be staying will you?'

There was a moment's silence, a moment in which the two women stared at each other. Then, with a little break in her voice, Gardenia said:

'But, Aunt Lily, I don't know what to do. I have nowhere, nowhere else to go!'

The Duchesse propped herself up on her pillows. Obviously the *cachet faivre* had begun to work and she looked slightly less exhausted.

'I think you had better start at the beginning of the story,' she said. 'What has happened?'

Gardenia, who was deathly pale, clasped her hands together, striving for self-control, trying to keep her voice steady.

'We have been desperately poor since my father died,' she said in a low voice. 'I often suggested to my mother that she should write to you and tell you the circumstances in which we found ourselves. But she didn't want to trouble you.'

The Duchesse gave a little cry.

'I never thought,' she said. 'How terrible of me! And I am so rich, I have had everything!' She put her hands to her eyes and said in a voice which trembled with emotion: 'You must forgive me. I am bitterly ashamed.'

'I didn't want to upset you,' Gardenia said, 'but when my father was alive it was different. He was proud, very proud.'

The Duchesse interposed eagerly.

'He resented my giving your mother expensive presents. She told me once that he minded because he wanted so much to give her everything himself.'

'That was true,' Gardenia said in a low voice. 'Yet it was not presents we needed, but food.'

'I never thought of that,' the Duchesse confessed. 'When your father died and your mother wrote and told me, I thought, "Now can I help Emily; now I can send her things." But I imagined it was only decent to wait a while and then . . . Yes, Gardenia, I admit it went out of my head.'

'We were in debt after my father died,' Gardenia said, 'with the doctors to pay, nurses and the chemist and all sorts of trades-people for the little delicacies which were all he could eat in the last months. We sold many things out of the house, silver and furniture. Of course, we didn't get very much for them. Actually, we hadn't got very much to sell.'

'It's humiliating,' the Duchesse whispered. 'How could I have been such a fool?'

'You couldn't have known,' Gardenia said. 'My mother wouldn't let me write and tell you, even though I did suggest it, not once but at least a dozen times.'

'If only I had known,' the Duchesse murmured.

'There was really no one we could turn to for help,' Gardenia said, 'and you know that Papa's family cut him off when he married Mama. He has never spoken to them nor seen them since.'

'That was not surprising,' the Duchesse said. 'They were furious. I remember seeing some of the letters they wrote, but I suppose from their point of view it was beyond the pale to jilt your bride two days before your marriage simply because you had met someone with whom you had fallen in love at first sight!'

'Mama used to tell me about it,' Gardenia said. 'She said that the moment she saw Papa she knew that he was the hero of all her dreams. Then he spoke to her and they both knew this was something different, something so wonderful that they could just stand and stare at each other.'

'It is what every woman prays might happen to her,' the Duchesse said with a little sigh.

'I suppose there was nothing else they could do but run away,' Gardenia said. 'There was Papa engaged to Lord Melchester's daughter and to be married in two days' time—and Mama was just a nobody.'

'I wouldn't say that,' the Duchesse said quickly. 'Your grandfather was a country gentleman and a Captain in the Hussars when he was young. He hadn't much money, but we were not poverty-stricken and we considered ourselves as good as anyone else in Herefordshire.'

'I am sorry,' Gardenia apologised with a smile. 'I didn't mean to be rude, Aunt Lily, but from the worldly point of view I suppose it was a very bad marriage, even though Papa was only a second son.'

'Your grandfather, Sir Gustus Weedon, was a stuck-up, pompous old snob,' the Duchesse said angrily. 'He was determined to make your father suffer for having married

38

the woman he loved. He cut him off without a penny and blackguarded him, even insisting that many of his old friends cut him.'

'I don't think Papa minded very much,' Gardenia said. 'He was so happy with Mama. At the very end of his life they used to hold hands and look into each other's eyes and forget that I existed.'

'I suppose in a way I was almost jealous of Emily,' the Duchesse said reminiscently. 'So many men have loved me and given me wealth, position and wonderful jewels; but I have never cared for one of them as your mother cared for your father.'

'That is why I know you will understand,' Gardenia said softly, 'when I tell you that Mama really died of a broken heart. It sounds sentimental, but it's true. When Papa died she just took no interest in anything any more. She wouldn't eat; I don't think she slept very much. She didn't even cry. She used to sit at the window looking out on to the garden, and I knew by the expression on her face she was thinking of him, perhaps talking to him. She was quite convinced that when she died she would find him again. She wanted to die. When she got ill because the house was so cold, and we couldn't afford to buy coal, she didn't try to recover. I used to try to talk to her about the future, about what we would do together; but all the time I knew she was slipping away, eager only to be with Papa and not really concerned about what happened to me.'

The Duchesse wiped the tears from her eyes.

'And what did happen to you, my poor Gardenia?' she asked.

'Mama died last Saturday,' Gardenia said with a little catch in her voice. 'At the last moment, after being almost unconscious all day, she suddenly opened her eyes and smiled. She didn't speak, she didn't see me bending over her. It was just as though she was looking straight at Papa and was glad to see him again.'

Gardenia's voice broke and for a moment she could not go on. Then, with an effort, she continued.

'The moment the news got out that Mama was dead, I received a letter from the firm which held the mortgage on the house, telling me that they wished to take possession as soon as possible. They were horrible people, always badgering and frightening us if we were a day late with the payments. I think they had had a prospective buyer for some time. Anyway, they made it quite clear that I could not stay. I didn't want to. As I had no money it was humiliating to face the trades-people.'

'I shall pay them, of course,' the Duchesse said, 'every one of them.'

'I hoped you would say that!' Gardenia cried. 'They have all been so very kind, allowing us credit week after week; and when Mama was so ill they sent her flowers, and even left special invalid food that I hadn't ordered in case it would help her.'

'I shall send them the money today,' the Duchesse said firmly. 'My secretary will write out the cheques. Oh, child, if I had only known about all this! Why didn't you write to me, whatever your mother might say?'

'You must remember, Aunt Lily, I had not seen you for seven years,' Gardenia replied, 'and I think I have only seen you twice in my life. The first time was when I was born, and I know it was due to you that I was christened Gardenia.'

'Yes, yes, of course,' the Duchesse interposed. 'I had forgotten. I came to see your mother a few days after you were born bringing with me an enormous basket of gardenias from a London florist, and when your mother saw them she laughed. "How like you, Lily," she said, "and I hope the baby's going to be as beautiful as you. We shall call her Gardenia." '

'My mother often told me of your gift,' Gardenia said, 'and she laughed because it was so absurdly extravagant and luxurious when she and my father were wondering how they were going to pay the doctor or the nurses, or indeed, for my layette which was not a very elaborate one.'

'So that was the reason!' the Duchesse said in a stricken voice. 'I didn't understand. I had been rich for so long. Everything I wanted was always poured at my feet, so that I had forgotten what it was to be poor. I was older than your mother, and by the time she grew up I was already married and living in Paris. I suppose the contrast of our lives never struck me. Oh, Gardenia, how thoughtless I have been! But I loved Emily, I did really!'

'You mustn't distress yourself,' Gardenia said soothingly. 'Mama never expected anything and she was so fond of you. She used to tell me how beautiful you were and how, when you went to church when you were girls, everyone's face turned towards you; and that the male members of the choir could hardly sing for peeping at you over their hymn books.'

'And the curate fell in love with me!' the Duchesse laughed. 'He used to come round to tea and go crimson in the face every time I spoke to him. I used to try deliberately to make him blush because I was just finding out how much power I had over men. Oh dear, what a long time ago those days were!'

She looked across the bed at Gardenia, and went on:

'At your age I was married. I wanted to get away from home. I also found Hugo Reinbard exceedingly attractive. I wasn't in love with him; he fascinated me. My father warned me against him, but I wasn't prepared to listen. What girl would have, when he offered me London and Paris, and all I had at home was the village life and the curate?'

'Mama used to say that you looked like an angel in your wedding-dress,' Gardenia said. 'She often talked about you. I longed to see you and when you came to visit us in June 1902—you see I remember the date—I thought she had not in any way exaggerated your loveliness. You were the most beautiful person I have ever seen.'

The Duchesse smiled appreciatively at this compliment and then she put her hands to her face.

'Seven years ago,' she said, 'and look at me now. I've grown old; my face is lined. Oh, don't bother to argue, my mirror tells me the truth. My beauty, Gardenia, is a thing of the past. But I try, and I shall go on trying, to recapture it. I have heard of a new discovery, something quite extraordinary that the Hungarians have invented. It is a special treatment to ...'

The Duchesse stopped suddenly, the eagerness fading from her face. 'But I don't want to talk about that for the moment. I want to discuss your position. You were right to come to me, absolutely right, dear child. There was no one else you could turn to, and I think it was very brave of you to make the journey alone.'

'There was nothing else I could do,' Gardenia said. 'I suppose I ought to have waited and written to you, but since the men were waiting to take over the house, I sold what was left of the furniture to our friends in the village. There wasn't much and I couldn't charge them a great deal as I owed most of them so much money. But I raised enough for my fare to Paris. Only just enough. I didn't dare spend any of it even on sending you a telegram.'

'And you arrived last night,' the Duchesse said. 'I could hardly believe it when Yvonne said that my niece was in the house.'

'It must have been a shock,' Gardenia said, 'but somehow I did not expect you to be giving a party. It was silly of me. I just thought I would arrive and I would explain what had happened and you would understand.'

'I do ... I do understand,' the Duchesse said, 'but now we have got to make some plans. As I have said already, I don't think you can stay here.'

'Not even for a little while?' Gardenia asked piteously. 'I realise that I shall have to get a job. I have been thinking about it all the time I was travelling, but what can I do? I am not clever enough to be a governess. My education was very sketchy. I speak French—Mama insisted on that. I play the piano and I can paint a little. My arithmetic was always terrible and I never could spell.'

'Being a governess is a terrible life for anyone,' the Duchesse said. 'Besides, you are my niece.'

'Yes, I know,' Gardenia said. 'But what else is there? A companion?'

'No woman should be a companion to another woman,' the Duchesse said. 'You will have to get married, my child.'

Gardenia flushed.

'I hope,' she said a little hesitantly, 'as of course all girls hope, that one day I shall fall in love. But, first with Papa so ill and then Mama, I haven't had much chance of going out or of meeting any men.'

'Yes, you must get married,' the Duchesse said firmly. 'The difficulty is how we are going to manage it.'

'Couldn't I stay here just a little while?' Gardenia asked nervously. 'I won't be a bother, Aunt Lily, and perhaps I could help you in the house in some way. I can sew and ...'

The Duchesse made a little gesture with her hands.

'My dear child, I have dozens of servants, dozens of them to do things for me. But I want to find you a husband and ...' She stopped, and it seemed to Gardenia there was an expression of embarrassment on her face.

'Oh dear!' the Duchesse exclaimed. 'I don't know what to say. I know of no one I can ask to chaperone you, no one who would accept a young girl on my recommendation.'

'I don't understand,' Gardenia said.

'No, of course you don't,' the Duchesse said. 'But there are problems. It's not that I don't want you to stay with me, but it is a difficult situation.'

'If you are frightened that I would get in the way of your parties,' Gardenia said, 'I would not come to them. I could hear how very gay it was last night; but when I wanted to come upstairs and tell you I had arrived, Lord Hartcourt persuaded me it would be a stupid thing to do.'

'Lord Hartcourt!' the Duchesse exclaimed. 'Have you met him?'

'Yes,' Gardenia said. 'I was waiting in the hall, and he and Comte André de——I've forgotten his name—spoke to me.' She decided not to tell her aunt how the Comte had behaved.

'That must have been André de Grenelle. Did you tell them who you were?'

'I told Lord Hartcourt I was your niece,' Gardenia said. 'Was that wrong?'

'No. No, of course not,' the Duchesse said. 'Did he seem surprised?'

'Well, it was rather awkward,' Gardenia explained. 'I fainted—I think it was because I had so little food on the journey—and he carried me into the sitting-room.'

'That was kind of him,' the Duchesse said. 'It is very unlike Lord Hartcourt to trouble with anyone. He is a very spoilt and rather difficult young man. When he comes to my parties I have the feeling he is looking down his nose at me.'

'Oh, Aunt Lily, how could he do that!' Gardenia exclaimed. At the same time she had a feeling at the back of her mind that that was exactly what Lord Hartcourt would do.

'So he has seen you,' the Duchesse said, 'and André as well. That makes things rather difficult.'

'But why?' Gardenia asked.

'You wouldn't understand,' the Duchesse said firmly. 'Well, we shall just have to make the best of it. But if I let you stay here, Gardenia, you must promise me to do exactly as I tell you. If I tell you to go to bed at a certain time you must go. If I tell you not to talk to certain people you must obey me.'

'Of course I would,' Gardenia said. 'Oh, Aunt Lily, does that mean you are going to let me stay?'

'I don't really see what else I can do,' the Duchesse answered. Then she smiled. 'Yes, dear child. It will be nice to have you; and, thank God, although you are young, you are not such a beauty that you will entirely eclipse me!'

'Me a beauty!' Gardenia threw back her head and laughed. 'Papa always said I never lived up to my name and looked like a modest hedge-rose or a common or garden English daisy, instead of anything so exotic as a gardenia.'

'Nevertheless,' the Duchesse said, 'you have possibilities: we will have to take you in hand and see what can be done. You can't wear your hair in that old-fashioned, untidy fashion, and as for that dress, well, it must have come out of the Ark.'

'It is rather old,' Gardenia admitted.

'And you can't wear black, not if you stay with me,' the Duchesse said. 'It is too depressing. It will make you look too like a poor relation, and that is enough to put any man off. No, Gardenia! If I am to find you a husband you will have to have proper clothes and look, as everyone will expect you to look, like my niece and, doubtless, as I have no children, my heir.'

'Oh Aunt Lily! I should not expect anything like that,' Gardenia protested.

'My dear, it is not such an asset as it sounds,' the Duchesse said. 'I may be a Duchesse and rich, but there are a lot of people in Paris who will not be particularly effusive at meeting you for that very reason.'

'But surely, Aunt Lily, as a Duchesse, you must be terribly important,' Gardenia said.

The Duchesse looked at her out of the corners of her eyes, seemed about to speak and then changed her mind.

'We shall talk about things like that in good time,' she said. 'At the moment we must be concerned with your appearance. I cannot even take you to see *Monsieur* Worth dressed as you are now.'

She touched a bell at her side and a few seconds later the door opened and the maid came in.

'Yvonne,' the Duchesse said, 'my niece, *Ma'm'selle* Gardenia, is going to stay with me. She will need clothes and a new hair style and many other things. As soon as I am

44

dressed I will take her to Worth's, but I cannot take her looking like this.'

'*Non, Madame, c'est impossible!*' the maid exclaimed.

'Very well, Yvonne, find something for her,' the Duchesse said. 'Perhaps some of my old gowns that I wore when I was thinner can be altered, at least until I can buy her some new things.'

'Oh, thank you, Aunt Lily!' Gardenia exclaimed, 'not only for the clothes but for saying I can stay. I can't tell you how wonderful it is for me. I was so frightened of being alone, of having no one. When Mama died I thought the end of the world had come; but now, because I've got you, it is different.'

'Because you've got me,' the Duchesse repeated in a strange voice. Then she bent forward to let Gardenia kiss her cheek. 'Bless you, my child. I suppose things will work out one way or another.'

'I will do everything you tell me, everything,' Gardenia said, 'and I do hope I shall be able to repay a little of your kindness.'

'That reminds me,' the Duchesse said. 'Yvonne, take *Ma'm'selle* to *Monsieur* Groise. She has some instructions to give him—please explain that they have my full authority.'

'Very good, your Grace,' the maid said stiffly, and rustled towards the door, obviously expecting Gardenia to follow.

Gardenia went a few paces and then looked back.

'Thank you, thank you, Aunt Lily,' she said. 'I didn't realise until this moment how terrified I was that you might turn me away.'

'Run along, child. Everything is going to be all right,' the Duchesse assured her.

As the door closed behind Gardenia and Yvonne, the Duchesse lay back on her pillows and closed her eyes.

'Poor child,' she whispered aloud. 'How can I ever explain to her? But undoubtedly she will find out sooner or later.'

In the meantime Gardenia, feeling elated, was following Yvonne down the staircase to the hall that she had entered so ignominiously the night before. There appeared to be a whole army of servants working in the Salon as they passed it, and there were cleaners on the stairs, brushing and scrubbing the carpet where food and drink must have been upset the night before. There were also men and women in aprons polishing the marble hall, and Gardenia could not help seeing that some of the pans into which they were brushing the dust contained broken pieces of a crystal-glass chandelier.

It seems strange, she thought, that Aunt Lily should give such rough parties; but, as she had told herself last night, the French were a very excitable race and not dull and stolid like the English.

Yvonne led her across the hall to a room opposite the one into which Lord Hartcourt had carried her when she fainted. She knocked. A voice said, '*Entrez*,' and Yvonne opened the door to disclose a grey-haired middle-aged man sitting at a big desk with piles of papers stacked in front of him.

Yvonne conveyed the Duchesse's instructions and obviously introduced her to *Monsieur* Groise, but she spoke so rapidly that Gardenia could not understand all that she said.

Monsieur Groise rose from the desk and held out his hand.

'*Enchanté, Ma'm'selle*,' he said in French and then continued in somewhat broken English. 'The maid has explained to me 'that you have something you wish to do and that it has her Grace's approval.'

'It is a number of bills that have to be paid,' Gardenia said a little uncomfortably. She drew the list from the pocket of her black skirt. 'I am afraid there are rather a lot,' she said nervously.

'On the contrary,' *Monsieur* Groise contradicted, 'it is a very small list. Are you quite sure everyone is included?'

'I don't think I have missed anyone,' Gardenia said, 'but if I have perhaps I could come and tell you later?'

'But of course, *Ma'm'selle*,' he replied. 'I am at your service. The cheques shall be sent today. These people shall all be sent money orders which are cashable at the nearest post office. That will make it easy for them, will it not?'

'It will be very kind indeed,' Gardenia said. 'I am most grateful.'

'It is a pleasure, *Ma'm'selle*' he replied.

'Thank you,' Gardenia said again.

Yvonne was waiting for Gardenia at the door of the secretary's room. Gardenia followed her out into the hall.

'We will now go upstairs, *Ma'm'selle,*' the maid said, but, as she spoke, Gardenia saw that the front door was being opened by a footman and she heard a voice which she knew only too well say:

'Is her Grace at home? Will you please tell her Lord Hartcourt and Mr Bertram Cunningham have called?'

'Her Grace is not at home to any visitors,' the footman said in French.

Gardenia could now see through the open door Lord Hartcourt standing on the doorstep and, fearing that he could see her, she felt the only thing she could do was to go forward and greet him. Shyly, with the colour rising in her face, she turned towards the door and held out her hand. 'Good morning, Lord Hartcourt,' she said. 'I feel I must thank you for your kindness to me last night.'

'I hope you are well this morning,' Lord Hartcourt said, taking off his top-hat. 'You must have been very tired after your journey.'

'I was very tired,' Gardenia confessed.

'It's not surprising,' a voice interrupted, and Gardenia turned to look at Lord Hartcourt's companion. She saw a tall, very elegantly dressed, dark-haired young man with a small dark moustache and an engaging smile which made her instinctively feel she should smile back.

'May I introduce my cousin, Bertram Cunningham?' Lord Hartcourt asked. 'I am afraid that in the unusual circumstances of our encounter last night I was not privileged to learn your name.'

'I am Gardenia Weedon,' Gardenia said, and she felt the warm pressure of Bertram Cunningham's hand on hers.

'I am so glad it was an Englishman who was able to welcome you to Paris,' Bertram said. 'My cousin was telling me how you arrived in the middle of the night. It must have been a ghastly experience, not knowing Paris and having to find your way alone. I insisted that we should call and see how you were this morning. But I can see from looking at you that you are none the worse."

'I am quite all right,' Gardenia said.

'Jolly good!' Bertram ejaculated.

Gardenia realised suddenly that he was still holding her hand and took it hastily away.

'My cousin and I wondered if you would like to come and drive with us,' Bertram suggested. 'I am just going to take my horses for a turn in the *Bois* and I feel sure the air will do you good.'

Gardenia looked to where in the drive there stood a very elegant dogcart in the very latest fashion, painted yellow and black, with the tandem of black horses with plaited manes and tails.

'How lovely!' she exclaimed involuntarily. 'How smart they look!'

'I am very proud of them,' Bertram said. 'All the same, if you prefer it, I have an automobile.'

'I much prefer horses,' Gardenia told him, 'but I am afraid I cannot come for a drive today. Aunt Lily has planned to take me . . .' She was going to say where they were going, but changed her mind. '. . . out with her.'

'You have seen your aunt?' Lord Hartcourt asked.

Gardenia felt that once again he was querying her reception, and remembering how greatly she had resented his advice the night before, she answered rather stiffly.

'Of course. I am glad to say Aunt Lily is delighted to see me. I am going to stay here with her.'

It seemed to her, and she didn't understand why, that on the last sentence Lord Hartcourt's face altered. It was almost, but, of course, that was absurd, as if there was a look of disappointment in his eyes.

'How delightful for you,' he replied in a rather bored tone, and turning to his cousin said: 'Well, Bertie, if Miss Weedon won't come with us we must be on our way.'

'Miss Weedon, I shall hope to see you again very shortly,' Bertram said. 'As a matter of fact, I believe your aunt has invited me to a party tomorrow night. I promise you, nothing shall keep me away.'

'I shall be very glad to see you,' Gardenia answered. 'Goodbye.'

Lord Hartcourt said nothing. It seemed to Gardenia that there was something almost aggressive in the manner he clapped his hat on his head, walked resolutely down the steps in front of Bertram and climbed into the dogcart.

Bertram made to follow him and then turned back.

'Quite sure you won't change your mind?' he said in a low voice to Gardenia. 'I would like to be one of the first to show you Paris.'

'No. I can't come today,' Gardenia replied, 'and anyway, I should have to ask Aunt Lily first.'

'Come tomorrow,' Bertram pleaded. 'I am sure the

Duchesse will not mind. I will fetch you about this time. Do you promise?'

'I can't promise anything,' Gardenia said, a little embarrassed by his insistence.

'But you must try and arrange it,' he said. And then, before she could answer, he had run down the steps and was climbing into the dogcart to take the reins in his hands. As the tandem drove off, Bertram waved at the turn of the drive, but Lord Hartcourt sat looking straight ahead of him. He did not look back.

'I think he is extremely disagreeable,' Gardenia said to herself. 'And I can't think why, but he seems to disapprove of me.'

As she followed Yvonne upstairs, she thought she would ask the Duchesse if she could go driving with Mr Bertram Cunningham the next day. It was not anything she would be allowed to do in England without a chaperone, but obviously, as he had invited her to go, things must be different in Paris. She had always heard there was much more license in the gay city and, after all, why should one need a chaperone to go driving in an open dogcart with a man who would be preoccupied with handling a tandem with skill? It might be different if he asked her to go out in his automobile.

Gardenia remembered she had heard all sorts of stories about girls who were enticed away on long drives by a man with a smart motor-car and then, after they had refused his advances, had been obliged to walk home. She somehow felt that Bertram Cunningham was not that type of man. He looked young and jolly and full of fun, and she thought rather wistfully it would be exciting to be with someone of her own age, to laugh and be gay and not have to worry about bills or where the next meal was to come from.

Yvonne was leading her up the stairs to the second floor. She passed her aunt's bedroom and went to the far end of the passage, where Yvonne opened the door of a room with the window overlooking the garden. It was a large room, and every wall was fitted with cupboards.

'This is her Grace's wardrobe,' Yvonne said, and started to open the doors to reveal more dresses than Gardenia imagined any woman would have in a lifetime, let alone have collected all at one time.

Driving towards the *Bois*, after negotiating the traffic round the Arc de Triomphe, Bertram exclaimed:

'An attractive little thing, and not at all the sort of niece one would expect the redoubtable Lily to possess.'

'You yourself told me she came from a decent family,' Lord Hartcourt reminded him.

'Well, that is what my father used to say,' Bertram replied. 'What do you think Lily will do with the girl?'

'Apparently Miss Weedon has every intention of staying with her aunt. I learnt last night that she was a very determined young woman,' Lord Hartcourt said drily.

'Determined?' Bertram exclaimed. 'That little English sparrow? Why, she looks as if she's only just fallen out of the nest. I don't think she's determined about anything. But she would be attractive if she were properly dressed.'

'I imagine the Duchesse will see to that,' Lord Hartcourt said.

'The whole thing seems a mystery,' Bertram continued. 'This girl comes over, she looks innocent, yet Lily accepts her, and apparently she is going to be one of the household. I shouldn't be surprised if André is right and the whole thing is a new stunt. It all seems a bit fishy to me.'

'I expect there is a perfectly good explanation, if we but knew it,' Lord Hartcourt said in a bored voice.

'Damn it all, Vane! You are never excited about anything,' Bertram complained. 'It will rather amuse me to show the girl a bit of life. I am fed up with all the blasé collection at Maxim's. Do you know, when Henry gave Yvette a diamond bracelet last week she handed it back to him and said the stones weren't big enough.'

'Well, Henry can certainly afford big ones.'

'Yes, but think of the ingratitude of it,' Bertram said. 'None of them are really pleased with anything. It's like Marie whom I took out for a while. She was always complaining: the caviar wasn't fresh, the champagne was corked, the seat was uncomfortable, the orchids I gave her were the wrong colour! I got fed-up and dropped her, and now poor old Oswald has taken her on. He doesn't know what he's in for! I don't mind girls costing money. After all, what else is there really to spend it on? But I do expect them to show some sort of appreciation.'

'Poor Bertie,' Lord Hartcourt replied. 'I cannot believe that all your efforts go unrewarded.'

'I suppose you will say I'm mean if I say I like value for

my expenditure,' Bertram said, turning his head to smile at his cousin. 'And I know you think I rush into affairs far too quickly. But the truth is, Vane, I haven't got your flair for choosing the right woman. My ladybirds always seem disappointing once I get to know them, while yours improve on acquaintance. If ever there was a high-stepper it's Henriette.'

Lord Hartcourt made no answer, and after a moment Bertram said plaintively:

'All right, Vane, I know that remark is not in good taste; but damn it all, a fellow has to talk to someone, and who better than a relation?'

'Who indeed?' Lord Hartcourt said. 'Very well, Bertie, cultivate the little English sparrow, as you call her. You have my blessing. Despite my misgivings, she may turn out to be amusing and worth the expense!'

Four

Gardenia burst into her aunt's bedroom impulsively.

'Aunt Lily, it is hopeless!' she exclaimed, and then stopped and gave a little exclamation. 'Oh, but how lovely you look!'

Standing with her back to the window, dressed in a sweeping silk gown of soft blue chiffon with a bunch of silk roses pinned with a huge diamond bow to her breast, and her golden hair covered with an enormous hat, the Duchesse did, in fact, look almost as beautiful as she had been when Gardenia had last seen her in England.

'Thank you, dear child,' Lily de Mabillon said, pleased with the compliment.

'Your dress is beautiful,' Gardenia said in an awed voice, 'and though I have read about them in the newspapers, I have never really seen a wonderful Merry Widow hat before.'

'Is that what you call it?' the Duchesse asked in an amused voice, glancing at her reflection in the mirror.

'At home, no one talks of anything else!' Gardenia exclaimed. 'It is Merry Widow gowns, Merry Widow hats, Merry Widow curls. My mother and I used to laugh as we glanced through the newspapers and magazines and wondered how we would look in the hats. I thought they might appear comical. Now I see that on you it looks right and terribly, terribly smart.'

The Duchesse was obviously pleased with Gardenia's enthusiasm. She turned to the two maids who had helped dress her and were now standing by the bed tidying away the wrappers, curling-tongs, hair-pins, lotions and creams which had obviously all been used in effecting the Duchesse's toilet.

'*Ma'm'selle* is delighted with my appearance,' she translated into French. The Duchesse moved a little as she spoke, and with the sunlight coming through the window Gardenia saw how much of the glowing pink and white skin was due to artifice. The Duchesse had covered her face with a mask of cream and rouge and now the sallowness which had been so obvious first thing in the morning was hidden.

'Well, now I am ready to go out,' the Duchesse said, with yet another look at herself in the mirror, touching as she spoke the dog-collar of pearls and diamonds which encircled her throat and hid the tell-tale lines of age.

'But, Aunt Lily, I have nothing to wear,' Gardenia said. 'That is what I came to tell you. Your dresses are lovely and I have never seen so many in the whole of my life, but they are all much, much too big. Yvonne says it would take hours, if not days, to alter them.'

'*C'est vrai, Madame,*' Yvonne said from the doorway. 'I have tried all of them on *Ma'm'selle,* and there is nothing, nothing she can wear which would not make her look ridiculous.'

The Duchesse looked Gardenia up and down. 'I cannot take you to Worth's in that coat and skirt,' she said. 'People would laugh. Even Yvonne is smarter on her days out.'

'Then I shall just have to stay at home,' Gardenia said miserably.

'You will do nothing of the sort,' the Duchesse interposed. 'Clothes you have got to have before we can make any plans, before we can arrange anything for you. Wait, I have an idea! It is a warm day, but I am going to wear my sables. There is always a slightly treacherous wind in the spring.'

Gardenia looked at her, bewildered. She could not see where this conversation was leading.

'Have you a gown amongst your luggage which is light, a summer dress for instance?' the Duchesse asked.

Gardenia nodded.

'Yes. I have one of pale pink voile which I made myself,' she said. 'It is not very smart, I am afraid, but I copied a sketch I saw in one of the fashion magazines.'

'Go and put it on,' the Duchesse commanded, 'and hurry.'

Just for a moment Gardenia hesitated. 'It is not mourning,' she said.

'I have already told you,' the Duchesse said almost sharply, 'that you cannot wear black. My friends in Paris will not be interested as to whether you should wear mourning or not.'

53

'Very well, Aunt Lily,' Gardenia said meekly. 'I will go and put it on.'

She ran from the room and fortunately found without much difficulty the new bedroom into which she had been moved. The saucy young chambermaid was still unpacking her things. The voile dress was creased, but once Gardenia was hooked into it, it did not look so old-fashioned as the black dress she had been wearing. Nevertheless, Gardenia could not help feeling sure she would look ridiculous beside Aunt Lily in her blue chiffon with its pink roses and pearl and diamond jewellery.

How marvellous to have beautiful clothes, she thought, and remarked how often her mother had sighed over the garments they must mend and patch and make do from year to year, simply because there was no money to buy any more.

Thanking the maid, who she discovered was called Jeanne, Gardenia ran down the corridor and back to her aunt's room. The Duchesse was seated once again at the dressing-table, adding a little more mascara to her eye-lashes.

Gardenia stared. She had always thought that it was only play-actresses who dared to wear cosmetics in the daytime, and she felt somehow at the back of her mind that her mother would not have approved.

Her aunt put down the tiny brush and turned to look at her.

'Heavens!' she exclaimed. 'I should have known that dress was home-made wherever I had seen it!'

Gardenia flushed.

'It was that or not having a new dress at all.'

The Duchesse gave a little exclamation.

'Oh dear. How unkind of me! I didn't mean to hurt your feelings, child. It was cruel when I think how easily I could have sent you and your mother boxes of clothes to wear. Think of all those things I have got upstairs! I have not the slightest idea what I can do with them.'

Two little dimples appeared in Gardenia's cheeks.

'You are laughing at me,' the Duchesse said accusingly. 'Why?'

'I can't help thinking how unsuitable all those glorious gowns would have been at home in the village,' Gardenia said. 'As for the ball-dresses, I think Papa would have had a fit if either Mama or I had appeared in them.'

The Duchesse had to laugh. She had seen the small manor-house in which her sister had lived, and the straggling hamlet with its village green and the grey, stone church. She knew that Gardenia was right when she said everything in her vast wardrobe-room would have been extremely out of place.

'I promise you we weren't envious,' Gardenia said quickly. 'Mama liked to think of you wearing gorgeous jewels and being the belle of every ball. She used to talk about you, and I would try to imagine the clothes you would wear to the opera or the diplomatic parties. Now I have seen them, I know that I just wasn't imagining the right thing.'

'You are going to have just as beautiful clothes yourself,' the Duchesse said firmly. 'Come along, Yvonne, put that hat on *Ma'm'selle's* head and bring the chinchilla cape.'

Yvonne hurried forward with a hat that was a smaller and more restrained edition of the Duchesse's. She set it on Gardenia's head and fastened it with two huge hatpins which were ornamented with tiny jewels. Gardenia felt that the hat was too large for her, but she hardly had time to glance at herself in the mirror before one of the other maids brought forward a long chinchilla cape, which she placed over her shoulders.

'But I can't wear this,' Gardenia protested.

'Why not?' the Duchesse asked. 'It will hide your dress, and though it is late in the season for furs, people who see you will be too impressed to worry about the weather. It is new, a present from a friend. Don't you admire it?'

'It is magnificent!' Gardenia exclaimed stroking the soft, shaded grey fur which felt almost like silk beneath her touch. 'It must be worth a fortune!' she exclaimed. 'I am afraid to wear anything so costly, Aunt Lily.'

'Nonsense!' the Duchesse said. 'It will establish you, if nothing else does. I have not worn it yet. I was keeping it for a special occasion—and that is now! Come along, child.'

Bewildered and at the same time feeling slightly foolish, Gardenia followed her downstairs, pulling the chinchilla around her shoulders and wondering if she was not dreaming and this was part of some strange Alice in Wonderland fantasy.

The car was waiting outside. With sable rugs over their

knees and with a uniformed footman sitting beside the chauffeur, they rolled slowly out of the pillared gates and into the roadway. The Duchesse lay back against the cushioned seat.

'Tomorrow,' she said, 'we will drive in the *Bois* and you will see how beautiful Paris can be in spring. Today we are too busy to do anything but think of clothes.'

As she spoke she waved her hand to several top-hatted men strolling beneath the trees of the Champs Elysées, who swept off their hats at the sight of her.

'They are friends of mine,' she said, 'but, alas, these days we go so fast. Just a few years ago I used to drive everywhere in a carriage, and then one could stop and talk to one's friends and also be seen. Now, one flashes by and people are out of sight before one has time to speak to them.'

'But it is very exciting to have a car!' Gardenia exclaimed.

'It is not so romantic,' her aunt answered, 'but at least one doesn't have to fuss about keeping the horses waiting. My husband, when he was alive, always complained if I was late because he was worrying about the horses. A motor-car, thank goodness, can wait indefinitely.'

'There are still many people who seem to prefer carriages and horses,' Gardenia remarked, looking at the traffic.

'Horses are still the vogue among the French aristocracy,' her aunt replied, 'and of course a lot of dashers like to be seen driving a pair or a tandem.'

'Oh! That reminds me,' Gardenia cried. 'I forgot to tell you. Lord Hartcourt called this morning and his cousin was with him. Mr Bertram Cunningham, I think his name was, and he asked me if I would go driving with him tomorrow. I said I would ask you if I could.'

'He asked you to go alone?' The question was sharp.

'I suppose that is what he meant,' Gardenia said. 'I knew it would not be allowed at home, but I thought that perhaps in Paris things were different.'

'You are quite certain he asked you to go alone?' Again there was that strange note in her aunt's voice which told Gardenia something was wrong.

'I thought that was what he meant,' Gardenia stammered. 'Lord Hartcourt might be there. I don't know.'

'Damn them, they waste no time,' the Duchesse said, almost beneath her breath.

'I am sorry if I have done anything wrong,' Gardenia said. 'I knew that in England I would have to be chaperoned.'

'You will not answer Mr. Cunningham's invitation,' the Duchesse said slowly. 'I will do that myself.'

'Yes, Aunt Lily. Of course, Aunt Lily,' Gardenia agreed. She felt she had done something very wrong, but she was not quite certain what it was.

Fortunately there was no more time for conversation. They drew up at what seemed to Gardenia to be a most impressive private house, not in the least like the shop she was expecting.

The footman drew the rug from their knees and helped Aunt Lily out. They walked up a blue carpet and into a magnificently furnished hall. It was only as they ascended the stairs that Gardenia guessed that they were in fact entering the Salon of the famous *Monsieur* Worth. The huge drawing-room on the first floor was arranged with Louis XIV sofas and chairs covered in oyster satin, with chandeliers hanging from the ceiling, and only when *Monsieur* Worth himself, resplendent in embroidered waistcoat, appeared, was Gardenia sure that this was not in fact a social call.

'*Madame,* you look enchanting,' he said to the Duchesse, kissing her hand. 'You give my creations a chic which even I could not put into them. Is this the first time you have worn it?'

'No, the second,' the Duchesse said. 'I can promise you that it was looked at with envy by a lot of female eyes, and with admiration by a lot of masculine ones.'

Monsieur Worth laughed, then turned his eyes on Gardenia.

'My niece,' the Duchesse said. 'I have brought her to you because only your magic wand can make her presentable, and until she is properly dressed I must keep her behind locked doors. Take off your coat, Gardenia.'

Gardenia did as she was told. Standing in the centre of the Salon in the cheap little dress she had made for herself, she felt almost naked under *Monsieur* Worth's scrutiny and wondered if the superior vendeuses watching them from the ends of the room were laughing at her embarrassment.

'Miss Weedon arrived from England unexpectedly last night,' the Duchesse said. 'She has come to live with me because her mother and father are dead. She is my closest relative and my heir. Will you dress her accordingly?'

Monsieur Worth was not looking at Gardenia's dress but at her face. She felt him take in every detail of her face, her eyes, her hair surmounted by the too large and too ornamented hat.

'Will you remove your hat, *Ma'm'selle*?' he asked.

She raised her arms and drew out the gigantic pins. Her hair, untidy from trying on all the dresses in the Duchesse's wardrobe, was curling rebelliously round her white forehead and at the nape of her neck.

'You do see,' the Duchesse murmured, 'she cannot appear looking like that.'

'She is very young,' *Monsieur* Worth said, almost as though he were talking to himself. 'How would you have me dress her, *Madame*? As a counterpart of yourself or as she is, very young, very unsophisticated?'

Gardenia could see that he was asking this question with a sudden urgency in his quiet rather deep voice. She felt, too, that something had passed between the couturier and her aunt and she could not understand. For a moment they seemed to look at each other; then the Duchesse, in a light and casual voice, said:

'I told my niece that we must find her a charming husband. She has had very little fun in her life, being little more than a nurse first to her ill father and then to her mother. I hope, *Monsieur*, that it will not be long before we ask you to make her a trousseau.'

'Exactly, *Madame*, that is what I would wish to do,' *Monsieur* Worth said.

Gardenia felt the question he had asked had been answered, and now he knew what to do.

He snapped his fingers.

'Bring me taffeta, tulle, white lace,' he said to the vendeuse who hurried up to him.

Bales of exquisite materials were brought from hidden cupboards. Meanwhile, *Monsieur* Worth just sat and looked at Gardenia till she felt the colour rise in her cheeks and she dropped her eyes in embarrassment. She had never been studied like this before. She had never thought that any man could sit for ten to fifteen minutes without speaking, just looking at her, seeming to take in every curve of her body, every movement of her shoulders and hands.

Three hours later she was beginning to feel that clothes were almost a disagreeable necessity. She stood, she turned, materials were pinned on her, taken away, sketches were brought and discarded, and yet not once was her opinion asked. *Monsieur* Worth talked to her aunt, and her aunt agreed with everything he said.

There were so many different gowns that Gardenia had lost count. Then they began to speak about accessories. Hats were brought in from the Salon next door and *Monsieur* Worth himself decided which Gardenia should have and which would go with the gowns he was creating for her.

Another hour passed and Gardenia was ready to drop with fatigue. She realised she had had nothing to eat since the rolls and coffee at breakfast and wondered if she dared tell her aunt she was hungry. To her relief her aunt looked at a little diamond watch which was pinned to her bracelet.

'Four o'clock,' she said. 'It is time for tea. I promised a friend that I would call in on her. Do you need Miss Weedon any longer?'

'One dress should be ready by now,' *Monsieur* Worth said. He signalled to one of the hovering minions, who ran hastily from the room.

'They have made something in this short time?' Gardenia asked breathlessly.

'It is something I would not do for anyone but her Grace,' *Monsieur* Worth replied. 'Always ladies come here and ask me for the impossible—a dress for tonight, a dress for tomorrow—and always I say, "*Madame,* God spent seven days in creating the world. You cannot expect me to rival such an achievement." '

'But the dress is ready, and in four hours!' Gardenia exclaimed, as she saw a woman bringing it down the Salon towards them.

'In this I think we have cheated a little,' *Monsieur* Worth said. 'To be honest, this gown was in fact already almost finished, but the Marquise de St Cloix is not expecting it for another week and by then another will be ready for her, with a few alterations, of course. I never make two gowns exactly the same.'

'But thank you,' Gardenia said a few minutes later. 'It is lovely, absolutely lovely!'

It was indeed a day-dress such as she had dreamed of possessing—of soft, very pale green crêpe, embroidered with braid and with draped chiffon. It gave her a diaphanous appearance as fresh and young as the spring itself. The hat to wear with it was of green straw, encircled with a small wreath of daffodils. It was very simple, very young, and made the Duchesse draw in her breath when she looked from it to Gardenia's shining eyes and parted lips.

'Youth,' she said with a sudden bitterness, 'is something not even you can create, *Monsieur* Worth.'

The couturier glanced up at her, saw the pain in the heavily mascaraed eyes and understood.

'But do not forget, *Madame*,' he said, 'that the French prefer experience, and that is something that can come only with the years.'

The Duchesse smiled.

'What a diplomat you are, *Monsieur*,' she said. She gathered up her sables from where they had been thrown on the sofa beside her. 'And now, if you are ready, Gardenia, I think we have done enough shopping for one day. Tomorrow you must have gloves, bags, shoes, and dozens of other things. Now I am tired and we can leave everything else in *Monsieur* Worth's most capable hands.'

She rose to her feet and held out her hand to the couturier, who bent to kiss it. 'You have promised my niece an evening gown by seven o'clock tonight.'

'It shall be done,' he answered, 'and your own robe will also be in time for your party tomorrow. I trust you will be pleased with it.'

'I am hoping it will be sensational,' the Duchesse said.

'And for *Ma'm'selle* Weedon something *pour une jeune fille*,' *Monsieur* Worth said.

'That is how I would wish it,' the Duchesse answered.

She swept from the room like a ship in full sail. Gardenia followed her, peeping at herself in the mirrors as she passed them, thrilled, hardly believing that this young, elegant creature with the tiny waist and closely fitted bodice could be herself. Downstairs, then they reached the doorway, she stopped to shake hands with *Monsieur* Worth.

'Thank you, thank you, *Monsieur* Worth,' she said. 'I don't know how to express my gratitude.'

'I want you just to be as lovely in yourself as the dresses I shall send you,' *Monsieur* Worth answered.

It was a surprising remark and Gardenia looked at him wide-eyed.

'Paris can spoil people. Don't be spoiled,' *Monsieur* Worth said. 'Remember, clothes, however gorgeous, are only a frame. I cannot re-make or create the person inside them.'

Gardenia felt he had some reason for making such remarks, and also he spoke in a low voice so that her aunt, who was already crossing the pavement, could not hear.

'I will remember that,' she said, 'and thank you, once again.'

'God help you,' he said softly to himself as Gardenia hurried after the Duchesse.

For some reason, *Monsieur* Worth's last words had damped some of the elation Gardenia had felt at wearing her new dress. She did not know why. Now she felt apprehensive about what lay ahead. Perhaps the parties would not be so much fun. Perhaps it was not going to be as easy as it seemed to please Aunt Lily, to do what was required of her. She didn't know what it was. She only knew that she felt solemn instead of being excited.

In the car Aunt Lily lay back against the cushions and shut her eyes.

'We are not really going anywhere,' she said, 'but I knew we would never get away and nothing would ever be finished unless I said we had an appointment. Jean Worth believes the whole world revolves around his Salon. He is not far wrong, but buying clothes is always exhausting.'

'How clever of him to fit me out so quickly,' Gardenia said.

'He can never resist anything new, a new face, a new kind of party, a new challenge, for that is how he thinks of it,' the Duchesse explained. 'Now sit up, Gardenia, and look about. You should take note of the people walking up the Champs Elysées at this time of the afternoon. We shall go slowly for I want them to see you.'

The Duchesse picked up the speaking-tube which was fastened by her seat at the side of the car and told the chauffeur, in French, to go slower. He was obviously used to such orders. Drawing in to the side of the kerb they moved so slowly that it was almost possible for people walking to keep pace with them. The Duchesse lowered the window and now it seemed to Gardenia that she knew everyone.

There were ladies in summer dresses and lacy parasols sitting under the trees, talking to men with their trousers creased down the side in the fashion that had been started by King Edward and wearing high satin cravats decorated with sparkling, jewelled tie-pins.

Gardenia noticed that everyone stared at her aunt and one or two people beckoned, quite obviously inviting the Duchesse to join them.

'They are curious as to who you are,' she said to Gardenia. 'A new face in Paris is always a novelty, but I am not going to gratify their curiosity now. They will all be tumbling over themselves to visit me tomorrow evening.'

'Do you have a party every night?' Gardenia asked, remembering what the Housekeeper had said.

'Not every night,' her aunt replied. 'At the beginning of the week people are often away, so Mondays I am not at home, nor on Tuesdays; but Wednesdays, Thursdays, and Saturdays my friends are always welcome.'

'What about tonight?' Gardenia asked.

'Tonight I have a small dinner party,' the Duchesse said, 'and afterwards we will be going on to Maxim's. But not you, dear child. You must go to bed. It is not at all a correct place for a young girl.'

'How disappointing!' Gardenia exclaimed. 'I have heard about Maxim's. It is very gay, and they sing a song about it in the *Merry Widow*!'

'I think even in the *Merry Widow* they make clear it is not for young girls.'

'Of course I have not seen the play,' Gardenia said. 'But some of the music was reproduced in the newspapers and Mama played it to me on the piano. Do you remember how beautifully she played?'

'Do you play?' the Duchesse asked.

'A little,' Gardenia replied, 'but not as well as Mama. Would you like me to play to you?'

'Some time when we are alone,' the Duchesse said hastily. 'In Paris people are not interested in amateurs performing after dinner as they are in England.'

'I was not so conceited as to think I could play to your friends,' Gardenia said, 'but Mama found it very soothing if I played to her when she had a headache, and Papa liked it too.'

'I will certainly let you play to me one day,' the Duchesse said in a tone which told Gardenia only too clearly she was not interested in such trivialities.

'Who is coming to dinner?' Gardenia asked.

'You will see,' the Duchesse said a little evasively, 'and now I am going to lie down. I nearly always try to get a rest after tea—which reminds me, you had no luncheon. How remiss of me! I always go without luncheon myself because of my figure. I am putting on weight I am afraid. Indeed, *Monsieur* Worth has spoken to me very severely about it. But you, poor child, must be hungry and there is no reason for you to try to get any thinner. Do forgive me! I must tell the servants that another day when I am fasting they must bring you something on a tray.'

'It is all right,' Gardenia said. 'I am not used to eating very much, but I would like some tea, if that is possible.'

'But of course,' the Duchesse said. She swept into the house calling the butler imperiously to bring tea up to her boudoir. 'And in future,' she added, *'Ma'm'selle* Weedon will have luncheon. Do you understand? A proper luncheon. I can't imagine why no one thought of it before we left the house.' She didn't wait for the manservant's apologies but swept upstairs to a room opening off from her bedroom.

Gardenia had heard talk of ladies' boudoirs but had never seen one. Everything in her aunt's seemed to be ornamented with cupids. The curtains were embroidered with flying cupids pointing their arrows; pelmets carved in moulded wood had the same motif; and the pictures, all by great Masters, depicted cupids with Venus in various states of nudity.

'It is lovely!' Gardenia exclaimed, feeling she was overworking that adjective, but finding no other word to describe it.

Her aunt did not answer and Gardenia saw that she was seated at a beautiful inlaid gilt and satin-wood secretaire writing a letter. Not liking to disturb her, Gardenia sat down on one of the brocade satin sofas and with satisfaction saw the footmen bringing in an elaborate tea which they set down on a table beside an armchair. There was a massive silver tray, laden with a silver teapot, kettle, tea-caddy, milk and cream jugs; but rather more satisfying were the plates of tiny triangled sandwiches of watercress, cucumber, honey, jam and Gentleman's Relish. There was also rolled bread and butter containing *pâté de foie gras* and asparagus tips. There were cakes of every description, cherry, madeira and rich fruit, as well as French patisseries filled with coffee-cream and nuts.

Since she did not like to start without her aunt's permission, Gardenia's mouth was watering by the time the Duchesse turned from the desk, having sealed her letter with a special little sponge kept in a gold and jewelled container.

She held it out to one of the footmen who was just leaving the room.

'Have this taken to the British Embassy at once,' she said. The man took it in his white-gloved hand and bowed his head in its powdered wig.

'Very good, your Grace.'

'And go at once,' the Duchesse said. 'There is to be no delay.'

'Very good, your Grace.'

Gardenia guessed to whom her aunt had been writing.

'Is that to Mr Cunningham?' she asked, a little nervously.

The Duchesse nodded.

'I told you I would answer your invitation for you, my child,' she said, 'and don't forget in the future to accept nothing unless you ask me first. It is very important, you understand?'

'Yes, Aunt Lily,' Gardenia said. 'But I don't think he meant anything wrong by inviting me.'

'Don't you?' the Duchesse queried. 'Well, let me give you some tea. Do you like milk and sugar? And help yourself to something to eat, you must be famished. I always have a real English tea and oh the trouble I have to teach these French chefs what I require! But now it is here I dare not touch a thing. I know it would put on pounds.'

Gardenia had no sooner finished her tea than the Duchesse sent her upstairs to rest. She was now not feeling tired and she stood for a long time in her bedroom admiring herself in the looking-glass. *Monsieur* Worth's words kept coming back to her. What had he meant by saying things like that? Was Paris such a wicked city that he really thought she might be spoilt by it? There was not much chance of that if she was going to be so strictly chaperoned by her aunt!

Gardenia felt disappointed that she was not to be allowed to go driving with Mr Cunningham in the *Bois*. It would be fun to sit on the high seat of his yellow dogcart and feel herself moving swiftly behind those high-stepping horses. But he had said he would see her the next day, and that meant that on Saturday night he would be coming to her aunt's party.

Tonight, Gardenia thought, he and perhaps Lord Hartcourt and all the other smart young men in Paris would be at Maxim's. It seemed unfair somehow that she was not allowed to go. She hummed to herself a tune from the *Merry Widow*. She wondered if she had brought the music amongst her other things, but even if she had not she could remember it. There was a piano in the grand Salon. She might go down and try to pick out the notes. It was such an appropriate song to sing when she was in Paris.

Her aunt was asleep; but since the Duchesse's windows faced a different way from those in the Salon there was no reason why she should hear the music if it was played very softly.

Gardenia opened the door to her bedroom. Everything was very quiet. She slipped down the stairs, opened the door of the Salon and went in. It had all been tidied and looked quite different from its appearance in the early morning. The green tables had been taken away, the carpets were down on the floor, elegant gilt-framed sofas and chairs were arranged in the conventional manner of any drawing-room. There were fresh flowers in the great vases which stood on the inlaid furniture and the evening sunshine coming through the window gave the room a warmth that had not been there before.

'I imagine things,' Gardenia told herself as she remembered her first impressions. She crossed the floor to the little anteroom in which the grand piano stood. It was open, and she sat down on the tapestry-covered stool and ran her fingers over the ivory keys.

It was a beautiful piano, and Gardenia, who loved music, started to play very, very softly one of Chopin's waltzes. Her father and mother had loved her music. Perhaps one day her aunt would also find it soothing. It would be something to offer her, some little gift in return for all her kindness—the beautiful clothes, the comfortable house, the excitement of meeting new people.

'I am grateful, terribly grateful,' Gardenia said aloud, 'and I am in Paris, the gayest city in the world.'

Music from the *Merry Widow* came flooding into her mind and she found she could remember every note, *'I'm going to Maxim's,'* she sang almost beneath her breath. Then a voice behind her said:

'And I hope I may be allowed to accompany you—whoever you may be.'

She swung round on the music-stool and saw a man standing looking at her. He was a tall, broad-shouldered man and she would have known his nationality even if she had not heard his voice. There was no mistaking the characteristics of his race in the harsh outlines of his hatchet-shaped face, his cropped hair and sabre-scarred cheeks. There was also something in the way he looked at her through an eye-glass with a faint smile on his thick lips which made Gardenia dislike him on sight.

'Who are you?' he asked in French with a guttural accent.

'I am Gardenia Weedon,' Gardenia replied, rising from the piano-stool. 'I am the Duchesse de Mabillon's niece.'

'Lily's niece, I don't believe it!' the man ejaculated in English.

'It happens to be the truth,' Gardenia said. 'May I ask your name?'

'I am Baron von Knesebech,' he replied, clicking his heels together, then unexpectedly taking her hand in his and raising it to his lips. 'I am delighted to make your acquaintance. Your aunt did not tell me that she had such a beautiful and accomplished niece.'

'I arrived very unexpectedly,' Gardenia said.

'And you are staying here?'

'Yes, I am staying.'

'Then that will be delightful,' the Baron said, 'for your aunt, of course.'

Gardenia realised he was still holding her hand. As she tried to take it away he raised it once again to his lips.

'We must be friends, you and I,' he said. 'I am a very old friend of your aunt's—a very dear friend, shall we say? We shall see a lot of each other, and so, little Gardenia, we two must get to know each other.'

His eyes seemed to flicker over her and there was something in the movement of his mouth which made Gardenia feel sick. She pulled again at her hand and he released it.

'I am afraid my aunt is resting now,' she said. 'Shall I tell her that you called?'

The twisted smile that he gave her was somehow insulting.

'Don't worry, little Gardenia,' he replied. 'I will tell her myself. You will be dining with us tonight? I will see you then.'

He clicked his heels together perfunctorily. It was more an instinctive reaction than that he wished to show her any politeness. Then he strolled away across the room and out through the door of the Salon.

Gardenia stood staring after him in perplexity. He was horrible, she thought. The sort of man she had always imagined the villain in every book she had ever read! And yet he was a great friend of Aunt Lily's and as such she must be nice to him. A great friend, indeed, when he could go upstairs, unannounced, to her boudoir when she was resting!

Five

Henriette Dupré picked up the emerald necklace and tried it against her white neck.

'How much?' she asked, in a voice she reserved for shopkeepers and servants, and which was very different from the soft, dulcet tones she used when speaking to her admirers.

'Ten thousand francs to Milord,' the shopkeeper replied. 'Seven-fifty for you, *Ma'm'selle.*'

'*C'est absurde.*' Henriette threw the necklace down on the dressing-table and rose from the low stool, her filmy, semi-transparent wrapper revealing the exquisite curves of her young body.

'Fifteen hundred francs!' she said.

'*Mais non, Ma'm'selle,*' the jeweller replied, spreading out his hands. 'That would leave me without profit. Seven hundred and fifty francs is fair. You will recall that I accommodated you over a bracelet. It was not worth my while to part with it.'

'Bah!' Henriette replied rudely. 'You are a rich man, *Monsieur* Fabian. You have made your money by taking huge profits and giving very little to those who bring you good business. Lord Hartcourt is rich and there are many, many important jewellers in Paris who would be only too pleased to find me a better necklace than this, and on far more advantageous terms to me.'

Monseiur Fabian, a small, grey-haired man, looked Henriette Dupré over shrewdly. He was used to dealing with the *demi-monde* and no one knew better than he how avaricious they were when it came to bargaining over their own commissions.

He suddenly decided he was bored with the eternal wrangling that every transaction entailed. Far better to sell something less spectacular to one of the nobility. The Duchess of Marlborough, for instance, only yesterday had bought a diamond ring without questioning the price. Of course, she was American, while *Ma'm'selle* Dupré was unmistakably and unforgettably of *Les Halles*.

'*Eh bien,*' he said. 'One thousand francs. *Ma'm'selle*—I can go no further. If Milord cuts the price, then naturally *Ma'm'selle* understands her commission will be cut accordingly. Even a jeweller has to live.'

'It would not be wise, *Monsieur* to quarrel with me,' Henriette said threateningly. 'I know that *Monsieur* Lucez would be very interested in obtaining my custom.'

Monsieur Fabian smiled. Picking up the necklace he started to arrange it in the pink leather case with its velvet lining.

'*Monsieur* Lucez is my cousin, *Ma'm'selle*. He also has had difficulty over the commissions of some of his favourite customers. We have therefore come to a little arrangement between us. The commission will be exactly the same, whether you buy from me or from any of my relatives.'

Henriette let out an oath of the back streets where she had been born.

'*Voyons, Monsieur,* you are a salesman,' she replied. 'Leave the necklace. I will see what his Lordship thinks of it.'

'*Ma'm'selle* is most kind,' *Monsieur* Fabian said. 'When his Lordship sees how greatly it becomes your exquisite skin, of which all Paris is talking, I have no doubt I shall receive his Lordship's cheque in due course. *Au revoir, Ma'm'selle.* As always, I am at your service.'

He bowed his way out of the room. Henriette made a little grimace and kicked a silk cushion, which was lying on the floor, in the direction of the door.

'*Cochon!* Parasite! Such vermin batten on one,' she grumbled. Then glancing at the necklace lying on her dressing-table in its open case, she smiled.

When Lord Hartcourt called he found his mistress lying on the satin-covered bed, wearing nothing except the magnificent emerald necklace which showed up the ivory whiteness of her skin . . .

It was some time later before the necklace was actually mentioned.

'What is this bauble?' Lord Hartcourt asked, touching one of the big stones with his finger, and lifting a glass of champagne which he held in his other hand to his lips.

'You like it?' Henriette asked. She had a habit of asking

a question and looking under her eyelashes as she did in a manner which was entrancingly provocative.

'Have you a partiality for emeralds?' Lord Hartcourt asked. 'I am quite prepared to admit they are becoming.'

'I love them,' Henriette said, and then with a sudden drop of her eyes, so that her lashes lay dark against her cheeks she murmured, 'but alas I cannot afford them.'

'They are expensive,' Lord Hartcourt commented a little drily.

'This, of course, is a bargain,' Henriette said quickly. 'It is supposed to have belonged to Marie Antoinette and to have been part of the jewels given by her Swedish lover. A gift of love, *mon brave.*' She leaned forward as she spoke, her lips very close to Lord Hartcourt, the exotic scent which perfumed her whole body seeming to envelop him. He touched the rounded column of her throat above the necklace.

'But still an expensive gift, Henriette,' he said. She pouted and drew back.

'Are you saying I am not worth it?' she asked. 'Are you bored with me? There are other men, men who are as rich and even as distinguished as you, but somehow ...' She paused.

'Go on,' Lord Hartcourt prompted, 'somehow what?'

'Somehow they don't make my heart beat any faster,' Henriette replied.

Again there was that provocative look from beneath her eyelashes. For a moment there was no answer and she pouted once again. She rose on her feet and walked across to the dressing-table. Every movement was one of grace. Her body was lean and lovely as that of a young tigress. She stood staring at herself in the mirror, noting how the emeralds accentuated not only her white skin but the vivid red of her hair. She put up her arms and as she pulled out the hairpins the long red tresses fell over her shoulders, down past her waist.

Lying against the pillows with a cynical expression on his face, Lord Hartcourt watched her. Then he said quietly:

'Your methods are very primitive, my dear Henriette. Very well, you can have the necklace.'

'I may?' The sulky expression vanished from her face. She turned and stood for a moment poised with her arms outstretched and ran towards him, a flashing, mercurial beauty of white and red and green. He felt her lips, the soft silk of her hair and her hands caress him.

'*Tu es charmant. Merci mille fois!* I am so happy, so very, very, happy!'

Driving back to the Embassy a little later, Lord Hartcourt reflected how very easy it was to give pleasure when it was only a question of money. His friends would doubtless condemn him for being an extravagant fool and envy him because he possessed the most glamorous and most talked of *demi-mondaine* in the whole of Paris. He wondered why in these circumstances he always felt slightly depressed when he left Henriette. She amused him, she made herself extremely charming, and she was in every way what a mistress should be, excitingly and unceasingly attractive. Why then, he wondered, did he often feel there was something missing? Something that should be there in their relationship but which was not.

There had been a great many women in his life, but no one quite as satisfactory as Henriette. Granted she was, as regards her profession, in a class of her own. He knew that she spoke the truth when she said there were other men only too willing to step into his shoes should their liaison come to an end. As far as Lord Hartcourt could see, there was no risk that it would: he had given her a very charming house, a car, a number of servants to wait on her; he paid bills that were out of all proportion to what any other man would have expected to spend on his mistress, and he paid them without grumbling. He had also provided her with some very fine jewellery.

The *demi-mondaines* had, as Bertie had said, become more and more demanding of those to whom they granted their favours. But Henriette, unlike some of the others, at least expressed her gratitude, and, though her demands were exorbitant, she made them with a finesse which took the sting out of the transaction. At the same time Lord Hartcourt knew he was not satisfied. What did he want? he asked himself.

The car turned into the Champs Elysées and he looked with an almost jaundiced eye at the elegance of those still sitting under the chestnut trees even though the period of *cinq-à-sept* was over and soon it would be time for dinner.

What do I want? he asked himself again. He felt bored

71

because he had promised after he had dined with the Ambassador to collect Henriette and take her to Maxim's. Friday night at Maxim's was becoming too much of a habit. The magic and excitement paled a little when one knew one would see the same faces, hear the same laughter, eat the same food, and listen to the same jokes.

'In fact, I am feeling bloody-minded about the whole thing!' Lord Hartcourt told himself.

He stepped out of the car and walked up the broad marble steps of the British Embassy.

'Mr Cunningham is waiting to see your Lordship,' the butler told him.

'Where is he?' Lord Hartcourt asked.

'Mr Cunningham went up to your Lordship's room.'

'Very good,' Lord Hartcourt said. 'What time is dinner, Jarvis?'

'At eight o'clock, m'Lord. You have exactly forty minutes.'

'Thank you,' Lord Hartcourt said. 'Are we wearing decorations tonight?'

'The Sultan of Morocco will be dining, my Lord. I have instructed your valet that decorations are required.'

'Thank you,' Lord Hartcourt said.

It was an unnecessary conversation he thought, as he climbed the stairs towards his own suite of rooms. His valet had been with him five years now and seldom made a mistake. He opened the door of his sitting-room and found Bertram lying on the sofa, with his feet on another chair, reading the English newspapers.

'Hello, Vane,' he said making no effort to rise. 'I want to see you.'

'I don't want to see you,' his cousin answered. 'I want a bath, and there is an official dinner tonight, so I have got to be downstairs at ten minutes to eight at the latest.'

'You have got time,' Bertie answered. 'I wanted to show you this.'

He got to his feet and drew a letter from his pocket.

'Read it, my dear fellow,' Lord Hartcourt said, opening the door into his bedroom. 'I dare not be late. Sir James has a stroke if we are all not grouped about like unnecessary pieces of furniture by the time the first guests arrive. What does it say, and who is it from?'

Bertram followed him into his bedroom and perched himself on the edge of the bed.

'It's from the Duchesse,' he said, 'and if you can tell me what it means I'll be very grateful. I'm damned if I can understand it.'

'Read it,' Lord Hartcourt commanded. He took off his coat as he spoke and handed it to his valet. He began to untie his tie.

Holding the letter almost at arm's length, Bertram complied with his cousin's request:

'Dear Mr Cunningham, I understand from my niece that you have kindly asked us to drive with you in the Bois tomorrow morning. I regret that, as my niece has only just arrived, we cannot accept your kind invitation. I hope, however, to see you tomorrow evening and that your cousin, Lord Hartcourt, will accompany you. Yours very sincerely, Lily de Mabillon.'

Bertram finished reading and throwing down the letter on the bed looked at his cousin.

'What the hell do you make of that?' he asked.

'It seemed quite an ordinary refusal to me,' Lord Hartcourt remarked.

'Ordinary!' Bertram ejaculated. 'From Lily de Mabillon! You realise she's saying that the girl ought to be chaperoned and I had no right to invite her to drive with me in the *Bois*. Lily de Mabillon, I ask you! And what's her little game? She can't keep the girl locked up; and, even if she does, nobody is going to believe that she is anything but Lily's niece.'

'After that quite incoherent statement,' Lord Hartcourt said, 'I imagine you are suggesting that the Duchesse should have welcomed you with open arms. My dear Bertram, she obviously has ideas for her niece: Marquises, Earls, Barons or Counts. They all take precedence over a mere Honourable who, as Lily knows only too well, is often rather short of ready cash.'

'You think it's money, do you?' Bertram asked.

'Well, I imagine so,' Lord Hartcourt said. 'After all, she would want the best for her niece. It's natural.'

'Damn it all, Vane, if you tell me I am not good enough for Lily de Mabillon's niece I really shall be offended!' Bertram expostulated. 'I may not be a Croesus when it comes to money, but I am a damned sight better than those ghastly creatures she has hanging round the gaming-tables.'

'Perhaps that is why she doesn't want odds and bods hanging round her niece,' Lord Hartcourt suggested.

'I think you are really being insulting,' Bertram said hotly. 'You are certainly not explaining the letter. You'd think she would be glad for the girl to get an invitation as soon as she arrived in Paris.'

'She will get plenty of invitations,' Lord Hartcourt said, 'especially when the Duchesse has dressed her up.'

Bertram let out an exclamation.

'That reminds me,' he said. 'I had something else to tell you, but you put it out of my head. What do you think is the latest rumour?'

'I seldom give credit to rumours of any sort,' Lord Hartcourt said in a bored voice.

His valet helped him into a dressing-gown and he turned towards the bathroom.

'No, wait. You must listen to this,' Bertram said. 'Two people have told me about it already. I am quite certain it is true.'

'Well, what is it?' Lord Hartcourt asked impatiently.

'They say,' Bertram said eagerly, 'that Lily took her niece to Worth's this afternoon and she was wearing nothing, nothing mark you, except a chinchilla cape worth millions of francs. She begged Worth to dress the girl, telling him that unless he did so, she had nothing, literally nothing, to wear.'

'I can guess who told you that,' Lord Hartcourt said. 'It is so obviously feminine.'

He walked from the bedroom as he spoke and shut the door of the bathroom firmly behind him.

'Damn it all, Vane, you can't go just like that!' Bertram expostulated. 'Do you think it's true?'

He went to the bathroom door and shouted:

'Do you think it's true, Vane? Everybody in Paris is going to say it is, aren't they?'

'I haven't the slightest idea,' Lord Hartcourt replied through the door. 'Go and dress for dinner, Bertie. If your little English sparrow goes out anywhere tonight she will be at Maxim's.'

'By Jove, so she will!' Bertram exclaimed with satisfaction. 'Thank you, Vane, I will see you later.'

There was a roar of rushing water behind the door which told him that his cousin could not hear him.

'Good night, Hickson,' he said to the valet who was tidying Lord Hartcourt's things.

'Good night, Sir,' the valet said respectfully; but when Bertie was out of hearing, Hickson muttered to himself: 'Women, they're all the same, women. They always cost a man more than he can afford.'

He glanced wistfully as he spoke at a pile of golden sovereigns which Lord Hartcourt had emptied out of his pocket on to the dressing-table. The French girl he had been taking around was costing Hickson far more than he could spare out of his wages. For two weeks he had missed sending a money order back to his mother and he felt bitterly ashamed of himself. There was something about the French girls, he thought, that got into your blood and under your skin and you just couldn't resist them.

Hickson stacked the little pile of sovereigns neatly and knew that he would never touch a farthing of Lord Hartcourt's money, however tempted he might be. At the same time, he wondered if he dared ask for a rise. He knew that the little he sent his mother made all the difference to her comfort, and yet he just could not resist that fascinating broken accent and the greedy little hand which seemed always to be held out for something.

The Embassy dinner was identical with every dinner which took place in the large panelled dining-room, with a footman behind every chair, the great golden ornaments and heavy chandelier interspersed with orchids and smilax.

Lord Hartcourt found himself seated next to the beautiful Countess of Warwick, who regaled him with titbits about the Court in England. She interspersed these with her revolutionary ideas on socialism, a creed which she had espoused much to the horror of her friends.

'How is his Majesty?' Lord Hartcourt asked.

'Getting plumper and at times very irascible,' Lady Warwick answered, but he still has an eye for the ladies, as Paris found last year. Mrs. Keppel keeps him amused. In fact, he goes nowhere without her. But, although he has aged, he still notices a pretty face.'

Lady Warwick, who had been one of the greatest beauties of her day, gave a little sigh.

'We are all getting older,' she said. 'It is very depressing. Make the most of your youth, dear Lord Hartcourt, it is something you can never have twice.'

'You will always be beautiful,' Lord Hartcourt said in the tone of a man who states a fact, rather than pays a compliment.

She smiled at him, a gracious, unembarrassed smile of a woman who has been fêted for many years.

'Thank you,' she said. 'And who are you in love with at the moment?'

'Nobody,' Lord Hartcourt answered truthfully.

'But what a waste of time!' Lady Warwick exclaimed. 'Men should always be in love, more in love than the women they court. It is the only way to preserve the balance of the sexes.'

'I must believe you as you speak from experience,' Lord Hartcourt said, his eyes twinkling.

Lady Warwick laughed.

'So much experience,' she said, 'that some day I must write a book. It is becoming the fashion. I shall put you in my book, Lord Hartcourt, as a very difficult and rather dangerous young man.'

Lord Hartcourt raised his eyebrows.

'Dangerous?' he questioned.

'Yes,' Lady Warwick answered. 'Because you are so reserved and controlled you will make women fall in love with you while you keep yourself severely in check. Then it is inevitable that their hearts will be broken.'

Lord Hartcourt's expression seemed to darken.

'I am afraid your Ladyship has a very poor opinion of me,' he said.

His voice was harsh, and Lady Warwick, who had been speaking lightly, was startled. Then, at the back of her mind, she remembered a whisper that someone, some great beauty older than himself, had treated Lord Hartcourt rather harshly when he was very young: she had led him on, enslaved him, and then cast him aside for someone more important—a Royal personage whom she had felt to be a more desirable and more important catch than the somewhat callow youth.

'So he has never forgotten,' Lady Warwick thought to herself. 'The wound still hurts. Perhaps that is why he looks so cynical.' Aloud she said:

'I am teasing you and you must forgive me. I am sure

76

you are always a model of kindness and consideration to the weaker sex.'

'That sounds infernally dull!' Lord Hartcourt retorted. 'I am afraid the references you are giving me are not particularly good ones.'

'If you will come and stay at Warwick when you are next in England I promise you that my assessment of your character will be couched in most glowing terms,' Lady Warwick smiled.

'I accept willingly,' Lord Hartcourt replied. 'I am told the pheasants are going to be particularly good this year.'

'You shall come when the King comes,' Lady Warwick said. 'You know how much he enjoys a good shoot.'

Lord Hartcourt thanked her, making a resolution at the same time that nothing would induce him to go to one of the huge pheasant slaughters which amused King Edward, but which many sportsmen found almost too much of a good thing.

It was a relief when dinner had come to an end and the Ambassadress was signalling to the ladies so that they could leave the gentlemen alone. Knowing that his job would be to talk to the Sultan, he moved his chair accordingly and poured himself out another glass of port.

The evening dragged on. When the gentlemen joined the ladies a singer from the Opera House regaled them with excerpts from *Carmen*.

Lord Hartcourt was relieved when the Sultan rose to go. He accompanied him to his motor-car and when he finally went back into the drawing-room he found the Ambassador yawning behind his hand.

'I think we did a good job tonight, Hartcourt,' he said.

'I hope so, your Excellency,' Lord Hartcourt replied.

'I think I managed to explain the English point of view very much more clearly than our pompous politicians had managed to do,' the Ambassador commented. 'Anyway, we shall wait and see results.'

'Yes indeed, your Excellency,' Lord Hartcourt said, not having much idea of what the Ambassador was talking about. He really had not followed the very intricate letters exchanged between Morocco and England.

'Well, good night,' the Ambassador said. 'I expect you are going out, Hartcourt—Maxim's, isn't it, on a Friday?'

'Yes, your Excellency.'

'Thank God I am too old for all that junketing,' the

Ambassador said. 'We've got the Germans to lunch to-morrow; if I don't have a good night's sleep I shall lose my temper with them and that would be fatal.'

'It would indeed, your Excellency,' Lord Hartcourt said, and this time he knew in every detail how much depended on tomorrow's lunch.

'Well, good night, Hartcourt. Enjoy yourself,' the Ambassador said, and Lord Hartcourt was free to take off his decorations and hand them to Jarvis. He picked up his top-hat, gloves and cane and stepped into the waiting motor-car which would carry him to Maxim's.

Henriette had sent him a message just before he went in to dinner to say she would meet him at Maxim's. He had smiled over the note, written in her somewhat illiterate hand and heavily scented with her favourite perfume. He knew only too well why Henriette wished to get to Maxim's before he did. She would tell him it was to save him trouble, but he knew it was really because she wished to show friends the emerald necklace and receive all their envious exclamations before he arrived.

He wondered to himself as the car carried him towards the Rue de Madeleine whether Henriette's friends thought him a fool or a benefactor. He was quite aware that had he raised his finger any one of them would have been only too willing to change places with Henriette. He was not so modest as not to apprise his own worth. There were many rich men in Paris, but the majority of them were not young, presentable and titled. What was more, a large number were married, and a wife always meant complications. It was unlikely that those of the social world and the *demi-mondaine* would ever come into contact, but there was always the feeling, or so Henriette once told him in an expansive moment, that the wife was an enemy working to destroy her husband's *chère amie*.

'It gives you, how shall I say it,' Henriette had gone on, 'a sinister feeling, as if someone is standing behind you with a knife, and knowing that she is praying always that you will have bad luck. It is so much more enjoyable that you are a bachelor.'

'It is time I settled down,' Lord Hartcourt had replied. 'I have a big house in England, a rich estate, and sooner or later I have got to provide an heir.'

'Do you think I would look pretty in a coronet?' Henriette had asked. 'You should marry me and find out.'

She had not been serious, and they had both laughed at the suggestion. The French *demi-mondaine* knew her place, and seldom, if ever, encroached on what was reserved exclusively for wives.

Now, annoyingly, it seemed to Lord Hartcourt, this conversation came back to him. An heir! Yes, he would have to be thinking of one very soon. His heart sank at the thought of the débutantes and the mamas who haunted the London ballrooms, and somehow, deep in his heart, he knew that Henriette was right when she said that it was tiresome to have a married protector. Married men should stay at home with their wives, but God knew he would find that boring enough with the type of girl he had encountered so far.

'What is wrong with me? Why am I being so serious tonight?' Lord Hartcourt asked himself. He knew that if he was honest he was not looking forward either to Maxim's or even to the pleasure of seeing Henriette sporting the emerald necklace which was costing him so much money.

The first person he found in Maxim's was his cousin Bertie, propping the bar and looking depressed.

'She has not come,' he told Lord Hartcourt.

Lord Hartcourt looked round the room as if he thought that Bertie must have overlooked the obvious.

'Surely that is the Duchesse over there?' he asked, seeing a large, noisy party in the corner and thinking it was impossible to miss seeing Lily de Mabillon with her faded blonde beauty, her spectacular jewellery, and Baron von Knesebech, with his sinister features, seated beside her.

'All the old gang. No little Gardenia!' Bertram said plaintively.

'I suppose the Duchesse has locked her up in her room to keep her away from just such wolves as you,' Lord Hartcourt teased. As he spoke he saw Henriette threading her way through the crowds towards him. She was looking beautiful, he noted with satisfaction. The white chiffon dress she wore showed off the emerald necklace to perfection, and there was a great osprey plume in her red hair and a fan of the same feathers in her hand.

'What can I do?' Bertie asked. 'You might help a fellow, Vane.'

Lord Hartcourt felt suddenly sorry for his cousin.

79

'Look after Henriette for a moment,' he said. 'I will go and find out what I can.'

He walked across the room and approaching Lily de Mabillon's table bent over her chair.

'May I thank you for a delightful party last night?' he asked.

The Duchesse looked round and gave a little cry of pleasure.

'Oh, Lord Hartcourt, how sweet of you. But I ought to thank you. I hear you were very kind to my little niece when she arrived unexpectedly in the middle of the night.'

'It was a pleasure to do what I could,' Lord Hartcourt said. 'I hope she is rested after her long journey.'

'Gardenia is much better today,' the Duchesse said. 'But of course she could not come here with me tonight. You do understand, it would not be *comme il faut pour une jeune fille.*'

Lord Hartcourt was too surprised to say anything, and after a moment the Duchesse went on:

'But you must come and see us and she must thank you herself for all you did. What about tea-time tomorrow? I promise you an English tea. I always have one myself.'

'I was thinking perhaps I might accept your kind invitation for the evening,' Lord Hartcourt said slowly.

'Of course I am expecting you then,' the Duchesse said, 'the evening would not be complete without you; but come to tea, quietly, just with Gardenia and myself, and we can talk about England. I am feeling homesick and I am afraid Gardenia will be too. At four-thirty—I shall be very disappointed if we wait for you in vain.'

She held out her hand and Lord Hartcourt knew himself dismissed. At the same time he was left in a state of bewilderment. Then it suddenly seemed to him that he saw the light! The Duchesse wanted the very best for her niece, and who better than himself?

Six

Gardenia decided that she disliked the Baron. She had the feeling that he was secretly amused by everything she said, and she loathed the manner in which he took her by the arm and paid her fulsome compliments with a note of insincerity in his voice.

But there was no doubt at all that Aunt Lily was delighted with him. Whenever he arrived she would run towards him with the eagerness of a young girl. She agreed with everything he said and kept looking at him in what Gardenia could only describe to herself as a peculiar way.

Of course, Gardenia told herself, Aunt Lily was old and she could therefore be friendly towards a man without it appearing fast or reprehensible as it might in anyone younger. At the same time, it did seem odd that the Baron should have so much freedom in the house. In fact this evening, for instance, Gardenia could not help feeling that he behaved in many ways as though he were the host.

It had all started when she had come down to dinner in the new gown which had been delivered from Worth's. It had arrived exactly an hour before dinner was due to start. Gardenia had been agitated and apprehensive that it was going to be late, that she would have nothing to wear and would therefore have to stay in her bedroom. When at last the box had been carried to her in triumph by Jeanne, she gave a cry of sheer relief.

'*Mon Dieu, c'est magnifique!*' Jeanne exclaimed as she opened the white tissue-paper to reveal a dress of white chiffon, skilfully embroidered with tiny diamond drops.

The two girls lifted it on to the bed. For the moment Gardenia just stood staring at it. She had never dreamt in all her life that she would ever own anything so lovely or so expensive. She could not help a sudden pang as she realised that even a hundredth part of what this dress had cost would have made all the difference to those last few months of poverty when she had had the greatest difficulty in procuring food for her mother.

Yet she was not bitter. She could so well understand how their difficulties had been forgotten by Aunt Lily, or, indeed, had never been understood by her. At the same time, she felt almost guilty now in allowing so much money to be spent on mere ornamentation. But what was the point of repining? She knew only too well that her mother would have been thrilled for her to have the opportunity of being in Paris, of wearing lovely clothes. At the same time, Gardenia could not help feeling that her mother would have been a little surprised at what she could only describe as Aunt Lily's way of life.

Yet, for the moment, nothing had mattered except that she should be dressed in time for dinner. Jeanne had done her hair and she looked very different from the shabby country girl who had left London. Jeanne had her instructions from Aunt Lily, who had taken them from *Monsieur* Worth himself, as to how her hair should be done. Instead of being frizzed and curled and built up on her head in the fashionable *Merry Widow* style, it was waved softly back from her forehead into a big coil which reached from the top of her head to the nape of her neck. It was a distinguished style and at the same time it made her look very young.

At first Gardenia wondered if she would not appear strange and old-fashioned; but when the dress was finally fastened it revealed the perfect curves of her breast and accentuated her tiny waist. *Monsieur* Worth had known what he was about: the whole effect was youthful, ethereal and at the same time subtly provocative.

'It is exquisite, *Ma'm'selle*,' Jeanne was murmuring in French, and Gardenia knew that the compliment was not flattering but completely sincere.

'All the men will be looking at you tonight,' the maid went on.

'I'm afraid I shan't know anybody,' Gardenia said.

'That won't matter. They soon get themselves introduced in this house,' Jeanne said, giving her a little sideways glance.

'I am sure my aunt will introduce me to the people she wants me to know,' Gardenia said, rebuking what she thought was a slight impertinence on Jeanne's part.

'Many won't wait!' the maid added irrepressibly.

Gardenia twirled herself round in front of the long mahogany-framed swing-mirror. The dress shimmered round her feet and the light caught the tiny drops of diamanté. It made her feel as if she were covered in dewdrops.

Now ready, she walked very slowly down the stairs to the small drawing-room on the ground floor where she knew her aunt was planning to receive the dinner guests.

As she reached the foot of the stairs, she saw the door of the drawing-room was open and heard voices. There was no doubt who was speaking. The deep, guttural tones of the Baron were unmistakable.

'This is ridiculous,' Gardenia heard him say angrily. 'You cannot expect a chit of that age to alter everything.'

'Not everything, Heinrich,' Aunt Lily replied. 'I just meant that we should be a little careful. She is very young.'

'Too young,' the Baron said. 'If you take my advice, you'll send her away.'

'No, Heinrich. I cannot do that. I loved my sister and the child came to me. I can't turn her away.'

'Very well then, she must put up with things as they are. No more dinner parties like this one or I warn you I won't come.'

'I'm sorry, Heinrich. I'm sorry.' Her aunt's apology was almost tearful and Gardenia realised she was eavesdropping.

Softly, hoping no one had heard her descending the stairs, she ran back up to the first floor to stand trembling, her hands locked together. What could that conversation mean? What was she disrupting, and why should the Baron so dislike her arrival? What right had he to interfere? He had seemed pleasant enough when he had arrived at five o'clock and gone up to Aunt Lily's boudoir as he had done the night before.

What was it they talked about? And why did he call so early in the afternoon and then return for dinner? They were questions to which Gardenia had no answer, and now realising it was nearly eight o'clock, she descended the stairs again, striving to compose herself and determined that none of her agitation and embarrassment should show on her face.

Fortunately, several guests arrived just as she reached the drawing-room. There was no time to say anything

83

except to listen to Aunt Lily's exclamations of delight over her dress.

'She looks charming, doesn't she, Baron?' she said in what was almost a pleading tone, and Gardenia realised that, while she had addressed the Baron by his christian name in private, in public she was correctly formal.

'Charming indeed,' the Baron said with one of his leering smiles, and Gardenia longed to throw his compliment back in his face.

More guests arrived, the men young, the majority of them English. There were, however, several Frenchmen and one vivacious Italian who Gardenia learned was a newcomer to the Embassy of his country.

The ladies were surprising: most of them were nearly the same age as Aunt Lily. The few young ones that there were seemed to be attached each to one particular man and not interested in talking to anyone else. The Baron, who had been given one of Aunt Lily's contemporaries to take in to dinner, was scowling, and Gardenia noticed as they reached the dining-room that Aunt Lily was talking rather too quickly and with an obvious pretence at brightness and gaiety.

Gardenia, however, was so preoccupied with seeing the table covered with gold ornaments, admiring the profusion of purple orchids which were laid between the dishes, and being overawed at eating for the first time off silver plate, that it was some time before she could look around her.

When she did she saw the Baron still had a disagreeable look on his face, but the rest of the party was brightening up considerably. The men all seemed at their ease, elegant in their high, stiff white collars, tail-coats and the red carnations which only the Englishmen sported in their buttonholes.

The ladies were laughing loudly and, in Gardenia's mind, rather noisily. She could not imagine her mother or any of her friends throwing back their heads in an almost abandoned manner at some joke, or leaning forward, their elbows on the table, which revealed an almost indecent amount of their snowy-white bosoms. But, of course, the majority of the women were French, and that, Gardenia told herself, accounted for a great deal.

She had an elderly man at one side of her at dinner and on the other side the young Italian from the Embassy. Her elderly partner obviously had no intention of exerting himself by talking to her until he had eaten a great deal and drunk even more. She made two or three tentative remarks to him, only to be received with grunts or a bare monosyllable in reply. He was rude, she thought to herself. He obviously considered her of no importance and was, therefore, determined to make no effort.

The Italian on the other side was all smiles and chatter.

'You are beautiful, very beautiful,' he told Gardenia. 'I did not expect to find so much beauty in Paris. Chic, elegance, yes! But not the beauty of a goddess.'

Gardenia laughed.

'I don't think you can have been here very long,' she said. 'I'm sure there are thousands of French women that you will be able to say that to in a week or so.'

He shook his head.

'The French are Latin, like my own countrymen,' he said. 'They are dark, very attractive and sometimes have the beauty of a madonna, but you, with your fair hair and white dress, you look like an angel!'

Gardenia laughed again. She could not take this young man seriously and therefore she was not embarrassed. He only amused her.

'At the moment I have no desire to be an angel,' she said. 'I want to enjoy Paris, I want to see it all, the beautiful buildings, the Seine, the parks and all the gay places too.'

'And you will let me be your escort?' the Italian asked.

'You will have to ask Aunt Lily,' Gardenia told him, and saw a look of surprise in his eyes.

'Can't you go anywhere, do anything that you like?' he enquired.

'Not without asking my aunt!' Gardenia exclaimed. 'You see, I am living with her. My mother and father are dead and naturally she is rather strict as to what I do and where I go.'

Now there was no mistaking the look of almost astonishment on the Italian's face.

'I do not understand,' he said, 'but I will speak to your aunt. She is really your aunt?'

'But, of course she is,' Gardenia said. 'What did you think she was?'

The Italian did not answer, but she had the impression that he could have told her what he had thought had he wished to do so.

As dinner drew to an end, the guests seemed to get noisier and noisier. The footmen in their gorgeous uniforms and powdered wigs were filling up the glasses as soon as they became empty, and now at last the Baron began to mellow a little and from the end of the table he raised his glass towards the Duchesse.

'To our charming hostess,' he said. 'I think that is a toast on which we would all agree, gentlemen.'

The gentlemen in question rose a little unsteadily to their feet.

'*La Duchesse,* God bless her,' they chanted, and swallowed the wine in their glasses in one gulp.

'Thank you,' Aunt Lily smiled. Gardenia noticed that now her face was flushed she looked younger and really remarkably beautiful. 'Thank you, and I hope you all have a good time tonight. A lot of friends will be coming in later and I hope that besides gambling some of you will dance. My niece is young. I know she will enjoy the music of Ventura's band.'

Aunt Lily rose as she spoke and started to shepherd the ladies out of the dining-room, but Gardenia heard the disagreeable man on her right murmur as she left:

'Ventura's band indeed! Flying a bit high, isn't she? I thought he only played for Royalty and embassies.'

A woman passing his chair heard what he said. Stopping, she bent down to murmur in his ear:

'Why should you complain? Have you not heard Lily de Mabillon is known as the Queen of *demi-Paris?*'

The old man gave a cackle of laughter which Gardenia could not help feeling was meant unkindly. But there was nothing she could say and, indeed, she did not understand what the woman had meant.

By this time her aunt had reached the door of the dining-room and the ladies were crowding out after her. Only one was left behind on the other side of the table. Before she moved she put up a long white arm, drew the head of the man sitting beside her down towards her own and kissed him passionately on the lips.

Gardenia stared in amazement. She had never imagined any lady would do such a thing at a dinner party or, indeed, anywhere where she might be seen.

The handsome young man sprawling back in his chair was apparently quite unperturbed by the kiss. He merely slapped the young woman on her behind as she moved away from him, swinging her hips as she did so, and Gardenia saw that her flame-red dress was cut daringly low both at the front and at the back.

'What would Mama have said?' Gardenia could not help the question springing once more to her mind as she followed the women upstairs to the bedrooms a little apprehensive as to what they might say and do. But Aunt Lily gave her no chance for conversation with any of them.

'Go and tidy yourself in your own room, Gardenia,' she said crisply, 'and then when you are ready come to mine.'

Gardenia could only obey her.

The men did not linger long in the dining-room—indeed, not as long as her father had done when they had had a dinner party at home—and soon the big Salon was filling up as more and more people arrived to shake Aunt Lily by the hand and then to rush, it seemed to Gardenia, towards the green-baize gaming tables.

The band was playing softly in the ante-room. The room itself, to Gardenia's surprise, had been almost transformed since she had seen it earlier in the day. There were fresh flowers everywhere, great garlands decorated the walls and the ceilings had been ornamented with tiny starlike lights which made the whole place mysterious and romantic. But nobody seemed interested and nobody listened to the superlatively good music which came from a dozen violins.

Gardenia thought that the Italian was certain to ask her to dance. But by the time she came down from her bedroom he was whispering in a corner with a very attractive woman who had come in after dinner wearing a skin-tight dress of black net and a diamond aigrette in her red hair.

'You are to stand beside me and help receive the guests,' Aunt Lily said. But she often made no effort to introduce a newcomer, and just waved him away towards the tables or the long bar at the end of the room where there were champagne and caviar.

Finally, when it seemed to Gardenia that they had been standing a long time, she saw a face she knew and realised that Lord Hartcourt, accompanied by his cousin, Bertram Cunningham, had just reached the top of the stairs.

She was glad to see them. Here were two people who

were not complete strangers, and also, woman-like, she wanted them to see her in her new gown.

Aunt Lily held out both white-gloved hands.

'Oh, Lord Hartcourt, how delighted I am to see you! I was very, very disappointed that you could not have tea with us this afternoon.'

'So was I,' Lord Hartcourt replied, 'but as I told you in my note, which I hope you received, I had work to do and could not get away from the Embassy.'

'You take life far too seriously,' Aunt Lily smiled. 'And how are you, Mr Cunningham? How nice of you to come.'

She put her hand on his arm and, while Lord Hartcourt was shaking hands with Gardenia, she said:

'Gardenia has been very good and helped me receive the guests. Do dance with her, Lord Hartcourt. Ventura will never forgive me if no one appears to appreciate his exquisite music. And you, Mr Cunningham, will you be so gracious as to give me a drink? My throat is quite dry.'

There was nothing either of the men could do but acquiesce in Aunt Lily's requests.

'Of course, let us dance,' Lord Hartcourt said in his serious voice to Gardenia, as Bertie Cunningham escorted his hostess to the bar at the end of the Salon.

As Lord Hartcourt put his arm round Gardenia's waist, she said a little nervously:

'I do hope I shan't tread on your toes. My mother taught me, but I haven't often danced with men. You must excuse me if I am clumsy.'

'I'm sure you could never be anything of the sort,' Lord Hartcourt said.

She found he was right and that as he danced simply and without any great pretensions she could follow him easily and they moved smoothly and rhythmically together.

'What a wonderful band!' Gardenia exclaimed. 'I never knew that dance music could sound so beautiful.'

After they had moved round the room several times Lord Hartcourt said:

'It's hot in here, isn't it? The scent of so many flowers is pretty overpowering. Why don't we go on to the balcony for a breath of fresh air?'

'Yes, of course,' Gardenia agreed, seeing the long windows opening out on to a wide balcony which ran along the back of the house.

They moved outside. There was a breath of wind and Lord Hartcourt turned his face towards it, saying:

'That's better. The French always keep their houses too hot.'

'But Aunt Lily is English,' Gardenia protested.

'So she is!' Lord Hartcourt exclaimed. 'I'm afraid I often forget and think she is French because she has a French title.'

'Of course,' Gardenia said.

She put her gloved hands on the balcony and looked out over the garden below them. The leaves of the trees were just stirring in the wind and behind them she could see the lights of Paris.

'Are you enjoying yourself?' Lord Hartcourt asked.

'It is all very exciting and quite different from what I expected,' Gardenia answered truthfully.

'You are looking different,' Lord Hartcourt said, also leaning against the balustrade and looking down at her. 'I suppose it is your dress. It is very unlike the one in which you arrived.'

'Aunt Lily has been so kind,' Gardenia told him. 'She took me to Worth's.'

'Yes, I heard she had,' Lord Hartcourt said.

'Fancy, he made this for me in twenty-four hours!' Gardenia went on. 'It seems incredible, doesn't it?'

'He must have liked you,' Lord Hartcourt said. 'I am told *Monsieur* Worth will never make for anyone in a hurry unless he likes them and thinks they will be a credit to his creations.'

Gardenia looked up at him with a little smile.

'And am I a credit?' she asked.

She felt almost coquettish as she spoke. Having watched the women at dinner, she felt that her stiffness and reserve were out of keeping in this strange atmosphere.

'You look delightful,' Lord Hartcourt replied. 'Are you going to be kind to Mr Cunningham?'

It was not what Gardenia had expected him to say. She looked at him with an expression of perplexity in her eyes.

'Kind to Mr Cunningham?' she echoed. 'I don't quite know what you mean.'

'I think you do,' Lord Hartcourt answered, 'but your aunt seems determined that he shall not get near you.'

'Aunt Lily would not allow me to go driving alone with him,' Gardenia said. 'That was because she said it was not done. It is my fault, I suppose, for even suggesting it, but I imagined things were different in Paris from what they are in England.'

'I think you know that that sort of thing is only pretence,' Lord Hartcourt replied. 'My cousin is very anxious indeed to be your friend. He is a nice boy—kind and generous. I don't think you would regret letting him be the first person to show you Paris.'

'Everybody seems to want to do that,' Gardenia said simply, and she thought that, although it might have been her imagination, Lord Hartcourt's face hardened.

'So poor old Bertie already has a rival, has he?' he asked. Gardenia did not understand.

'I expect the truth is,' she said, 'that Aunt Lily wants to show me Paris herself. I couldn't help thinking tonight that it was sad she had never had any children of her own. If she had had a daughter or son it would have been such fun for her. It must be amusing to give parties for one's friends, but much more enjoyable to give them for one's own family.'

Lord Hartcourt said nothing and after a moment she turned her head to look up at him, her eyes very wide in her small face. He looked down at her; then after a moment he reached out his hand, took her chin between his fingers and turned her face even further up to his.

'Are you a fool or really as innocent as you sound?' he asked.

Gardenia wanted to answer him back and tell him that she resented being called a fool; but instead something in the expression in his eyes which she could see quite clearly in the light of the windows made her catch her breath. They just stood looking at each other. She could feel the warm strength of his fingers on her chin and somehow, unexpectedly, it made her tremble.

Then a voice from the window made them both start.

'Ah! Here you are!' Bertram Cunningham exclaimed. 'I've been looking for you everywhere. I couldn't think where you had got to.'

'It's too hot to dance,' Lord Hartcourt said, taking his hand away from Gardenia's chin and turning to face his cousin.

'I don't mind the heat if I'm enjoying myself,' Bertram

90

Cunningham answered. 'Come and dance with me, Miss Weedon. One doesn't often have as good a band as this at Mabillon House.'

'I would like to,' Gardenia answered, 'but it seems rather rude to leave Lord Hartcourt here all alone.'

'Don't worry about him,' Bertram laughed. 'He'll find someone to cheer him up, that is if he stays, which I very much doubt.'

'Now don't push me, Bertie,' Lord Hartcourt said. 'You begged me to come with you tonight and I certainly don't intend to go jaunting off just because you've got Miss Weedon to yourself.'

'Don't let us go and dance for the moment.' Gardenia pleaded. 'Let us stay here and talk. It is so cool and the lights of Paris are the loveliest things I have ever seen. I feel frightened when I get amongst Aunt Lily's guests: they are so noisy!'

Gardenia remembered as she spoke what it had been like the night she had arrived, and she felt herself shudder a little. If it was going to be like that tonight she would go up to bed and lock herself in her room.

'Miss Weedon's right, you know,' Bertie said. 'It is certain to be rough here a little later on. I saw André de Grenelle arrive just now and he is pretty bosky already.'

'What does "bosky" mean?' Gardenia enquired. She spoke to Lord Hartcourt, but Bertram Cunningham answered her.

'Drunk, tipsy, had too much to drink,' he said. 'It's a ritual with him. Most Frenchmen hold their liquor well, but André's not one of them. It makes him want to break things.'

'I do hope he won't break Aunt Lily's lovely furniture,' Gardenia said anxiously. 'Yesterday morning I saw that a Dresden china vase had been smashed. It must have cost a lot of money, but I never heard Aunt Lily complain.'

'Perhaps she doesn't mind,' Bertram suggested.

'But of course everyone minds their home being knocked about,' Gardenia said. 'I should mind very much. I think it is very ungracious of people to come here and accept my aunt's hospitality and then behave like that. I don't believe it would happen in England.'

'It does, though,' Bertram Cunningham answered. 'Don't you remember, Vane, that party at the Cavendish

91

one night? Rosa was furious next morning and put about twenty pounds on to everybody's bill.'

'Who is Rosa?' Gardenia asked.

'Rosa Lewis, a great character,' Bertie replied. 'She keeps a hotel in Jermyn Street.'

'But one can hardly compare her with Aunt Lily,' Gardenia said. 'Smashing up a hotel is rather different from doing the same thing in a private house.'

There was a moment's silence. Then Bertie gave a hoot of laughter.

'You are magnificent, you really are! No wonder André said you would be the talk of Paris.'

Before Gardenia could speak, Lord Hartcourt said:

'I think Miss Weedon is talking complete sense. This is a private house and people should remember it.'

His cousin looked at him, seemed about to speak and changed his mind. Then, before they could say anything more, Comte André de Grenelle came through the French windows and on to the balcony.

'I guessed this was where I would find you, Cunningham,' he said. 'I heard you were here and couldn't see you in the room; so knowing the English passion for fresh air I thought to myself the balcony is where he will be!'

'And you were right,' Bertie said a little curtly.

The Comte was not listening to him. He had seen Gardenia. He moved towards her and, taking her hand in his, raised it to his lips.

'The little nun!' he exclaimed. 'I knew next time that I saw you you would be wearing something sparkling, but there is rather a lot of it, too much in fact.'

'Listen, Comte,' Lord Hartcourt said, and his voice was very firm, 'Miss Weedon is a niece of the Duchesse and has come over from England to stay with her. When she arrived the other night you made a mistake. I think you owe her an apology.'

'A niece of Lily de Mabillon?' The Comte had drunk a lot but his brain was still working. 'Is that the truth?'

'It is indeed,' Lord Hartcourt said.

'Then I apologise, most sincerely I apologise,' the Comte said, turning to Gardenia. 'But I am still sorry I didn't kiss you.'

Once again he raised her hand to his lips. She took it away a little nervously.

'Come and dance, Miss Weedon,' Bertie said, and Gardenia was glad to escape.

Bertie swept her around the dance floor. He danced better than his cousin, but at the same time she could not help wishing her dance with Lord Hartcourt had been longer. It was because he was slower, she told herself, that he had given her the confidence to be able to follow his steps.

'I say, this is wonderful!' Bertie whispered in her ear. 'I have been longing to get you to myself. What do you say we slip away when no one is looking and go to Maxim's for an hour or so? I'll bring you back before your aunt notices you are missing.'

'But I couldn't do that,' Gardenia said surprised.

'Why not?' he asked. 'Your aunt's being rather a dragon, you know. I am not as rich as my cousin or as distinguished, but I would look after you and give you a good time, I promise you that.'

'Lord Hartcourt said that you wanted to show me Paris,' Gardenia said in a low voice.

'Well, what about it?' Bertram asked.

'I don't think Aunt Lily would allow it,' she said.

'Oh really!' Bertie expostulated. 'You can't go on saying that. What are you waiting for? One of the Grand Dukes?'

'I'm not waiting for anyone,' Gardenia replied.

'Then let's have a little bit of fun, shall we?' Bertie coaxed. 'Come along. We'll slip away now. Get your coat—no, don't bother, it's a warm night. My motor-car's outside.

'I couldn't possibly do that,' Gardenia protested. 'You don't understand. Aunt Lily has been so kind to me, she trusts me; and if she says I'm to be chaperoned as if I were in England, then of course I must agree. After all, I am entirely dependent on her.'

'That's just what I am trying to say to you,' Bertie said. 'You don't have to be dependent on her. I have got enough as long as you are not too greedy.'

'Let's go out on the balcony,' Gardenia said a little breathlessly, moving out of his arms. She felt her head was whirling like her body. She couldn't understand what he was trying to say.

By this time other people were dancing. One of the couples stopped beside Bertie and started to talk to him.

Gardenia reached the balcony to find the Comte had disappeared and Lord Hartcourt was there alone. He looked up as she approached.

'Enjoy the dance?' he asked. He had lighted a cigar and the fragrance of it hung in the air.

'I don't know,' Gardenia answered. 'Mr Cunningham has been trying to persuade me to go with him to Maxim's, but I'm sure Aunt Lily would not approve. I ought not to go alone, ought I?'

It was the question of a child and her eyes were innocence itself as she raised them to Lord Hartcourt.

He stood staring down at her and again it seemed as if there was nothing that need be said. They could only look at each other. Then, almost harshly, he turned his head away.

'I think that is a decision you have got to make for yourself,' he said.

'But Mr Cunningham doesn't understand!' Gardenia said. 'I tried to explain to him that Aunt Lily has been so kind, and as I am entirely dependent on her I must do what she wants.'

'And what does she want?' Lord Hartcourt asked. There was a faint and cynical smile on his lips.

Gardenia did not answer. She suddenly remembered her aunt saying: 'I have asked Lord Hartcourt to tea alone. He is very rich and eligible. There has never been any scandal about him. I want you to make yourself very nice to him. It is most important.'

'Well?' The monosyllable woke Gardenia from her daydream.

'I think . . .' she said slowly, telling the truth because he had asked the question, 'my aunt wants me to be friends with you rather than with your cousin.'

'So that's it, is it?' Lord Hartcourt answered. "Well, let me make this very clear. I am not in the running. Do you understand? I am not in the running.'

As he spoke, he threw his cigar over the balcony into the garden and walked away, leaving Gardenia alone on the balcony staring after him. She must have said something wrong, but even if she had, she couldn't understand his leaving without saying goodbye. It was a rudeness that she felt was uncharacteristic of him.

As she watched him disappear into the big Salon, somehow the elation and excitement that had been hers all the

94

evening faded away. She felt lonely, afraid, and perilously near to tears.

Lord Hartcourt walked down the stairs into the hall and ordered his car. The whole situation was ridiculous, he told himself. If the Duchesse wanted a protector for her niece, why on earth should she choose him? Certainly, with the girl looking so pretty, she could find someone richer than Bertie. But at the same time as she was so young one would have thought that it was better for her to have some decent and clean-living young man than one of the well-known *roués*. But doubtless the Duchesse was prepared to sell the girl to the highest bidder. It was always the way with the *demi-monde*. All they thought about was money and, although from all reports the Duchesse had a packet of her own, it was unlikely that she would be prepared to spend much of it on her niece, apart from setting her up with grand clothes.

'I'll drive myself,' Lord Hartcourt said to his chauffeur. The man took off his cap respectfully as the motor-car moved away.

Lord Hartcourt had a sudden desire for fresh air. There had been something cloying and over-fragrant in the ballroom, and something nauseating in the thought of Gardenia being pushed first on to this man and then another until the Duchesse could find someone of whom she approved. Was this one of the Baron's ideas? Lord Hartcourt wondered.

He disliked the Baron even more than Gardenia did. Having encountered him for over a year now in the Diplomatic Service, he knew he was a bully and brute and extremely unscrupulous when it came to women. How any woman, even one as *déclassée* as the Duchesse, could take up with von Knesebech was beyond his comprehension.

He felt as though he was being involved in a plot to which he could not yet see the finish. He remembered again Gardenia's cry for help when the Comte had tried to kiss her in the hall when she first arrived. He remembered how frail and helpless she had looked lying on the sofa, her eyelashes long and dark against the pallor of her cheeks. He had to admit to himself that she looked very different and very lovely tonight. There was something about those wide innocent-seeming eyes and that small, piquant face which made one feel that she must be telling the truth however incredible she might seem.

Of course that was ridiculous. She must by this time have guessed what her aunt was. She couldn't imagine the women she had met at dinner or seen in the Salon came from Parisian society, or indeed that any respectable woman would cross the threshold of Mabillon House. Her air of innocence must be an act, Lord Hartcourt told himself. She knew what she was saying when she told him her aunt wanted him to be her friend. Of course she did! Well, he just wasn't having any of that! He had Henriette, she satisfied him, and what man could ask for more?

He must have driven for some miles without realising where he was going, for he found himself in the *Bois,* nearing one of the restaurants which he often patronised. He drew up outside, thought he would go in for a drink, then decided it looked too full and noisy. The band was certainly raucous after the delicate tones of Ventura's violins.

He suddenly decided what he would do. He would visit Henriette. He felt a sudden need for her. At least she was not complicated. There was no pretence about what she was and what she was not.

'*Des fleurs, Monsieur?*' The throaty question came from an ancient flower-seller, carrying a large basket filled with flowers.

'*Non, merci,*' Lord Hartcourt answered. Then he changed his mind. 'Give me those!' he said, pointing to a large bunch in the corner of the basket.

'They are not yet arranged, *Monsieur,*' the flower-seller explained. 'They are for the buttonholes. My daughter has only just brought them to me from the country.'

'I'll buy the lot,' Lord Hartcourt said.

He gave the man a five-franc note, which brought a spate of '*merci beaucoups.*'

The bunch of white flowers was handed over and Lord Hartcourt set them down beside him on the seat. It was only as he drove away that he realised that they were gardenias. With their green leaves not yet trimmed away, they made a bouquet, the fragrance of which wafted to his nostrils. Gardenias! They made him think of that damn girl again.

He put his foot hard on the accelerator. The sooner he

got to Henriette, the better. She was not expecting him, but that would make their reunion all the more enjoyable. He had been with her between five and seven, and when he had left she had clung to him a little and begged him not to go so soon. He thought of her with affection as he drove back through the *Bois.*

He turned down the small unfashionable *boulevard* where he had bought a house. The whole place seemed deserted. He left his car under the trees in the centre of the street, walked across the pavement and opened the door with his latch-key. It gave him an amusing sense of adventure to be stealing in unexpectedly to see Henriette. Usually there was a trim little maid whom he also paid to open the door and take his hat. Henriette would be waiting for him upstairs, sometimes dressed exotically, at others sensationally naked, as she had been last night when she wished him to buy her the emerald necklace.

The carpet was soft and the lights were out in the hall and on the stairs. The street-lamps shining through the window showed him the way. He was well aware that Henriette's room would not be in darkness. She had a horror of the dark and a light was always kept burning by her bedside. When she was a child, her father, to punish her, had shut her up in a dark cupboard and now she had claustrophobia. At the mere idea of being in the dark she became hysterical.

Softly Lord Hartcourt turned the handle of Henriette's bedroom door, holding the bouquet of gardenias in his hand. He thought whimsically he would scatter them over her pillow, so that her head would be scented with them. As he had expected, the light was on, shaded by a pink shade but revealing quite clearly the big satin-covered bed at the far end of the room.

Lord Hartcourt could see Henriette's red hair trailing over the pillows. Then he stood very still! There was a strange naked arm thrown over Henriette's shoulders and another head close beside hers. Henriette was not alone!

He must have stood there motionless for perhaps three or four seconds before Henriette opened her eyes. She gave a scream, a scream of sheer terror.

'You must forgive me if I intrude,' Lord Hartcourt said in an icy voice which seemed to freeze the very air of the room.

'*Mon Dieu!* But you said you were not coming tonight!' Henriette gasped.

The man beside her moved and half raised himself in bed. He was middle-aged, with greying hair and thick, dark eyebrows. He stared at Lord Hartcourt with an almost ludicrous expression of embarrassment on his face.

Lord Hartcourt turned on his heel.

'May I wish you both good night?' His voice was resonant with sarcasm. Then he went out of the door and closed it very quietly behind him.

As he went downstairs he could hear Henriette screaming. Her voice was shrill and unpleasant and he knew she would both scream after and berate her lover, whoever he might be.

Lord Hartcourt got into the car and drove away. He drove furiously, making for the woods, away from the streets and houses of Paris. He was furious not only with Henriette but with himself for having been made to look such a fool. It would have been better, he thought, if the man with whom she had been unfaithful to him had been young and attractive; but a middle-aged lover could only mean one thing—that she wanted more money, more jewels, that her greed was insatiable. He despised himself for being mixed up with anyone so avaricious, so utterly without scruples.

When he thought of the bill that he would have to pay for the emerald necklace he had given Henriette the night before, his foot clamped down on the accelerator and he went faster still. It would be easy to refuse to pay the bill, to tell the jeweller he had not sanctioned the gift and that it must be returned. But he knew he would grit his teeth and pay. He had given his mistress a gift and as a gift she could keep it. He only hoped that eventually it would throttle her. Yes, she could keep her jewels, but he would instruct his attorney to turn her out of the house immediately.

He thought to himself bitterly it would be a long time before he allowed himself to be caught up with such an obvious trollop again. He knew now he had never cared for Henriette, except as an acquisition which was the envy of his friends. She was attractive, of course, it was part of her stock-in-trade. She amused him at times, but he found almost to his relief that he had no affection for her. All

98

that was left was the pique of knowing that she had made a fool of him.

Dawn was breaking as Lord Hartcourt drove back to Paris. He was suddenly very tired, his anger had burned itself out and all he wanted was his bed. Tomorrow would be time enough in which to think what he would tell his friends.

'You have finished with Henriette?' they would ask. 'Why, what has she done?'

Of one thing he was quite certain: he was not going to tell them the truth. It might be conceit, it might seem childish, but he just could not bear them to laugh at him.

He had reached the bottom of the Champs Elysées before he was aware of a fragrance beside him. He must have unconsciously carried the flowers he had bought for Henriette back into the car and set them down beside him.

The big fountains of the Place de la Concorde were in front of him. They were iridescent in the morning sunshine, catching the first gleams of gold which were creeping up the sombre sky. Lord Hartcourt drew the car to a standstill; then, picking up the bouquet, he leant over the door and threw the flowers into the water.

They landed with a splash in the middle of the basin. The string that tied them together must have come loose, for they floated away singly, their white faces turned towards the sky, their green leaves encircling them. They looked very fragile and Lord Hartcourt saw that some of them were not yet in bloom but were only half-open buds.

Annoyingly, aggravatingly, they reminded him of Gardenia!

Seven

Lord Hartcourt returned to the Embassy late on Monday afternoon. He had spent Sunday in the country in an ancient château.

He enjoyed the company of his French friends and he had been annoyed to find that on this occasion they had other English visitors besides himself. He had met Lady Roehampton several times before in England, but he had not expected to find her in Paris or that she should be accompanied by her débutante daughter.

Lord Hartcourt had not been a few hours at the château before he realised all too clearly that Lady Roehampton looked on him as a very desirable son-in-law. She was charming, and no one knew better how to charm than Lady Roehampton, who had been a great beauty in her time, but on this occasion she was doing her best to attract Lord Hartcourt not for herself but for her daughter.

The Roehampton girl was dull, shy and obviously determined to make as little effort on her own behalf as possible. After enduring her company for several meals and on some very obviously manœuvred walks in the garden, Lord Hartcourt found himself longing passionately for Paris, and for any gay, uninhibited spot where débutantes and their matchmaking mamas were not likely to be found.

He therefore left on Monday morning earlier than he had intended, making as excuse the amount of work he had to do at the Embassy. But as the journey back to Paris was slow, and the day hot, he arrived in an exceedingly bad temper.

He stalked up to his rooms on the second floor of the Embassy building, knowing that no one expected him back until the next day and feeling that Paris on a warm day was a waste of time when he might have been in the country. However, anything was better than Lady Roehampton's machinations.

He flung on to a chair the dustcoat in which he had driven his car, and walked across to look at the pile of mail waiting for him on his writing-desk.

His room at the Embassy was charming. It constituted a self-contained flat, and, although he could enter from the main building, he could also use a small staircase with a private door which led into the garden and to which only he had a key.

His secretary had placed the letters in the usual three piles which he knew so well. On the left hand were those which were personal and unopened; in the centre were those of diplomatic importance, which were also unopened; and on the right were those which the Ambassador had sent him to deal with and which were opened and neatly clipped together.

One glance was enough to tell Lord Hartcourt who had written the majority of letters in his personal pile. There was no mistaking the mauve writing-paper with the flamboyant monogram. There was also Henriette's familiar scent which seemed to percolate the room. One, two, three, four letters! She must, Lord Hartcourt thought, have written feverishly the whole of yesterday and sent them round at varying intervals.

He stared at her large, slightly illiterate writing and, with a little gesture of disgust, picked up the letters one by one and dropped them into the wastepaper-basket. He then walked across the room and opened the window; the light breeze coming from the Champs Elysées seemed to sweep the last vestige of Henriette from the room and from his mind. The past was closed, he had no intention of reopening it.

He poured himself a glass of Perrier, drank it and sat down at the desk. As he was there he might as well do some work. It was too early to go out in search of amusement and, besides, for the moment at least, he had lost all interest in women.

He opened the rest of his private mail. There were innumerable invitations to parties, receptions, dinners, soirées—all socially very gratifying, but Lord Hartcourt knew only too well how the same formula would be repeated on each occasion. The same people would greet him and sit next to him at dinner, they would mouth the same platitudes, and the same entertainment would be provided by each hostess in varying degrees of expenditure.

He yawned and began to slit open the diplomatic letters. There was a knock at the door.

'Come in,' Lord Hartcourt called out without turning his head.

'I have just heard that you have returned unexpectedly,' said a well-known voice.

Lord Hartcourt jumped to his feet.

'Good evening, your Excellency. I didn't realise it was you.'

'I was not expecting you until tomorrow,' the Ambassador replied, 'but I am glad you are back. I have various things to discuss with you.'

'Why didn't you send for me?' Lord Hartcourt enquired.

'I have just come back from a luncheon at the Travellers',' the Ambassador answered. 'Jarvis told me you were here, so I thought I would come and visit you. Do you mind?'

'No, I am always delighted to see your Excellency,' Lord Hartcourt said with obvious sincerity.

The Ambassador settled himself comfortably in one of the deep armchairs.

'Things are bad, Hartcourt,' he said.

Lord Hartcourt raised his eyebrows.

'Worse than usual?'

'Much worse,' the Ambassador replied. 'The Kaiser is playing a double game. You remember when the King went to Berlin in February he said quite openly that his Majesty was merely coming to "thwart and annoy"? Well, the Germans have decided to annoy us. They are building more dreadnought battleships.'

'Not more, surely, your Excellency?' Lord Hartcourt ejaculated.

'Four more is what I am told. You know that Reginald McKenna, speaking for the Sea Lords, has demanded that we should build four to be equal with them? The King now wants eight!'

'England can't afford it,' Lord Hartcourt protested.

'That is what the Opposition say,' the Ambassador answered wearily. 'They want the money spent on social services. But battleships we will have whatever the cost! They will, I believe, be more cheap in the long run.'

'What do you mean by that?' Lord Hartcourt enquired.

'Anstrudter returned from Berlin last night. He told me that it is now absolutely confirmed that at all their regimental dinner parties the Germans raise their glasses and toast "*Der Tag*".'

'Meaning the day they fight us?' Lord Hartcourt said drily.

'Exactly,' the Ambassador agreed. 'The Germans have always loathed us.'

'I'm surprised anyone should have thought otherwise,' Lord Hartcourt said slowly.

'God knows the King has done all he can to improve the relationship between our country and theirs,' the Ambassador said. 'But things are looking serious. I thought you ought to know.'

'Thank you, your Excellency. I'm grateful for your confidence,' Lord Hartcourt said.

The Ambassador rose to his feet.

'Incidentally, the Germans have changed their Codes, so, naturally, we have had to change ours. Only the new Naval one has arrived so far. I don't suppose we shall have much use for it. The Diplomatic one has been promised in a few days.'

'How long will it take us to break their new ones?' Lord Hartcourt asked with almost a boyish grin.

'I can't answer that question,' the Ambassador replied in all seriousness. 'Our Secret Service has been extraordinarily inefficient lately. Anstrudter tells me it is getting more and more difficult to employ anyone in Berlin. The contacts we have got are small people of little importance. I think I had better have a talk with M5 next time I go to England.'

'I think that would be a good idea, your Excellency,' Lord Hartcourt said. 'I suppose the French Government are aware of all these developments?'

'The French don't trouble to disguise their hatred of the entire German race,' the Ambassador answered. 'In a way it makes it easier for them. We have to pretend to be friends, realising all the time that the hands we clasp are just waiting to point a pistol at our belly.'

'A charming thought,' Lord Hartcourt said drily.

'Anyway, if Tubors from the French Secret Service calls you can be comparatively frank with him,' the Ambassador said. 'He is a good man and there is not much he misses. I wish I could say the same of all our chaps.'

He walked to the door.

'Do you like your new job, Hartcourt?' he asked as he reached it.

'Very much, your Excellency. I find it most interesting.'

The Ambassador's tired face seemed to brighten.

'I am glad about that. I like having you here.'

He walked briskly away and Lord Hartcourt shut the door after him.

For the moment he felt cheered by the kindness in the Ambassador's voice; then he frowned as he walked back to his desk and sat down to study the new Naval Code.

He had not been working for more than half an hour when the door was thrust open and Bertie came hurrying into the room.

'Jarvis has just told me you are back!' he cried. 'I wasn't expecting you until tomorrow. What happened? Country turn out to be a dead bore?'

'Extremely dull,' Lord Hartcourt replied.

'Well, have you heard what has been happening here?' Bertie asked.

'No. What in particular?' Lord Hartcourt enquired.

'Well, Henriette called no less than four times yesterday. She was absolutely determined that you were not away. Jarvis had a hell of a time with her.'

'Really?' Lord Hartcourt drawled the word.

'That isn't all,' Bertie went on. 'It's rumoured all over Paris that she tried to commit suicide last night. They say she took an over-dose of sleeping pills and has been taken off to hospital.'

If Bertie expected his cousin to look stricken or excited by the news, he was disappointed. Lord Hartcourt only raised his eyebrows and started tidying the papers on his desk.

'Damn it all!' Bertie exclaimed, sitting on the corner of the flat-top desk. 'You might seem a bit more interested. After all, she is your *chère amie* and she wouldn't commit suicide unless she was upset about something.'

Lord Hartcourt sat back in his seat.

'Listen, Bertie,' he said. 'You haven't been in Paris very long. I can assure you this is the oldest trick in the world. It is tried by every member of the *demi-monde* who can't get her own way or finds herself laid aside by her current

104

protector. They take a few sleeping-tablets, not enough to kill them, just enough to induce a heavy sleep or a light coma. They notify their friends first, who most conveniently find them before it is too late. Then they are carried off to hospital surrounded by flowers and they wait, frilled and perfumed, for the recalcitrant male to come crawling back with his apologies.'

'Good Lord! Do they really go to such a length?' Bertie asked.

'Ask André de Grenelle. He will tell you it is a very ordinary occurrence in Paris. In fact, it happens to be the fashion! I should have thought that Henriette had more sense!"

'So you have given her the chuck,' Bertie said.

'I didn't say so,' Lord Hartcourt replied.

'But it's obvious, isn't it? She was happy enough with you on Friday night at Maxim's. She wouldn't be committing suicide forty-eight hours later unless you'd upset her.'

Lord Hartcourt did not reply and after a moment Bertie said irritably:

'Oh do come off your high horse, Vane, and be a bit more human! You know perfectly well I'm bursting with curiosity and so is the whole of Paris. You've got to say something, whether you like it or not.'

'Very well,' Lord Hartcourt answered. 'My liaison with Henriette has come to an end. Did you really want me to put it in the newspapers?'

'But why?' Bertie asked. 'You were so fond of her. You gave her that whacking great emerald necklace on Friday. Something must have happened. Do tell me, Vane.'

'I have no intention of discussing my private affairs with anyone,' Lord Hartcourt replied. 'Most people would have the good taste not to press me.'

Bertie grinned.

'Well, I haven't any taste,' he said. 'I'm only damned curious. What the hell happened?'

'That is something you will never know,' Lord Hartcourt answered. 'Now, let's change the subject.'

'Curse you! You are an obstinate fellow!' Bertie exclaimed. 'I was certain you'd tell me.'

'Then you were wrong,' Lord Hartcourt said.

'I don't know what's got into you,' Bertie complained. 'You used to be a damned good fellow when we first knew each other.'

'Was I?'

'I don't mean when we were children and our time at Eton, but when I grew up. I was younger than you, but you took me around London and showed me a friendliness I shall never forget. I thought it would be the same in Paris when I came over here. Now you seem quite unaccountable. I don't know where I am with you.'

'I am just the same,' Lord Hartcourt said patiently, 'but you must learn, Bertie, not to interfere in things which don't concern you. I never have discussed my women with anyone and I don't intend to start now.'

'Regimental honour and all that sort of thing?' Bertie teased. 'Well, you are right, I suppose. But I can't understand what is happening, and that's the truth. First there's Henriette banging on the door and making a regular nuisance of herself while you skip off to the country; and then after you left the party on Saturday night everything seemed to go wrong.'

'What do you mean by that?' Lord Hartcourt asked.

'Well, by the time I reached the balcony you had gone and Miss Weedon seemed almost in tears. She wouldn't talk and wouldn't dance. What did you say to upset her?'

'Was she upset?' Lord Hartcourt asked evasively.

'Well, I thought so. Two or three people joined us and quite suddenly she said she had a headache and slipped away. I don't know what you have done. You certainly spoiled my evening.'

'I'm sorry about that,' Lord Hartcourt said gravely.

'As a matter of fact, I did meet a rather attractive little thing who had come to the party with one of the Russian envoys—all big eyes and high Slavonic cheek-bones, you know the type. She was quite amusing! I took her home, as her escort seemed to have disappeared, and I must say the Russians have something these French girls haven't got.'

'Well, I am glad you enjoyed yourself,' Lord Hartcourt smiled.

'Not as much as I would have enjoyed it had I managed to have a proper talk with the little British sparrow,' Bertie said. 'You know, I'm sure the Duchesse is determined I shan't get near her. Look at the way she behaved when we arrived, taking me off to get her a drink and telling you to dance with Gardenia.'

'I am afraid the Duchesse doesn't consider you sufficiently rich or important enough,' Lord Hartcourt said.

'You really think it's going to be a case of the highest bidder?' Bertie asked. 'It's pretty disgusting, isn't it?'

Lord Hartcourt shrugged his shoulders. Then in a voice which suddenly seemed to rasp he said:

'For God's sake, Bertie, let me get on with my work. If you are going to stay here, you must be quiet. If you're going to chatter, you must go away.'

'Oh, very well then,' Bertie said huffily. 'If that's going to be your attitude, I'll take myself off. I have a good mind to go round to Mabillon House and see what the girl is doing. The Duchesse can't shut me out all the time unless she keeps Gardenia under lock and key.'

'I expect that is exactly what she will do when she sees your bank balance,' Lord Hartcourt said disagreeably.

His cousin went out of the room and slammed the door.

Lord Hartcourt, with a heavy frown between his eyes, sat down to his correspondence.

Gardenia was in fact at that moment receiving a lecture from her aunt.

'You must make more of an effort to be charming,' Aunt Lily was saying. 'It is no use being shy and tongue-tied. Men in Paris have no use for that sort of thing. They want to be entertained and if you don't entertain them they will find someone who will.'

'I do try,' Gardenia said miserably.

'I thought you were being very off-hand to Comte André de Grenelle when we met him in the Park just now. He is a rich young man and comes from one of the best families in France.'

'He drinks too much,' Gardenia said. 'He was insulting to me on Saturday night. I didn't quite understand what he was saying, but I know it was insulting.'

The Duchesse lay back in her armchair and suddenly looked very tired.

'One has to learn to handle men,' she said. 'They are not all perfect. Some of them drink too much, some gamble, some are just difficult.'

'I'll do my best,' Gardenia said in a stifled voice, and then impulsively went and knelt by her aunt's chair.

'I am so grateful to you, Aunt Lily,' she said. 'I am thrilled with all my wonderful clothes and I love being here with you. But somehow I feel out of place. I expect it's because I have lived such a quiet and sheltered life. I don't understand half the things people are saying to me and I don't think that the Baron likes me.'

She said the last words nervously. She was well aware she was being daring in voicing what was in her mind, but she felt that somehow she must bring into the open that undercurrent of suspicion that she felt existed between her and the man who incessantly was in and out of the house.

'What has the Baron said to you?' the Duchesse's voice was sharp.

'Nothing, nothing in particular,' Gardenia replied. 'I just feel . . .'

'Then don't feel anything!' the Duchesse said sharply. 'The Baron is a difficult man, Gardenia, but he is very clever, very important and has very big responsibilities in Paris. Sometimes even I find him hard to understand. You must accept him as he is; try to make things easy for him when he comes here to relax.'

'Hasn't he got a house of his own?' Gardenia asked.

'He lives in his Embassy,' the Duchesse replied.

There was a little pause, then Gardenia asked:

'He isn't married?'

The Duchesse rose from the chair and walked across the room.

'Yes, of course he is married,' she said at last, casually. 'His wife is in Germany managing the very big estates that he owns in North Prussia. They have four children. He is a very respected man.'

'I see,' Gardenia said.

She still didn't understand why, if the Baron had a wife and children, he was always hanging around Aunt Lily. Why, when she had come unexpectedly into the small drawing-room last evening, had he hastily taken his arms from around the Duchesse's shoulders? Her face had been turned adoringly up to his as though he had just been kissing her. Gardenia had been shocked. Surely Aunt Lily was too old for that sort of thing?

Then, when she had thought about it later, she had decided that Aunt Lily was thinking of marrying the Baron. After all, there was no reason why she should not marry again and, though it was unfortunate she should like such a man, and a German at that, at least the Baron was someone to look after her. He might prevent her from spending so much money on the parties which must be an incredible expense and to which such strange and noisy people were invited.

Gardenia rose from her knees. Aunt Lily was making a pretence of rearranging some carnations in a vase by the fireplace.

'I think, Gardenia, I should explain,' she said in rather a strange voice. 'I have often been very unhappy and lonely since my husband died. The Baron has been very kind to me. He has helped me with my very difficult legal affairs. He has given me his advice when I have most needed it.'

'Yes of course I understand,' Gardenia said quickly. 'It just seemed strange that he should come here so often. I didn't realise that he was helping you.'

'You must see how it is,' her aunt went on, her head bent over the flowers. 'He too is lonely, his wife and family are far away and the French don't like the Germans. He is sensitive and it hurts him when people are rude and inhospitable where he is concerned.'

Gardenia said nothing. Somehow she could not imagine the Baron having hurt feelings or being anything but autocratic and overbearing. But perhaps, she thought to herself, she was being uncharitable and, after all, Aunt Lily did know him well.

'I'm sorry if I appeared curious, Aunt Lily,' she said. 'You must forgive me. It is intolerable of me to be asking questions. It is just that I want to understand and not to make mistakes.'

'Of course, child, and if you want to please me,' the Duchesse said, 'you will be kind to that nice Lord Hartcourt. He is such a charming man and very rich.'

Gardenia felt her face burn.

'That is something I wanted to speak to you about, Aunt Lily,' she said timidly. 'You see, from something Lord Hartcourt said to me the other night, I think he now imagines that you are running after him.'

'Did he say so?' the Duchesse said in a voice that was suddenly sharp.

'Yes, he did in a sort of way,' Gardenia faltered. 'It was my fault. I told him you wanted us to be friends. Afterwards I realised how silly I had been and I felt ashamed. I don't want to marry anyone, Aunt Lily, unless I fall in love with them.'

'Gardenia, you have got to be married,' the Duchesse

109

said. 'All I want to do is to find you somebody rich and eligible who will look after you and with whom you will be happy. There is nothing else, can't you understand? You talk of being a governess or companion: what sort of life is that? You would hate it. Besides, it is degrading, a life in which you grow old without any happiness. Women were made for marriage and you have got to be married as quickly as possible.'

'But why so quickly?' Gardenia asked. 'Someone will come along that I can love. I shall meet someone one day.'

'You can't wait for someday,' the Duchesse said, 'and that is a fact. I am not going into details, Gardenia. You must believe I know best. I want you married as soon as possible. I will give you a good allowance, a magnificent trousseau and when I am dead you shall have all the money that I have left. That ought to be enough to attract any normal man . . .'

She paused a moment, and stood looking at her niece.

'You are very pretty,' she murmured. 'I would like you to marry well, really well. It will be such a slap in the eye for . . .'

She stopped suddenly.

'There is no point in talking about it. If you want to please me, if you want to show your gratitude, you will make yourself very pleasant to the men I point out to you. To de Grenelle, for instance, and of course, to Lord Hartcourt. Don't let them know you are running after them, just make yourself indispensable, just be there when they want you.'

Gardenia said nothing. She felt there was nothing she could say. How impossible it was to describe her dreams: how she had hoped one day to meet a man and to know that because he loved her she could love him in return. She wanted to give her heart willingly without weighing up the worldly advantages of her future husband's wealth and social position. Almost because she knew it would annoy her aunt, she asked:

'What about Mr Bertram Cunningham? May I not be nice to him?'

'I suppose he might be better than nobody,' her aunt said in an exasperated voice. 'He is only a cousin of Lord Hartcourt's and he comes from a good family, but he is only a second son. It seems a pity when you are so pretty to throw yourself away unless there is no alternative.'

'He is very anxious to be friendly,' Gardenia said.

'Then be friendly with him,' the Duchesse said unexpectedly. 'I'll tell you what you can do. He asked you to go driving in the Park, didn't he? Very well, you can go, but someone else has got to be there too. You needn't be chaperoned by a woman, a man would do, Lord Hartcourt for instance.'

The frown which had creased the Duchesse's face suddenly vanished. She smiled and seemed suddenly pleased with herself.

'Does that please you, you silly child?' she asked. 'Go and write Mr Cunningham a nice letter. Say that I have changed my mind and that you can go for a drive with him, so long as it is not alone. I shouldn't suggest that Lord Hartcourt should accompany you the first time; just wait and see who Mr Cunningham brings. I have a suspicion it will be his cousin.'

Gardenia poised her lips to say that she did not wish Lord Hartcourt to go with them after the way he had behaved last night. But she knew that it would annoy her aunt. Besides, Aunt Lily might enquire more closely as to what Lord Hartcourt had actually said, and Gardenia knew that she couldn't remember and somehow couldn't explain. It was all too muddled and she didn't want to talk about it. It made her hot and embarrassed. What was more it made her feel again that strange unaccountable throbbing of her heart when Lord Hartcourt had walked away and left her alone on the balcony.

'Now go and write the letter,' the Duchesse was saying. 'I will send it round to the Embassy.'

'Very well, Aunt Lily,' Gardenia agreed meekly.

She went into the writing-room which lay off the drawing-room, took one of the crested and heavily engraved pieces of writing-paper from its holder, and laid it on the blotting-paper. Then she sat staring across the room.

Somehow this was wrong. It was not how an ordinary girl of her age would behave in England, writing to a man to ask for an invitation, even though she had refused him once. Gardenia was sure her mother would not have approved. She was certain of that, just as she was certain her mother would not have approved of the party on Saturday night, of the Baron, of the strange, noisy women

111

at dinner, or the people that her aunt had talked to in the Park when they had gone driving that afternoon.

They had drawn the car up under the chestnut trees and quite a number of people had come up for a chat. The men had been distinguished, there was no doubt about that. But there was something too intimate and too familiar in the way they spoke to Aunt Lily, and when she was introduced, Gardenia knew that the way they stared at her was insulting. It was almost as if they undressed her with their eyes until she was naked. What was wrong? Why were things so different from what she had thought they would be?

The house was magnificent, the furniture and furnishings were all in exquisite taste; it gave her a thrill even to look at them. But Aunt Lily's guests, with their spangled dresses and vulgar jewellery, were out of place. Surely all French women were not like that? Perhaps Aunt Lily had got to know the wrong people; yet, as a Duchesse, the very élite of society would flock to her house?

'I don't understand, I don't understand,' Gardenia whispered to herself. This letter to Mr Cunningham—what could she say? What would her mother have wanted her to say?

Gardenia gave a sigh. It was all too difficult. Her mother was dead and Aunt Lily was very much alive. Slowly she wrote:

Dear Mr Cunningham,
My aunt has told me that I may reply to your kind invitation to go driving in the Bois. She asked me to say that I may not go alone and that if we could be accompanied by another friend, she would be pleased to give her consent.

Yours sincerely, Gardenia Weedon

Gardenia read it again and again. She wished it could be stiffer and even more formal, but she felt she could not improve on it. Finally, she put the letter in an envelope and addressed it. Carrying the letter, she walked towards the drawing-room. As she reached the connecting door, which was only partially closed, she realised that her aunt was no longer alone. She heard the deep, guttural tones of the Baron and knew it must be after five o'clock.

'Oh, Heinrich,' she heard her aunt say. 'I am so glad to see you. I've had such a difficult afternoon.'

'Then if you are glad to see me, what are we waiting for?' the Baron enquired.

The Duchesse gave a little laugh. It sounded young, gay and almost excited. Gardenia heard them cross the room and their footsteps going upstairs. For the moment she could only think of what her aunt had said. 'A difficult afternoon!' Difficult because she had been with her. Perhaps because she had asked questions. Again there was that horrible feeling of knowing that something was wrong and yet not being able to put her finger on it.

Why, she asked herself, should she be so introspective? Why did she keep asking herself questions instead of accepting things as they were?

Firmly and deliberately she walked into the hall. There were two footmen on duty. She held out the letter to one of them.

'Have this taken immediately,' she said, 'to the British Embassy.'

'Faster, faster!' Gardenia cried excitedly as Bertie drove his splendidly matched tandem along the dusty, almost empty roads which criss-crossed the *Bois*.

'If you want to go so fast you should have let Bertie drive you in his Peugeot,' Lord Hartcourt remarked drily.

'Horses are much more fun,' Gardenia asserted positively. 'Besides, one feels as if one is going faster.'

Bertie laughed.

'It all comes down in the end to imagination,' he said. 'I have been imagining myself flying an aeroplane.'

'An aeroplane!' Gardenia ejaculated.

'I was talking to a chap called Gustav Hammel last night,' Bertie went on. 'He is determined to beat Blériot and get to England in half the time. There is something in the idea, you know, Vane. We may all be flying in a few years' time.'

'How exciting!' Gardenia said. 'I remember Mama and I were very thrilled when we read about *Monsieur* Blériot crossing the Channel. The French always seem to think of something ahead of every other country.'

'Not always!' Bertie objected. 'There's life in the old lion yet. Don't you agree, Vane?'

'I hope so,' Lord Hartcourt said surlily, 'but we have to admit the French have beaten us so far when it comes to progress in the air.'

'I would love to meet *Monsieur* Blériot,' Gardenia said. 'Do either of you know him?'

'Well, I can introduce you to Gustav Hammel, who will introduce you to Blériot,' Bertie said, 'and there is an Englishman who has done a lot for flying—Claude Graham-White. You know him, Vane?'

'I have met him,' Lord Hartcourt replied. 'But I imagine the days when ladies take to the skies is very far off.'

'Don't be so damping,' Gardenia pleaded. 'If you talk like that I shall join the Suffragette Movement and scream for women's rights!'

'That is the most awful lot of nonsense I have ever listened to,' Bertie said. 'Women are making a blasted nuisance of themselves—forgive my language, Gardenia—tying themselves to railings, screaming outside the Houses of Parliament. It makes one quite ashamed of the fair sex!'

'I personally don't want a vote,' Gardenia said, 'but I think women have a very raw deal all round. Look how they are ordered about, first by their parents, and then by their husband. A woman never has a chance to think for herself or do anything she wants to do.'

'I will let you do anything you want to do,' Bertie said in a low voice.

'You are very kind,' Gardenia said lightly, 'but I couldn't have come out today if Aunt Lily had said no.'

'What made her change her mind?' Bertie asked, guiding his tandem with really exquisite skill past two stationary cars.

'I can't think,' Gardenia said quickly, not anxious to pursue the subject. 'It must be because women are unpredictable.'

'That is for us to say,' Bertie laughed. 'I have always found them so. What about you, Vane?'

Lord Hartcourt seemed uninterested in the subject. Instead he asked:

'What do you think of Bertie's horses, Miss Weedon? Don't you agree they are perfectly matched?'

'Of course I do,' Gardenia answered, 'and I think it is so marvellous of Mr Cunningham to keep to horse-flesh rather than go in for all those noisy, smelly cars. All the men in Paris seem to have them.'

'Except the nuts,' Lord Hartcourt said teasingly. 'The really slap-up toffs are all tooling the reins. You will see several tandems rivalling Bertie's and some very fine pairs too.'

'I am quite content to be behind these,' Gardenia smiled.

'Are you really?' Bertie said eagerly. 'That is jolly nice of you. I don't get many compliments these days and I value the ones I have.'

'Don't encourage him,' Lord Hartcourt urged with mock seriousness. 'If you do, he will want to drive a coach-and-six, and heaven knows in that case we shall never squeeze through the Arc de Triomphe.'

Gardenia laughed. She was enjoying herself more than she had thought possible. There was something exhilarating in driving in this fashionable yet quite idiotic vehicle, perched up high above the passers-by and with what she thought secretly to herself to be two of the handsomest men in the world on either side of her.

She had put on her most attractive gown for the occasion, and she knew that the rose-pink crêpe, with its touches of azure-blue ribbon on the neck, the wrists and on the wide tight waistband, was exquisitely becoming. Her almost childish hat, trimmed with a wreath of roses, framed her excited face and sparkling eyes. She would not have been a woman if she had not realised that everyone they met turned to look at the picture they all made.

'I am so happy!' she exclaimed and Lord Hartcourt, who was not immune to the tremulous emotion in her voice, looked down at her and smiled.

'I'm beginning to think it takes quite small things to make you happy,' he said.

'It is often the small things that can make one unhappy,' Gardenia answered. 'One can somehow stand up to the really big disasters and catastrophes in life, but small things reduce one so easily to tears.'

There was a little throb in her voice which made him feel guilty. He had been annoyed at being cajoled by Bertie into playing the part of a 'gooseberry,' but now he banished his ill-humour and settled down to be as pleasant as only he knew how.

'You must come,' Bertie had insisted. 'You know damn well the Duchesse won't let Gardenia out of her sight unless she thinks there's a chance of her being with you. We'll fix something else later on; but just this first time be a sport, Vane, and let me write and tell the old girl that we will both pick Gardenia up tomorrow morning.'

'Why should I be a nursemaid to this budding romance?' Lord Hartcourt asked bitterly.

'Only because there won't be a romance or anything at all unless you help me,' Bertie said plaintively.

It was impossible to be ill-humoured in the face of such frankness and so, in the end, Lord Hartcourt had laughed and consented to make what he called the unwelcome third.

He was, however, annoyed when the time came at not being able to play polo; but when Gardenia had come

116

running down the steps of Mabillon House looking like a rosebud about to burst into bloom, he found it hard to resist not so much her loveliness as the fact that she was so genuinely excited and thrilled at just being taken for a drive.

'We had such a horrid party last night,' she chattered. 'I can't think why you didn't come.'

'To a horrid party?' Bertie enquired. 'Surely you wouldn't wish that on us?'

'It wouldn't have been horrid if you had both been there,' Gardenia replied.

She had forgotten Lord Hartcourt's unkindness, and that on Saturday night she had gone to bed in tears. She could only remember that these two Englishmen were her friends and they were the only people in Paris she could talk with naturally.

'Why was it so horrid?' Lord Hartcourt asked in his deep voice.

She turned her tiny pointed face up to his.

'I wish I could answer that question,' she said, 'because I have asked myself what was wrong and couldn't find the answer. The guests were so strange and Aunt Lily sent me to bed very early, in fact very soon after dinner.'

'Now don't tell me you didn't find all those glamorous dark-eyed, compliment-paying Frenchmen delightful,' Bertie said teasingly. 'All women love Latins because they pay such fulsome and extravagant compliments.'

'One just cannot believe them,' Gardenia said scornfully. 'They don't even sound sincere.'

'Do I sound sincere when I pay you a compliment?' Bertie asked.

'I think all compliments are rather embarrassing,' Gardenia replied, 'and all Frenchmen are not young and exciting-looking. There was a horrid man who came to dinner last night. I couldn't bear him.'

'Who was that?' Bertie asked.

'I think his name was Gozlin,' Gardenia answered. 'He was very ugly and growing bald, fat and rather oily, and, would you believe it, the Baron said that Aunt Lily and I were to be very nice to him.'

'Gozlin, did you say?' Lord Hartcourt asked. His voice was suddenly sharp.

As if she knew she had been indiscreet Gardenia did not answer.

'Was that the name?' Lord Hartcourt persisted.

'Yes,' Gardenia replied a little hesitantly. 'Pierre Gozlin, I think it was, but I shouldn't have spoken so disparagingly about him. I'm sure he is all right really.'

'You don't have to pretend in front of us,' Bertie said, flicking his whip in an expert manner. 'We are countrymen and friends, at least I hope we are and it would be a poor thing if we can't be frank with one another in this land of frogs. Tell us all about this *Monsieur* Pierre Gozlin. Whatever you say will go no further. Vane and I are not chatterboxes.'

'No, I am sure you aren't,' Gardenia said, 'but it seemed rather ungracious and ill-bred of me to abuse one of Aunt Lily's guests, especially when he was such an important one.'

'Why was he important?' Lord Hartcourt enquired.

'I really don't know,' Gardenia said evasively. She was not going to tell them how before dinner the Baron had come into the little drawing-room and said:

'I have invited Pierre Gozlin tonight. Make a fuss of him, Lily. You know he adores you.'

'Oh not that terrible man again!' the Duchesse had exclaimed. 'It is too bad of you, Baron! You know how I dislike him: he gets so terribly drunk. In fact, after his last visit I made up my mind to tell the Major-Domo that in future I was not at home to *Monsieur* Gozlin.'

'You will do nothing of the sort!'

It was an autocratic command.

'Pierre Gozlin is important,' the Baron continued, 'very important to me and he is penitent, extremely penitent, if his behaviour last week upset you. He explained to me he had been over-working and had had very little to eat and the wine—your very good and expensive wine, my dear Duchesse—went to his head.'

'I am not interested in his apologies,' the Duchesse said petulantly. 'He is a revolting little man. I always feel he says one thing and means another. Besides, he has wet and flabby hands.'

'I still tell you to be nice to him,' the Baron said tersely.

To Gardenia, sitting quietly in the corner of the room, it seemed an impertinence.

'And if I refuse?' she heard her aunt ask.

The Duchesse threw up her chin as she spoke and stood looking at the Baron almost defiantly. She was looking

118

particularly beautiful that night and in the softly shaded light in the drawing-room the lines on her face, the sallowness of her skin, were not noticeable. The great diamonds in her necklace glittered round her throat. Her dress was cut to show her figure to its very best advantage, cleverly disguising where she had thickened and fattened with age. As Gardenia had discovered, a tremendous amount of lacing must go on before the Duchesse could be literally dragged into her gowns by Yvonne and the other maids.

The Baron did not answer the Duchesse's question. Now, impatiently, she tapped one of her slim satin-clad feet so that the diamond buckle sparkled.

'Well? Suppose I refuse?'

The Baron drew a step nearer to her.

'Then, my dear Lily,' he said very slowly, forgetting for once to address her formally, 'then—I would have to take him elsewhere.'

There was no disguising the threat in his tones, and Gardenia to her consternation saw her aunt crumple as if he had hit her.

'No, Heinrich, no! You wouldn't do that! But of course I was only joking. I will be nice to *Monsieur* Gozlin . . . I will be charming to him . . . I promise you.'

'That is goot!' the Baron's voice rang out triumphantly, and before any more could be said the butler's stentorian tones announced from the door:

'*Monsieur* Pierre Gozlin.'

Gardenia could see at once why her aunt disliked him. He was very unlike a Frenchman, bloated, oily and somehow resembling one of the frog-footmen in *Alice in Wonderland*.

He came sliding over the polished floor, took Aunt Lily's white-gloved hand in his and covered it with kisses.

'Forgive me,' he said in French. 'I apologise, I grovel at your feet, *Madame*. I was a fool, an ingrate. My good friend, the Herr Baron, tells me you have forgiven me.'

'We will not speak of it again,' Aunt Lily said.

'You are enchanting, an angel from heaven itself,' Pierre Gozlin enthused, in enraptured tones.

'He is ridiculous,' Gardenia thought. Then she saw the expression in his eyes and she felt as though a sudden cold wind had made the gooseflesh rise on her bare skin. 'No, he is evil,' she decided, and was thankful when she found at dinner that Pierre Gozlin was placed on Aunt Lily's right and a long way from where she was sitting.

He had drunk a lot at dinner, but not enough for anyone to say he had too much. Gardenia had felt that in some sinister way he overshadowed the whole party. It was not so much what he said, but it was the way he looked. 'He is evil,' she had repeated to herself, not once but many times during the evening . . .

'I have met *Monsieur* Gozlin,' Lord Hartcourt now said in his quiet voice. 'I advise you to steer well clear of him. He is not, as you say, a pleasant character.'

'I was not wrong, then,' Gardenia said. 'I just felt there was something . . . bad . . . about him.'

'Keep away from him,' Lord Hartcourt warned.

'I can't understand why the Baron likes him so much,' Gardenia said, speaking more to herself than to her companions, 'but then he always seems to like strange people.'

'Do they appear to be close friends?' Lord Hartcourt asked. 'I mean the Baron and *Monsieur* Gozlin?'

'Oh, very close!' Gardenia answered. 'The Baron seemed to be watching all the evening to see if *Monsieur* Gozlin was amused, if Aunt Lily was making enough fuss of him, and just as I went up to bed I saw him stop dancing with Aunt Lily himself and hand her over to *Monsieur* Gozlin. I thought she couldn't be very pleased about that.'

She stopped speaking, feeling once more she was being indiscreet. She wondered why Lord Hartcourt was so interested in the horrible froglike Frenchman.

'But I shouldn't be speaking like this,' she said quickly. 'Forget it, please forget it.'

'It is of no importance, of course,' Lord Hartcourt replied soothingly, but she had the feeling that to him it was important. There was something new and alert about him which there had not been earlier in the drive, and she thought she had interpreted a warning expression in his eyes as he looked over her head at his cousin Bertie. Still, she might have been mistaken. Why should they be interested in Aunt Lily's guests? She wished she had not said so much about the Baron. Perhaps they did not know that the Baron was there so often or on such familiar terms. She had much rather they did not know.

They drove round the *Bois* and finally stopped at the

restaurant in the centre where there were coloured umbrellas over small tables in the garden and where a number of people were sitting sipping aperitifs.

'How pretty it is!' Gardenia exclaimed.

Lord Hartcourt helped her dismount. Then, as she walked through the white gateway, he saw the old flowerseller from whom he had bought the gardenias for Henriette which he had finally left floating in the marble basin of the fountain in the Place de la Concorde.

'*Bonjour, Monsieur,*' the old man quavered as they passed him.

Gardenia stopped.

'How lovely lilies-of-the-valley smell!' she exclaimed.

Lord Hartcourt's lips twisted in a cynical smile. The little British sparrow might appear innocent, but she certainly knew the tricks of the trade, although he doubted whether, like all the other ladybirds, she knew enough to come back for her commission later on.

'I will buy you some,' Bertie said eagerly.

'No, no! Let me have the privilege,' Lord Hartcourt claimed with an ironic note in his voice.

Gardenia looked at them wide-eyed.

'Please, I don't want you to buy me anything, I just couldn't help remarking on the fragrance of the lilies. You see, we had a bed of them at home and they were my mother's favourite flowers.'

Bertie didn't seem to hear her. He was bringing a golden sovereign out of his pocket and finding that was all the change he had.

'I will buy them,' Lord Hartcourt said good-humouredly, and added in a low voice which Gardenia could not hear: 'Go and find a nice table, Bertie. I must say she occasionally does it over brown.'

'I believe every word she says!' Bertie exclaimed.

'I'm sure you do,' Lord Hartcourt said in an amused tone. 'Don't quarrel with me, my dear fellow. I'm putting myself out a great deal to be with you this afternoon.'

'And I've never for a moment stopped saying I'm grateful,' Bertie retorted as he hurried after Gardenia.

He found her a table with a big orange sunshade by the side of a tiny ornamental fountain.

'What would you like to drink?' he asked. 'Champagne?'

'Good gracious, no!' Gardenia laughed. 'I couldn't drink

121

champagne at this time of the day. Do you think they could possibly provide a cup of tea?'

'Most unlikely,' Bertie answered, 'but I'll try.'

Lord Hartcourt was still buying the lilies-of-the-valley.

Bertie bent towards Gardenia and said: 'You are lovely, you know, lovelier every time I see you. Gosh, I'm glad you were able to come out this afternoon! We've got to make plans, you and I.'

'Plans about what?' Gardenia asked.

'How we are going to see each other,' Bertie answered. 'I can't get Vane to chaperone us every time. He has interests of his own.'

'What sort of interests?' Gardenia asked.

'Well, as a matter of fact, he is a bit freer than usual,' Bertie confided. 'He's had a row with his *chère amie.*'

'What does that mean?' Gardenia asked.

'I thought you spoke French,' Bertie said. 'You know, his particular girl friend. Very pretty she was too.'

'You mean he was engaged to be married?' Gardenia asked.

'Oh, now really!' Bertie expostulated. 'You aren't as green as all that! He certainly had no intention of marrying Henriette. She's one of the *demi-monde*. Paris is full of them. One night you must get your Aunt Lily to bring you to Maxim's: you'll see the lot.'

Gardenia felt the colour rise up her face. So Lord Hartcourt had a *chère amie*. She had never thought of that, somehow. She had always seen him unattached, but, of course, naturally, she would not have been likely to meet this Henriette at one of her aunt's parties. She did not know why, but she felt a sudden depression. The sun seemed to have gone out.

Gardenia chided herself for being foolish. Men like Lord Hartcourt, and she supposed Mr Cunningham as well, obviously had French lady friends whom they entertained and took out to dinner. How childish and foolish Mr Cunningham must think her to have spoken of marriage. Of course, she knew there were women who were not received in respectable society, who were gay, fast and very attractive to men. But somehow Lord Hartcourt had seemed so staid and conventional that she had not expected him to be what her father called a 'Stage-door Johnny.' She had a sudden curiosity to know what Henriette was like. What did Lord Hartcourt admire in a woman, what

122

did he find attractive? But naturally she knew that it would be extremely ill-bred to question Mr Cunningham on such a matter or, indeed, to mention it at all. As her mother would have said only too firmly, ladies did not talk about such things or such people.

Bertie had already forgotten the subject, being far more intent on his own affairs.

'When can I see you?' he said insistently. 'Can you creep out one night? I could wait for you a little way down the road and we would go somewhere amusing. You would love the Moulin Rouge! Although it is a bit noisy at times, I would look after you.'

'I couldn't possibly do anything like that,' Gardenia said. 'You know quite well that Aunt Lily has only just come round to allowing me to come out with you as long as Lord Hartcourt is there.'

'I wasn't suggesting you should ask your aunt,' Bertie said in an exasperated voice. 'Why should she know? She sends you off to bed early: creep out and meet me. It would be quite easy; once one of those noisy parties is in full swing nobody would hear you if you let off a bomb!'

'I couldn't, I couldn't really,' Gardenia protested. She didn't understand why Mr Cunningham kept pressing her to do things which she knew were wrong and involved disregard of any older person, let alone anyone who had been as kind as Aunt Lily.

Before she had any time to say anything more, Lord Hartcourt came back to the table with an enormous bunch of lilies-of-the-valley, in fact the flower-seller's whole stock.

'How very, very kind!' Gardenia exclaimed. 'but you shouldn't have spent all that money on me. I feel ashamed now of drawing attention to the flowers. Thank you so much!'

She buried her face in them and when she raised her head they saw her eyes were misty with tears.

'It seems so ungrateful,' she said in a very low voice, 'but sometimes I'm terribly homesick for England.'

Lord Hartcourt had a sudden vision of his own home in the spring, the great banks of rhododendrons, the lilac blossom heavy on the trees, and the pink cherry looking faintly oriental against the first green foliage of the English spring. He found himself wondering why he stayed in this foreign land when he might be at home. His horses were waiting for him; the gamekeepers would be eager to tell him how the pheasants were hatching out. There would be innumerable problems concerning the estate which in the past he had found tedious, but which he thought now would seem interesting.

'I have a good mind to go home,' he told himself. Then he knew that the house, large and lovely though it was, could be lonely. It was different if the place was filled with his friends, but one couldn't have party after party, and a man, if he was going to live in the country for any length of time, required a wife. He thought of the Roehampton girl and shuddered. He was getting maudlin, he told himself. What he needed was not a wife but another Henriette, and the sooner he started looking for one the better.

'Keep Miss Weedon amused,' he heard Bertie say, breaking into his thoughts of home. 'I see Archie Claydon over there. I want to ask him if he's got a tip for the Derby. He's usually pretty well informed.'

Bertie rose as he spoke and wended his way through the tables, leaving Gardenia and Lord Hartcourt alone.

She tried to find something to say, but she could only think of what she had just heard about him. Then she raised her downcast eyes to look straight into his. It appeared to her that there was a question he was asking her, but she was not certain what it was.

'Still happy?' he enquired.

'Of course,' she answered, a trifle untruthfully.

'You look very pretty,' he said, and somehow the compliment meant far more than Bertie's more fulsome admiration. 'Your dress is charming too.'

'Aunt Lily has been very kind,' Gardenia faltered.

'She is not the only person who would like to be kind to you,' Lord Hartcourt replied. Quite unexpectedly he put his hand over hers as it lay on the table. She had taken off her gloves and now she felt the warm hardness of his fingers. A sudden tremor went through her, quite unlike anything she had experienced before.

Now she saw that his eyes were on her lips. She felt herself blush, not because she understood, but rather because of the strange feeling which ran through her at the touch of his hand and something magnetic and exciting which was passing between them. She felt his fingers tighten.

'You know,' he said softly, 'the choice is entirely up to

you. No one can persuade you to do anything you don't want to do. You must make up your own mind.'

His words bewildered her. She did not understand what he was trying to say. It was a part of the whole incomprehensible relationship between herself and these two men who had come into her life so unexpectedly. She didn't understand one half of what they were talking about. She only knew now that her heart was beginning to throb in a very strange way, and she felt her breath coming quickly between her parted lips.

'You are so young and so unspoiled,' she heard Lord Hartcourt say. 'I think something ought to be done about you very quickly.'

She wanted to ask him what was the hurry; but, before she could say anything, Lord Hartcourt took his hand away and sat back in his chair. So she knew without looking round that Bertram Cunningham was coming back to the table.

He sat down, putting his top-hat on the empty chair beside Gardenia.

'Archie says Minorin is almost certain to win,' he announced.

'The King's horse!' Lord Hartcourt ejaculated. 'Well, it certainly might have a chance.'

'Archie says it is almost a certainty. I shall put my shirt on it and, if it comes home, Gardenia shall have the best and nicest present in all Paris.'

Gardenia flushed. He had used her christian name, but she thought that it would seem stiff and old-fashioned if she rebuked him. She also thought Aunt Lily would not be pleased if she accepted presents from a young man, but it seemed rude and ungracious to say so. Perhaps the horse would lose, she told herself.

The time passed quickly and finally Gardenia rose to her feet.

'I am sure it is time I was going home,' she said. 'We are going to the theatre tonight—the *Comédie Française*. For the first time I shall see a French play and I certainly don't want to be late.'

'Who is taking you? Bertie enquired.

'The Baron,' Gardenia answered. 'He said he was bringing another man to make us four. I do hope ...' she stopped suddenly.

125

'... that it is not Pierre Gozlin,' Lord Hartcourt finished. 'Well, I hope so too for your sake.'

'I couldn't bear it!' Gardenia exclaimed. 'It would spoil everything. No, I'm sure it will be somebody different.'

Nevertheless, feeling rather miserably that she might be wrong, she sat in silence as Bertie drove them back to Paris.

'Don't forget what I asked you,' Bertie whispered in her ear as they stopped outside Mabillon House. 'I shall be coming to your aunt's party on Thursday and I have a plan all worked out. But even that is too long to wait. I will call tomorrow afternoon in case there is a chance of seeing you.'

'I don't know what Aunt Lily's plans are,' Gardenia replied.

'Damn Aunt Lily!' he said irritably. 'I must see you.'

Gardenia smiled, and as she climbed out of the dogcart Lord Hartcourt helped her to the ground.

'Thank you so much,' she said. 'It was a lovely afternoon. I have enjoyed it so much.'

Lord Hartcourt shook her by the hand and the two men swept off their top-hats.

Gardenia ran up the steps and into the house. Glancing at the clock as she went through the hall she saw it was just after six o'clock. That meant Aunt Lily would be resting. She went up the stairs and, as she did so, the Baron came out of Aunt Lily's boudoir, shutting the door carefully behind him.

'Ah, there you are, Gardenia,' he said. 'Your aunt was expecting you back earlier.'

'I had a lovely drive,' Gardenia replied.

'With the two Englishmen?' the Baron enquired.

Gardenia nodded.

'Yes, Lord Hartcourt and his cousin Mr Bertram Cunningham. We drove in a dogcart and tandem. It was very, very smart!'

'Ha! These Englishmen, they are always affecting something new for the sport,' the Baron said scornfully. 'Such frivolities, such a waste of money! My countrymen have more serious things to think about!'

'One doesn't always want to be serious when it is the spring and one is in Paris,' Gardenia protested.

She had enjoyed herself so much that she was not going

126

to let the Baron spoil it with his criticisms and his insinuations. She had heard him before say that the English were effete and wasted their whole lives looking only for amusement.

'And what did you talk about to Lord Hartcourt?' the Baron enquired.

'Nothing very important,' Gardenia parried.

'You like this Lord?' the Baron asked.

The question was unexpected and to her annoyance Gardenia felt herself blushing.

'I like both Lord Hartcourt and his cousin immensely,' she replied. 'At least we all speak the same language.'

It was a rude retort, but the Baron seemed unperturbed.

'That is goot,' he said. 'You must make friends with nice young men. That is what your aunt wants for you, and especially she likes Lord Hartcourt, eh?'

'I must go and dress,' Gardenia said hastily, 'or I shall be late for the theatre. I am looking forward to it so much.'

'Ah yes, the theatre,' the Baron said, as though it had just come to his attention. 'I am bringing my friend with me whom I think you met last night, *Monsieur* Pierre Gozlin.'

'Oh no!' Gardenia ejaculated involuntarily before she could stop herself.

The Baron raised his eyebrows.

'You do not like him? Your aunt feels the same. He is not a very prepossessing man but clever, very clever. One cannot always have both looks and brains. As you grow older you will understand that. But in fact *Monsieur* Gozlin wishes to speak not with you but with your aunt. You can talk with me. That will be pleasant, eh?'

'Very pleasant,' Gardenia replied through stiff lips.

The Baron chuckled and stepping forward put his thick fingers under her small chin and turned her face up to his.

'Very pleasant,' he repeated, and before she could move or even realise what was happening, he bent his head and his lips were on hers. She recoiled from him, wrenching herself free; then, without a word, she was running swiftly up the stairs, frantically scrubbing her mouth as she did so with the back of her hand.

As she went she heard the Baron laugh, a throaty, guttural laugh, which made her loathe him as she had never loathed any man in the whole of her life.

Nine

That evening Gardenia kept to her bedroom. She felt she
could not face the Baron. The memory of his kiss seemed
to sear her lips so that, even though she rubbed them until
they were raw, the horror and the indignity of it remained.

'I hate him!' she stormed, walking up and down her
room, and then knew with a sudden feeling of utter
helplessness there was nothing she could do about it. How
could she go to Aunt Lily and complain? And there was
no one else. Never before in her life had she felt so utterly
alone. With tears in her eyes, she thought how this was the
lot of all women, that they were at the mercy of men.

Suffragettes, with their screaming for equality, might
have made themselves laughing-stocks, but in many ways
they were right; for, however much people might talk of a
woman's influence and her inspiration to men, in actual
fact she was a chattel, a second-class citizen without rights
or privileges unless they were granted to her through the
benevolence of her father or husband.

Half an hour before dinner was due, Gardenia sent a
note to her aunt saying she had a headache. Then she lay
down on her bed, knowing that it was in fact the truth,
except that she had a heartache as well.

She suddenly felt not only disgust with the Baron but
with everyone else she had met in her aunt's house:
fulsome, overvoluble Frenchmen, drunk and noisy women,
the sinister frog-like Pierre Gozlin, and, to crown all, the
guttural brutish boorishness of the Baron.

It was with a sense of relief that her thoughts dwelt on
Lord Hartcourt. His reserve, his dignity and, especially,
his reticence made her feel proud that he was her country-
man. She found herself thinking of that surprising moment
when his fingers had touched hers, and she had felt some
strange and almost magical communication. Perhaps, she
thought, she had misunderstood him when he had seemed
to be rude to her on the balcony at the party. She wanted

to make excuses for him; she wanted to cling to him as a person of integrity and strength amidst the crowd of strange and unpleasant people she had met since she arrived in Paris.

What was wrong? Why was this house so different from what she had expected? Why did her aunt encourage the attentions of such a man as the Baron? Why did Aunt Lily have to be kind to a man like Pierre Gozlin? It was all too incomprehensible. Gardenia only felt lost and unhappy and, like a child, found the tears running down her cheeks as secretly she cried for her mother.

Gardenia went to sleep in tears, but with the elasticity of youth she woke in the morning feeling the cloud of depression had gone, that she was strong enough to cope with everything.

She woke early and decided that while the house was sleeping she could no longer lie in bed. She had found out by now that even the servants kept late hours because there was no one up early enough to hustle them about their duties and because, in fact, most of them had gone to bed very late.

Gardenia knew that it was not correct for her to go out walking by herself, that a maid should accompany her; but she doubted if Jeanne was awake yet and, even if she was, she had no desire for her company.

She dressed and slipped down the stairs. She undid the bolts and locks on the front door herself and pulled it to behind her with a decisive little bang.

There was something exciting and adventurous about being abroad in Paris at this hour of the morning, and she felt that, however much she might be scolded for her escapade, it would be worth it.

The sun was shining, there was a scent of flowers in the air, and she felt as though she moved along the pavements with winged feet. She reached the Champs Elysées; the blossoms on the chestnut trees were like pink and white candles against the blue of the sky.

There were none of the fashionably and elegantly dressed persons of the *beau monde* sitting under the trees and at the little tables. They would be all fast asleep in bed. Instead there were men in shirt-sleeves sweeping up the debris of the night before, and numbers of women of all ages, black shawls over their heads and carrying huge baskets, which told Gardenia they had come from the market having made their purchases for the day. There were workmen of every type hurrying off to their jobs or driving their carts down the roads, some of them pulled by dogs.

It was all fascinating and thrilling, and Gardenia moved amongst the trees hardly aware of the curious glances which followed her. Wearing her dress of green she looked like some tree-nymph, with her face alight with excitement, her eyes shining, and her fair hair only partially concealed by her straw hat with its wreath of flowers.

She must have walked for an hour before she realised she was hungry and should retrace her steps. She had just turned for home when there was the sound of a horse's hooves beside her and she glanced up to see a handsome face leaning down towards her and heard a voice exclaim:

'*Ma'm'selle* Weedon, this is a surprise!"

It was the Comte André de Grenelle and she was not too pleased to see him.

'Good morning,' she said stiffly.

'You are up early,' he said, 'and you look as beautiful as the spring itself. May I compliment you, *Ma'm'selle,* both on your looks and your gown?'

'You may if you want to,' Gardenia replied crushingly, 'but I'm afraid I cannot stop and listen; I am in a hurry to get home.'

'I doubt if you will go faster than my horse,' he retorted with a whimsical smile.

There was no reply to this and Gardenia walked swiftly along, aware that he was keeping level with her and feeling that his intrusion spoiled her enjoyment of the morning.

'Do you always rise so early?' the Comte enquired.

'It is a chance to be by myself,' Gardenia said with meaning.

'You are very unkind to me,' he complained.

She refused to look at him, keeping her eyes staring straight ahead of her. After a moment he added:

'All I want is to be your friend.'

'I have no need for any further friends,' she answered, and wished that it was the truth.

'You are interested only in my Lord Hartcourt and his young cousin,' André said. 'But I assure you, they can't offer you anything more than I can offer, and perhaps less. Will you not please smile at me, *Ma'm'selle?*'

Gardenia thought he was talking nonsense and kept on walking. She could not help feeling at the same time that when he was sober the Comte was rather charming. He was so handsome and with the supple grace of a perfect equestrian he looked his very best on a horse.

The Comte was silent for a moment; then he said:

'Tonight when I come to your aunt's party I will bring you a present. It will be something which I know you will like. Something to match the grey of your eyes. Will you promise me that we may go somewhere quiet so that I may give it to you?'

'It is kind of you,' Gardenia answered, 'but I am sure my aunt would not wish me to accept presents from a stranger.'

'But I am not a stranger!' the Comte expostulated. 'Besides, why should your aunt object?—she herself accepts very beautiful presents and makes no fuss about it. I heard you were wearing one the other day.'

'I was?' Gardenia exclaimed in surprise. 'I don't know what you are talking about.'

'The magnificent chinchilla cape which I am told you were wearing the first day when you went to see *Monsieur* Worth,' the Comte said. 'That was a present to your aunt, and I can guess who gave it to her.'

'Indeed?' Gardenia's reply was frigid.

She felt this was dangerous ground. What right had the Comte to gossip about her aunt? What right had he to insinuate something unpleasant? At the same time, she would have been inhuman if she hadn't been curious. The chinchilla cape was worth thousands of pounds. She realised that. And who could have spent such a sum on her aunt—except perhaps one person? She felt the blood rising in her cheeks, and because she couldn't bear to hear the Comte say the words she turned suddenly and twisted her way through a labyrinth of small tables where she knew he could not follow.

She heard him call after her: '*Ma'm'selle* Gardenia, where are you going? Wait for me!' Then rounding the side of a small kiosk which sold newspapers and tobacco, she started to run, wending her way through the trees and keeping well away from the paths which could be used by a horse.

She ran swiftly without looking behind her, and when finally a few minutes later she reached Mabillon House she was out of breath and her heart was beating suffocatingly.

Only when she reached the safety of the drive did she look back to see the Comte was no longer in sight. He had spoiled her morning with his gossip, his insinuations and, most of all, his suggestion that she would be willing to accept a present from him! Why would Aunt Lily with all her money take presents from any man? Here was another bewildering question to which Gardenia longed and at the same time feared to know the answer.

The front door was opened to her by a footman, who looked at her in surprise, but without saying a word Gardenia ran up the stairs and reached the sanctuary of her own room. Was this the only place, she asked herself almost sadly, where she could find safety?

She was not able to see her aunt till lunchtime, and after Gardenia had apologised for being unable to go to the theatre the night before they went for a short drive, called at several shops and returned home in time for tea.

As her aunt went up to rest, Gardenia was well aware that it was dangerous to hang about in case the Baron should appear. He was not likely to arrive so early, but she was taking no chances. She slipped downstairs to the library to find a newspaper to read, prepared if necessary to go through the hidden door and up the back staircase she had used the first night of her arrival, rather than encounter the Baron in the hall.

She had not been in the room more than a few seconds when she heard the front-door bell ring. It was unlikely to be the Baron, but picking up the newspaper she sought for the hidden spring which the Housekeeper had used to usher her up the back stairs. To her dismay it was not where she had expected it to be. She thought she had memorised the spot so clearly, but it was not there. While she was still hurriedly pulling one or two books out of the case, the library door opened and she heard the Major-Domo's voice saying, 'I think *Ma'm'selle* is in here, Herr Baron.'

She turned round startled, her face suddenly pale, her eyes wide with apprehension. The Baron, looking larger and more formidable than usual, came into the room.

'Ah, here you are, Gardenia,' he said. 'The Major-Domo said he thought he had seen you.'

'I have nothing to say to you,' Gardenia said defiantly.

133

'My dear child,' the Baron made a gesture with his hands. 'You must allow me to apologise. I am afraid that I frightened and distressed you yesterday. It was stupid of me. You must understand that I look on you as a child, just a child, who might be the daughter of my very dear friend, the Duchesse. When I kissed you, and I am afraid it was that that has incensed you, it was the kiss of a father or an uncle. I assure you it was nothing more.'

Gardenia had thought at the time it was a great deal more, but she told herself now that she was too inexperienced to judge. Perhaps German fathers or uncles did kiss their children on the mouth. It was not the English way. But, as she had so often before thought, foreigners were different. She felt herself relax. It was difficult to stand there defiant and antagonistic when the Baron was prepared to apologise so abjectly.

'We must be friends,' Gardenia, he was saying, and she knew he was making every effort to make his voice beguiling. 'We both love the same person, we both wish for her happiness. Is that not true? I am referring naturally to your beloved aunt.'

'Yes, of course,' Gardenia agreed.

'Then we must not quarrel,' the Baron went on. 'She is fond of you. Indeed, she loves you; for she has told me so. You are taking the place in her heart of the child she never had. As for me I am of no importance, but all I want is her happiness, her contentment. Can you understand that?'

'Yes, of course,' Gardenia said again.

'Then you forgive me,' the Baron asked.

'I forgive you,' Gardenia replied. There was really nothing else she could say.

'That then is finished,' the Baron said positively. 'And now, my dear Gardenia, sit down for a minute; for I have something of importance to say to you, which is why I have called so early this evening. I wanted to see you without your aunt knowing anything of our conversation.'

Gardenia stiffened again.

'Why?' she asked.

'Sit down and I will tell you,' the Baron replied.

She obeyed him, sitting very gingerly on the edge of the chair, her hands folded in her lap, her back very straight. Though she had forgiven him, she liked him as much as anyone could like a rattlesnake. 'I don't trust him,' she thought. His eyes were shifty and she felt as though every time those thick lips moved they lied.

'I have told you,' the Baron said, 'that your aunt loves you. Can you tell me what are your feelings for her?'

'Of course I love Aunt Lily,' Gardenia said defensively. 'She has been so kind to me. Besides, she is my only relation. I have no one else in the world.'

'Very sad,' the Baron commented, 'and who would want more than an aunt who is so devoted, who has taken you into her house and into her life, and wants only that you should be happy.'

'No one could be kinder,' Gardenia murmured.

'I agree,' the Baron said, 'and that is why I want you to do something in return for your aunt.'

'But of course,' Gardenia answered. 'What can I do?'

'Something a little difficult but something which will give her great happiness,' the Baron said. 'You are prepared to do it?'

'Naturally,' Gardenia answered. 'There is no question about it. Why didn't Aunt Lily ask me herself?'

'Ah! That is the point,' the Baron said. 'Your aunt must know nothing of what I am saying to you. That is very important! For if she knew I was asking you, she would, because she is so unselfish, because she thinks of everyone but herself, tell you to do nothing.'

'I am sure that is true,' Gardenia agreed.

'Well, this is the position,' the Baron went on. 'Your aunt has a protégé, a young man for whom she has an affection because his mother was a close friend. He is an orphan, and when his parents died your aunt made herself responsible for him financially. He was English and he was very anxious to go into the English Navy. Your aunt arranged it and he is at present at sea with the British fleet!'

'How old is he?' Gardenia asked, not because she particularly wanted to know, but the Baron seemed to expect some comment from her.

'About seventeen or eighteen, I think,' the Baron answered vaguely. 'He is, of course, only a midshipman or whatever you call the very lowest officer in the British Navy.'

'Yes, that is right, a midshipman,' Gardenia said.

The Baron screwed his eye-glass tight into his eye.

'What is worrying your aunt,' he said, 'is that she thinks this boy, David is his name, is in some sort of trouble.'

'Why does she think that?' Gardenia asked.

'Because she has had various messages from him,' the Baron answered. 'But here is the difficulty; they are smuggled out to her by other young men in the Navy and they are written in code.'

'In code!' Gardenia ejaculated.

'That is what we think it must be,' the Baron explained, 'and naturally your aunt doesn't understand it.'

'But I can't understand why he should write in code.' Gardenia said.

'Nor can your aunt,' the Baron said with a gesture of his hands. 'That is why she thinks David must be in some terrible trouble, imprisoned on the ship for some misdemeanour. Maybe he dare not let his messages be read by those who smuggle them to your aunt.'

'It sounds very strange,' Gardenia said.

'That is what your aunt keeps saying,' the Baron agreed, 'and you can imagine how desperately it worries her. She doesn't sleep, for she has told me so. David's dilemma is at the back of her mind all the time.'

'She has said nothing to me,' Gardenia said.

'I know,' the Baron said, shaking his head. 'She would not wish to worry you; and, besides, she is afraid, afraid for little David.'

'In what way?' Gardenia asked.

The Baron lowered his voice. 'Can't you see that if a lot of people are told of what he is doing it may make things worse for him? If he is imprisoned and if he has been told he is not to write letters, which seems likely, then to say anything would be to draw attention to him, perhaps to make his punishment worse.'

'Yes, I suppose I can understand that,' Gardenia agreed. 'But what can I do about it?'

'That is just what I am coming to,' the Baron answered. 'I believe you can help your aunt. I believe you can put her out of her misery if only you will do what I say.'

'Of course I will try,' Gardenia told him.

'You promise that you will not say anything to her of all this? She would be angry with me, very, very angry, if she knew that I told you. But I can't bear to go on seeing her suffering.'

'I promise,' Gardenia answered, 'but how can I help?'

'You can do exactly as I tell you to do,' the Baron said, 'and then your aunt will know what is hidden in these messages.'

'I can't find an answer to the code,' Gardenia said. 'I don't know anybody who has codes.'

'Indeed you do,' the Baron said almost triumphantly, 'Lord Hartcourt has them!'

'So you want me to ask him?' Gardenia enquired.

The Baron threw up his hands in horror.

'No, no, a thousand times no! How can you be so stupid, so insensitive? Can't you see, if Lord Hartcourt thought David was using the Naval Code to write to your aunt it could be disastrous? He might even report him to the Captain of the ship on which the boy is serving. Whatever punishment David is enduring now, it would be much more stringent if it was discovered what steps he was taking to get in touch with the outside world.'

'Yes, I can see that,' Gardenia said, and it did appear to her that the Baron's story was logical.

'What you must do,' the Baron went on, 'is to get a look at the book in which Lord Hartcourt has the Naval Code.'

'How do you know he has it?' Gardenia asked.

The Baron smiled at her.

'My dear child, everybody knows that in Lord Hartcourt's new position at the Embassy it is his job to decode all the cables and letters which come to the Embassy.'

'I understand,' Gardenia said. 'So if we could see his book we could decode David's messages.'

'That is right,' the Baron said.

'But I am not likely to see it, am I?' Gardenia asked. 'I don't suppose he brings it out to dinner with him.'

'No, but it will be in his apartment at the Embassy,' the Baron replied.

'Then how can I see it there?' Gardenia asked. She thought now the Baron was talking nonsense and what he had suggested didn't make sense.

'That is the difficult part,' the Baron said, 'and that is why I am going to ask you, for your aunt's sake, to go to Lord Hartcourt's rooms.'

Gardenia rose to her feet.

'But of course I couldn't do that,' she said quickly. 'I don't know how you can suggest such a thing. I know my mother would not approve of my going alone to any man's rooms, and I don't think Aunt Lily would approve of it either. I am afraid, Baron, the answer must be no.'

The Baron rose also.

'I am sorry,' he said. 'I thought you were fond of your aunt. I thought you were grateful for all she had done for you since you came to Paris, desolate, orphaned, with the idea, I think, of becoming a governess, or was it a companion? But I was mistaken. The young have no gratitude and little interest in anything except themselves. I thought you were different.'

'That is not fair,' Gardenia said hotly. 'You know I would help my aunt if I could. You know I am grateful to her. But how can I go alone to any man's rooms? What would Lord Hartcourt think?'

'Lord Hartcourt would not know,' the Baron replied, 'but don't talk about it any more. You are right and I am wrong. I am just an old fool who doesn't like to see a woman suffer, and I know how deeply your aunt is suffering. Forget it, please don't mention it again. Let us both behave as though this conversation had never taken place.'

He made as though to walk to the door.

'You say that Lord Hartcourt will never know?' Gardenia said in a low voice. 'But surely that is impossible.'

'Well, he might know,' the Baron conceded, 'but he would not be there at the time. He would only learn about it afterwards and then think it of little consequence.'

'I don't see how you can arrange that,' Gardenia said.

'I have an idea, a very simple one,' the Baron replied. 'But you have already said you do not wish to help your aunt.'

'I didn't say anything of the sort,' Gardenia said with a touch of anger in her voice. 'I merely said it was impossible for me to go alone to a man's rooms.'

'But if the man is not there and the rooms are empty, what then?' the Baron asked.

'How can you be sure of that?' Gardenia asked.

'I can be sure, absolutely certain,' the Baron said. 'But don't let's talk about it. Let your aunt be unhappy, let the boy remain imprisoned or whatever is happening to him. I expect there will be a solution in time. Time usually settles everything. But I couldn't bear your aunt to be ill, and that is what I am afraid she will be if she goes on like this. Forget about it, Gardenia. Go and put on one of your pretty dresses and enjoy yourself.'

'No, wait a minute,' Gardenia said. 'Tell me exactly what you have in mind.'

With a little smile on his lips the Baron shut the door which he had already opened . . .

An hour later Gardenia drove in the carriage up to the door of the British Embassy. It was only just half past five and the Baron had assured her that Lord Hartcourt was playing polo at that very moment on the other side of Paris. Nevertheless her lips felt dry and her voice quavered a little as, when the door was opened, she asked:

'Can I see Lord Hartcourt, please?'

'His Lordship is out,' the footman informed her.

'I am sure there must be some mistake,' Gardenia protested. 'I made an appointment to meet Lord Hartcourt here this evening. I have brought an aquarium which he asked me to bring.'

She held a small glass tank in her hands, and the man could see the little fish darting backwards and forwards in the water.

'Please wait a moment, Miss.' The footman pulled the door wider open and another man appeared dressed like an English butler. It was not the redoubtable Jarvis whom everybody in Paris knew, because the Baron had told her that today was Jarvis's day out. It was another Englishman, his assistant, who had only recently arrived at the Embassy.

Gardenia raised her large eyes to him.

'Lord Hartcourt asked me particularly to come here this evening,' she said, 'at half past five and bring him this aquarium. I am afraid he must have forgotten our appointment.'

'His Lordship is playing polo, I think, Miss,' the butler said, and Gardenia's heart gave a little throb of relief.

'In that case perhaps I could put the aquarium up in his sitting-room,' she said. 'I am afraid I must carry it there myself because it is very easy to upset the water, and that disturbs the fish.'

'Very well, Miss. If you will come this way.'

The new butler didn't hesitate as an older man would have done about the unconventionality of a young lady going up to his Lordship's private rooms.

He led the way and Gardenia followed him slowly. The

water in the tank was inclined to slop over. At the same time she was terribly afraid that they might meet someone.

'Don't worry,' the Baron had assured her. The Ambassador and Ambassadress are attending a reception at the Persian Embassy. I know, because I was invited there myself.'

They reached the second floor and the butler opened the door. Gardenia entered Lord Hartcourt's sitting-room and walked across to put the small aquarium, which by this time seemed very heavy, down on a table in the centre of the room.

She arranged it first this way and then the other and then said:

'I will just leave the instructions for Lord Hartcourt as to how he must feed the fish. Do you think I could write him a note?'

'But of course, Miss,' the butler said. He drew a piece of crested writing-paper from the leather-covered case which stood on the writing-desk. He placed it on the blotter and pulled the ink-pot with its attached glass pen-tray, in which there was a confusion of different pens, a little nearer.

'You can write here, Miss,' he suggested.

'Thank you so much,' Gardenia smiled at him. 'I am afraid it will take me a minute or two. Don't wait if you are busy.'

'You can find your way down, Miss?'

'Yes, quite easily,' Gardenia smiled. 'I will prop the letter against the aquarium so that his Lordship will see it as soon as he arrives back.'

'Very good, Miss.'

The butler, who was not particularly interested in the aquarium or in Lord Hartcourt's reaction to it, obviously wanted to get back to the hall and went out leaving the door ajar.

Gardenia, waiting until she heard his footsteps dying away, sprang from the writing-table and closed the door quietly. Her heart was beating suffocatingly. She opened the drawers of the desk.

'Look at the back,' the Baron had said. 'Englishmen are so untidy and careless, they always shove anything of importance at the back of a drawer.'

It was actually true, Gardenia knew. Her father always

140

used to put the letters of importance or the bills he found unpalatable at the back of the drawer in his desk. She remembered that her mother had to ferret them out and get him to pay them when he was in a good mood.

There were various small books and letters and a profusion of other papers at the back of Lord Hartcourt's drawers, but not the book for which she was looking.

'It is likely to be small with either a grey or blue stiff cover,' the Baron had instructed her. 'It may have nothing written on the outside, more than likely not. Just open it, glance inside, and find only one letter, or two or three if you can, and what is written against them. That is all I need. I can then set your aunt's mind at rest.'

It sounded quite a simple thing to do. But Gardenia, concerned at the impropriety of entering Lord Hartcourt's room, could only search with trembling hands, anxious to find what she was seeking and to be gone.

There was only one drawer left, the lowest one on the left-hand side. She had to kneel down to open it and put her hand at the back. She was in this position, her skirts billowing out round her, when she heard the door behind her open. She turned her head, for the moment too paralysed even to jump to her feet. Then, as she saw who stood there, she felt the blood drain from her cheeks and her heart almost stopped beating.

Lord Hartcourt came into the room. He was wearing his white polo-breeches and his peaked cap was in his hand. He looked at her and the expression on his face was the most frightening she had ever thought to see on any man's.

'Good evening,' he said. 'You appear to be searching for something. Can I help you?'

The Baron had told her that if by any chance she was disturbed by a servant she was to say that she was looking for an envelope. But now everything he had told her went out of Gardenia's head. She could only stay where she was, kneeling on the floor and staring at Lord Hartcourt as if he was an apparition from some other world.

'I had no idea that my possessions, meagre though they are, would be of such interest to you,' Lord Hartcourt said. 'May I enquire what particular object you had in mind?'

'I thought you were playing polo,' Gardenia said, almost idiotically.

'That was obvious,' Lord Hartcourt said. 'And now are you prepared to give me an explanation or do I ask one of the footmen to fetch the police?'

'The police?' Gardenia got slowly to her feet. Her face was very white and she was trembling.

'I can't explain,' she said. 'It ... it would get someone into trouble.'

'I'm sure it would,' Lord Hartcourt said easily, 'but I'm afraid you have got to give me an explanation; otherwise, as I suggested, I must send for the police and accuse you of stealing.'

'But I haven't stolen anything,' Gardenia expostulated.

'How can I know that?' Lord Hartcourt replied. 'I personally am not prepared to search you, and you are here in my rooms under false pretences. You told the butler that you had an appointment with me.'

'Yes, I know that was not ... true.' Gardenia faltered miserably, 'but I had to come.'

'What for?' Lord Hartcourt's question was like a pistol-shot.

'I can't tell you,' Gardenia replied. 'You see, as I have already said, it would be getting someone into trouble.'

'It is going to get you into a great deal of trouble, I'm afraid,' Lord Hartcourt said. 'Very well, if you won't tell me, I will send a footman for the nearest policeman. I think there is usually one on duty outside the Embassy.'

'No, no, please!' Gardenia cried. 'It would cause a terrible scandal, and what would Aunt Lily say?'

'I should think she would say a great deal,' Lord Hartcourt answered, 'but not half as much as I am going to say. What are you doing here in my rooms? Who sent you? What are you looking for? Who's paying you?'

As the questions came out fast and furiously, Gardenia took a step backwards, recoiling from him, her hands going out trembling to seek the support of the desk.

'Nobody's paying me,' she protested. 'Of course they're not.'

'Do you expect me to believe that?' Lord Hartcourt asked. 'Spies are always paid and paid heavily, I believe.'

He spoke with so much scorn in his voice that Gardenia felt almost as though he had flayed her with a whip.

'But I am not a spy,' she said. 'I swear I am not spying.'

'Then what have you come here for?' he enquired.

She opened her lips to speak and realised suddenly, as

142

though someone had hit her with a blow between the eyes, what was the truth. Her eyes widened and suddenly her fingers crept up towards her beating heart.

'I didn't know. I didn't realise,' she said. 'Oh God, what am I to do? I must have been crazy to have listened to him!'

'To listen to whom? The Baron?' Lord Hartcourt asked.

'Yes, but I didn't realise what he was asking of me. I thought it was strange, but he told me my aunt was unhappy and worrying. He said that if I cared for her at all, and the way he put it it seemed such a little thing, such a very little thing . . .' Gardenia's voice broke. She was on the verge of tears.

'Suppose you sit down and tell me all about it,' Lord Hartcourt said in a very different voice.

Almost as though she obeyed him in a dream, Gardenia crossed the room to the sofa by the fireplace. She sat down, pulling her hat from her head as she did so, and the evening sunlight coming in through the window touched the gold of her curls and turned them into fire. She clasped her hands together and raised a white and frightened face to Lord Hartcourt.

'I believed him when he told me about this boy, a midshipman in the Navy, and now I wonder if he really exists at all. Perhaps he just invented him. How could I be so stupid, so foolish?'

This time the tears broke her voice. She clenched her hands together, fighting for self-control.

'Start from the beginning,' Lord Hartcourt said quietly.

In faltering, trembling tones, Gardenia told him exactly what had happened, what the Baron had said about the imprisonment of the midshipman, how she had said it was impossible for her to visit a man's rooms and how he had told her to forget about it as obviously she did not care for her aunt.

'I am grateful, terribly grateful to Aunt Lily,' Gardenia went on. 'The way the Baron put it, it seemed so ungracious, so unkind of me not to try to help her.'

'You're a little fool,' Lord Hartcourt said, and now there was no anger in his voice. 'But I believe you.'

'I see now how stupid I was,' Gardenia went on brokenly. 'Of course the boy would not write in such a way, even if he was imprisoned. I don't suppose a midshipman can even get at the Naval Code.'

'Of course he can't,' Lord Hartcourt agreed.

'I didn't stop to think,' Gardenia went on. 'The Baron made me hurry upstairs and get my hat; when I came down he had the little aquarium waiting for me and the carriage was outside.'

'The Baron knows his job,' Lord Hartcourt said. 'Shock tactics should always be carried out at the double. Act first and think afterwards, at least as far as the truth is concerned. The German High Command always do their thinking well in advance.'

'Everything he said was right,' Gardenia murmured. 'You were playing polo, there was a new butler, the Ambassador was out.'

'They are very thorough,' Lord Hartcourt agreed. 'But he didn't anticipate the game would be over early owing to an accident.'

'How can I ask you to forgive me?' Gardenia asked with a little throb in her voice. 'I am ashamed, deeply ashamed, at being so stupid. If you had sent for the police how could I have explained that I was looking for the Naval Code? They would have thought that I was a spy.'

'They would have indeed,' Lord Hartcourt said rather grimly. 'France is very sensitive as regards foreign spies at the moment, perhaps because they are everywhere.'

'You mean Germans are spying on the French?'

'But of course,' Lord Hartcourt said, 'and on the British. They can think of nothing else. No pawn is too small, and you would have played your part in their game of intrigue if it had come off. I am sure Herr Baron really imagines that in my usual careless, soft British manner I leave the Code Book lying about on my desk. It would have been a tremendous feather in his cap if you had found it. If you failed, well, I should merely have been surprised that you had come to call at the Embassy, and there was the charming little present, for which I would have to thank you, and a note which would have accounted for your presence in my sitting-room.'

'It is clever, terribly clever,' Gardenia said, 'but if I had any wits about me I would not have fallen into his trap so easily.'

'The Baron is a very experienced and clever man,' Lord Hartcourt said. 'It is not the first time he has brought off a coup of this sort.'

Gardenia looked startled.

'You mean he is a spy?' she asked. 'Then why, why don't you arrest him?'

'My dear, we are friends with Germany. They are our cousins, we are devoted to them,' Lord Hartcourt said with heavy sarcasm. 'We should never do anything so gauche as to make accusations we could not prove against anyone so important as the Baron von Knesebech.'

'But you can prove them!' Gardenia exclaimed. 'He sent me here.'

'And suppose he denies it?' Lord Hartcourt asked. 'It is only your word against his, and who do you think is going to be believed?'

'But I would say that he insisted I came, that he gave me the aquarium.'

Lord Hartcourt smiled.

'And you, young and attractive, went to the rooms of a man whom you knew very slightly, in whose company you had been seen on several occasions alone. What explanation do you think the world, the sensuous world of high society, would put on that?'

'Oh!' The exclamation came involuntarily from Gardenia's lips. Her two hands pressed against her cheeks as if to hide the flooding colour which rose from her tiny chin to the top of her little forehead.

'Exactly,' Lord Hartcourt said. 'That is what they would think, Gardenia, and what a pity it is not true.'

He was no longer angry and his voice had almost a caressing note in it.

Gardenia got quickly to her feet.

'I must go home,' she said.

Lord Hartcourt, who had seated himself beside her on the sofa, reached out his hand, caught hers and drew her back.

'Not yet,' he said. 'Why waste this delightful interview which the Baron has arranged so skilfully?'

Gardenia, because the pressure of his hand compelled her, sat down on the edge of the sofa.

'Please, please don't tease me,' she begged. 'I am so unhappy, so worried and so ashamed. Just forgive me and tell me what I must say to the Baron.'

'Tell him the truth,' Lord Hartcourt said. 'No, I have a better idea.'

He got to his feet and wrote down three letters on a

145

piece of paper with a corresponding letter opposite each of them.

'Give him this,' he said. 'Tell him this is what you discovered in a little book.'

Gardenia looked at it suspiciously.

'What is it?' she asked.

'The Code for which you were looking,' Lord Hartcourt replied.

'But it is the wrong one,' Gardenia said positively.

'Of course,' Lord Hartcourt told her. 'It is the old one which is no longer in use. The Baron will be delighted with you until he discovers that your information is out of date.'

'I would rather not do it,' Gardenia said. 'I don't want to give him anything. I don't want to speak to him again. I have always hated him since I first saw him, and now I know he is a spy, that he wants to hurt my country . . .'

'Then help your country by doing what I tell you,' Lord Hartcourt said. 'Perhaps you can give us some information. It would be a change to have someone in the enemy's camp.'

Gardenia threw the piece of paper on the floor.

'I won't, I won't!' she cried passionately. 'You know as well as I do that I would not have come here if I had had the sense to understand what he was suggesting. I won't spy for anyone or anything. It is low and degrading. It makes me think of reptiles and serpents and I won't be a spy. I won't have anything to do with treachery.'

Lord Hartcourt laughed, but gently so that somehow she was not offended.

'You look lovely and your eyes flash when you are annoyed about something,' he said. 'I have never met a face which can show so many different emotions so quickly. You are a strange person, Gardenia.'

'I only feel unhappy at the moment,' she said. 'I have got to go back and face the Baron. I would like to tell him the truth, that you found me and that you know he was trying to make me spy against my own country.'

'No, don't tell him that,' Lord Hartcourt urged. 'It will do no good and only put him on his guard. Tell him nothing and give him the piece of paper as I have suggested.'

'No!' Gardenia said positively. 'He might try to thank

me before he realises that the information is wrong, and that I couldn't bear.'

She shuddered as she spoke and Lord Hartcourt looked at her with suddenly perceptive eyes.

'You hate him,' he said. 'Has he tried to make advances to you in any way?'

'He kissed me,' Gardenia said, the words slipping out almost before she was aware she had uttered them, 'and I wanted to kill him! I tried to hide from him, I stayed in my room all last evening and would not go down to dinner. Today he caught me unawares in the library, and he played on my feelings, I see that now, until I consented to come here. I can't, oh I can't keep seeing a man like that!'

'You will have to leave your aunt's house,' Lord Hartcourt said.

'How can I?' Gardenia asked piteously.

'Quite easily,' he replied. He bent forward and before she realised what he was doing he had slipped his arms round her and drawn her close to him. Suddenly she found his lips were close to hers and a quick tremor of excitement ran through her.

'Let me take you away, Gardenia,' Lord Hartcourt said very softly, 'I will keep you safe from all the wicked Barons in the world. I will look after you and I think we would be very happy together.'

She heard his words almost in a dream; then his lips were on hers and the world stood still. She felt his lips hard, possessive, take her mouth captive and she felt a sudden flame run through her, searing its way through her body and up her throat until she knew that without her conscious will or volition she was giving herself to him utterly and completely in a kiss which seemed to join them, man and woman, for all time. It was so beautiful, so utterly and completely wonderful. She remembered nothing save that she was safe at last.

The strong arms that held her kept out fear, and the wonder of his kiss had evoked an ecstasy in herself which was beyond anything she had ever imagined in her wildest dreams.

'I love you.'

She heard herself murmur the words against his mouth, and then he was kissing her again, wildly, passionately and with a fervour which made her feel the whole world was

147

alight with golden stars. Only when she felt his hand moving against the soft curve of her breast did she awaken to a sense of propriety. With difficulty she forced herself from his arms.

'I must go,' she said. 'I must not stay here. It is wrong. You must see that.'

She looked so lovely, with her eyes alight and her lips open where he had kissed them, that Lord Hartcourt sat looking at her as though he had never seen her before.

'I must go,' Gardenia repeated. 'Please, my aunt will be wondering what has happened to me.'

Lord Hartcourt glanced at the clock. In a short while he also had to be on duty.

'When can I see you again?' he asked. 'Alas, I can't come to you tonight. I have three different parties I have to attend with the Ambassador. It will be two o'clock in the morning before I am free.'

'Come tomorrow,' Gardenia said. She put her hands into his. 'I am happy, so terribly happy,' she whispered.

'And so am I,' Lord Hartcourt said. 'Are you going to tell your aunt?'

'No, no, of course not,' Gardenia said. 'She would tell the Baron and she would ask . . . oh, let us keep it secret, just you and I, until we have time to make plans.'

'That is right,' Lord Hartcourt smiled, 'we will make plans tomorrow. I will come and collect you about twelve-thirty. I think I can get away for lunch. We can go somewhere quiet and talk about everything.'

'That would be wonderful, utterly wonderful!' Gardenia cried.

She bent and picked up her hat from where she had thrown it on the ground. Then she stood for a moment, looking up at him. Her head only reached his shoulder.

With a look on her face that he had seldom seen on any woman's, she said very softly: 'It is true, isn't it, that we love each other?'

'Of course. You are very, very sweet, Gardenia, and I am a very lucky man.'

Then, as she gave a little sigh of utter content, Lord Hartcourt said in a sensible, business-like voice: 'We must get you out of here. Where is your carriage?'

'Outside the door,' Gardenia said. 'Does it matter?'

Lord Hartcourt's lips tightened for a moment, and she

loved him more because he was thinking of her reputation.

'We will have to brazen it out,' he said. 'Put your hat on and your gloves and speak to me as coolly and distantly as possible. If you had not brought your carriage I could have let you out by the side door.'

Gardenia did as he said, arranging her hat in the mirror over the mantelpiece, then walking across to the door where he was waiting.

He stood looking down at her and bending his head kissed her once again on the lips. She wanted to cling to him, she wanted to stay there in that enchanted room where she had found a new happiness; but the door was open and there was nothing she could do but walk sedately down the wide blue-carpeted staircase towards the front door.

Only as they went did she whisper to herself: 'One day I will come here quite openly; one day I will come as his wife, and walk beside him without fear of being seen, without being nervous in case we are overheard.'

As they reached the front door, Lord Hartcourt helped her down the steps into her carriage.

'Goodbye, Miss Weedon,' he said in a loud voice, taking her hand. 'Thank you very much for calling and for the very charming aquarium. It was most kind of you to bring it.'

He stood there as the carriage drove off. She had one last glimpse of him walking up the steps, his back towards her. She felt a sudden pang of unhappiness because she must leave him, because she felt as though he had already forgotten her. Then she told herself she was being childish. He had kissed her. She loved him and he loved her. Oh God, how she loved him!

Ten

Gardenia ran down the steps of the house to where Lord Hartcourt was waiting for her in his grey motor-car. She felt that the glory of the day dazzled her eyes and made it difficult to see him. The happiness welling up inside her turned everything to gold. She had woken this morning feeling as though she must cry out at the loveliness of the world just because she was so happy.

She had dressed with extra care, putting on a new dress which had arrived from *Monsieur* Worth, which seemed to give her a new radiance. It was pale cyclamen in colour with faint underlying touches of turquoise blue, very young and very simple in design. She looked like a lovely flower as she raised her face to Lord Hartcourt.

'You are punctual,' he said with a smile, 'the only woman I have ever known who does not keep me waiting.'

'I have been ready for over half an hour,' Gardenia replied. She was too unsophisticated and too overwhelmingly in love to pretend to him or be in any way coquettish.

She got into the motor-car and put her hand on his arm.

'I thought the hours would never pass till I could see you again,' she whispered.

He looked down at her, the expression on his face unusually tender.

'I wanted to see you too,' he said simply.

He started the car and they drove off.

'Where are we going?' she asked.

'To a little restaurant by the Seine,' he said. 'I think it will amuse you. You can watch the barges moving up and down the river and the food is superlative. In a month or so it will be spoiled, but at the moment only the discriminating few like myself know about it.'

Gardenia laughed.

'It makes you sound very conceited,' she said, 'but I

150

know exactly what you mean. Once everyone goes there it will no longer be amusing.'

'And no longer the place for us,' he said.

Gardenia resisted an impulse to press her face against his shoulder.

'Say that again,' she begged him. 'For the moment it seems to be the most wonderful word in the world—us—just you and I.'

'Just you and I,' he repeated. 'What a child you are, Gardenia! There is so much I want to teach you.'

He drove skilfully through the traffic. They reached the restaurant and Gardenia saw with pleasure that there were very few cars or carriages outside.

It was small and not expensively furnished, but she realised that Lord Hartcourt was an honoured guest and noticed they were taken to the best and most discreet table in a small alcove.

Gardenia drew off her gloves and the waiter handed her a large menu.

'Now don't hurry,' Lord Hartcourt advised. 'We must discuss the dishes. Always remember that food is a religion to the French and they take it very, very seriously.'

Gardenia wanted to say that she was not hungry because she felt as if she had already been fed on ambrosia. But she knew that that would spoil the meal for Lord Hartcourt, so, instead, she said:

'You choose, I know I shall like to eat whatever you do.'

Lord Hartcourt nodded his approval. It was what he had expected her to say. He took a long time discussing this dish and that with the waiter and even longer over the wine list. Finally it was all done, and he sat back and held out his hand to Gardenia. She put her fingers into his and felt the familiar little thrill run through her at his touch.

'I have splendid news for you,' Lord Hartcourt said.

'What is it?' she asked.

'A friend of mine has a flat on the left bank of the river which he is leaving tomorrow. He has been sent to Sweden and wants someone to take over the rest of his lease. It is furnished quite charmingly and has a magnificent view overlooking the Seine and Notre-Dame. Would you like that?'

'But of course,' Gardenia answered.

'A little later on I will have a house,' Lord Hartcourt

went on, 'but it is not yet available. The flat will be all that is necessary for the moment, and, as I say, it is available from tomorrow.'

'How marvellous!' Gardenia exclaimed. 'But surely we won't want it quite as quickly as that?'

'Today, if it were possible,' Lord Hartcourt said firmly. 'I will not have you living any longer in a house where the Baron is a frequent visitor. When I think what he asked of you I could murder the man with my own hands.'

His face darkened and Gardenia said quickly:

'Yes, you are right, of course you are right. He is a horrible man and I long to see the last of him—but I don't want to upset Aunt Lily.'

'Your Aunt's behaviour is something which I think we had best not discuss,' Lord Hartcourt said coldly.

Gardenia gave a little sigh.

'She has been very kind to me.'

'That is a matter of opinion,' Lord Hartcourt replied, 'but let us talk of something else. Shall we go and see this flat after luncheon?'

'Oh, may we?' Gardenia asked eagerly.

'I thought that was what you would like,' he said.

'I would love to see it. I am sure I will like it if you do, and, after all, you are the person who must be comfortable.'

'On the contrary, it is you who have got to be considered, you funny little thing. I shall not be able to be with you all the time, you know.'

Gardenia looked at him in surprise. Then she said:

'Oh well, you will have to go to work, of course. I understand that. But I will be able to cook your breakfast for you before you go. I hope you will think I am a good cook.'

Lord Hartcourt looked at her with a little frown between his eyes.

'I shan't be able to stay with you every night,' he said, 'only very occasionally in the week and sometimes at weekends, and then we might go away into the country. There are lots of charming little inns about twenty or thirty miles out of Paris . . .'

He stopped, realising Gardenia was looking at him with a very strange expression on her face.

'But surely . . .' she began, but at that moment there was an interruption.

While they had been talking the restaurant had been filling up, and now the door had opened to admit yet another couple, and the woman, having looked around her, had come straight up to their table.

Gardenia looked up to see one of the most attractive women she had ever seen standing staring at Lord Hart-court. Dressed in green, with a huge hat covered with green ostrich feathers, she carried a parasol of green chiffon and lace. It was a striking ensemble, but what held Gardenia's attention was the woman's face. She had never imagined anyone could have such a white skin or that her eyes, with their long artificially darkened lashes, should look so elegant, or indeed, in their own way so beautiful.

'Vane, I must speak to you.' The newcomer's voice was soft and beguiling. She spoke in French and one hand in a pale green suède glove went out towards him appealingly.

Lord Hartcourt rose very stiffly to his feet.

'I am sorry, but there is nothing to discuss.'

'But there is, you know there is. I want to tell you what happened. I want to give you an explanation, if you would only listen to me! You have not answered my letters—that is cruel and unlike you, Vane.'

Gardenia thought she had never heard a voice that could be so beguiling. She wondered how Lord Hartcourt could resist this woman's pleas.

'I am sorry, Henriette, I have nothing to say,' Lord Hartcourt said.

Gardenia felt herself go rigid. So this was Henriette, this was the *chère amie* of whom she had heard, this beautiful, exquisite, almost overwhelmingly attractive woman.

Lord Hartcourt resumed his chair.

'Goodbye, Henriette,' he said sharply. 'There is no point in prolonging this discussion.'

Henriette stood there and Gardenia saw her clench her fingers together.

'So that is all you have to say to me!'

Now her voice had changed, it was no longer beguiling but fierce and spiteful, and there was something in the way she spoke that reminded Gardenia of a snake.

'You can't get away with this,' she snarled. 'You can't treat me as though I was some dirt that you had picked up in the street. Your attorney came to see me this morning and told me to get out of the house. I'll move

153

when I am ready and not before. You can sue me; but you would not be likely to do that, would you, your important Lordship? They don't like scandals at your Embassy, but if you aren't careful I'll cause one.'

Lord Hartcourt looked up at her coolly. The venom and spite in Henriette's voice obviously had no effect on him.

'Either you leave this restaurant or I do,' he said. 'Do you wish me to call for the proprietor?'

For a moment Gardenia thought Henriette was going to strike him. It seemed as though there was a battle of wills between them.

'I have left you in possession of the emerald necklace,' Lord Hartcourt said, 'but I have not yet paid for it. If there is any trouble, Henriette, of any sort, scandals or a refusal to leave the house, then I will not be responsible for the bill. Is that clear?'

Henriette was beaten and she knew it. There was no chance of Lord Hartcourt returning to her, and she was well aware it might be a very long time before she found anyone else willing to spend such a large sum of money on her. Giving him a look of venomous hatred, she turned to leave the table, when she saw Gardenia as if for the first time.

'Perhaps you are the reason he is so eager to be rid of me,' she said to Gardenia in the same malevolent voice she had used with Lord Hartcourt. 'Well, he is certain to be bored within a few weeks. You're not his type, I can tell you that! And you can tell that old trollop your aunt the same thing!'

'Henriette!' Lord Hartcourt interrupted in a voice of thunder, but Henriette had already gone, walking back towards the door to the man who had brought her there.

'Come, we won't stay here,' she said in a high voice. 'The place is full of rats which have been swept out of *les Halles*. I wouldn't wish to eat amongst them.'

Several people looked up with angry expressions at the slang that was used only in the gutters of Montmartre; but Henriette had already gone, leaving behind her a disrupted atmosphere and an overpowering fragrance of expensive perfume.

Lord Hartcourt gave a little sigh of relief.

'I apologise,' he said to Gardenia. 'I didn't expect to

find her here. I would not have subjected you to that scene for anything in the world.'

Gardenia's face was very white.

'I'm sorry,' Lord Hartcourt said again, realising she was upset. 'Let us have a drink and you will feel better. I was a fool for ever getting mixed up with such a woman. People reveal their true character when things go wrong.'

He raised his hand and signalled to the *sommelier*.

'Open the champagne!'

The wine-waiter hurried to his table and poured out two glasses of champagne. Lord Hartcourt drank half his glass down quickly as if he was in need of sustenance, but Gardenia did not touch hers.

When the waiter had gone she said in a low voice, almost as though she forced herself to speak:

'You said that the flat was available from tomorrow, didn't you?'

'Yes, of course I did,' Lord Hartcourt said quickly, glad to change the subject to anything that did not concern Henriette.

'If I were to go there tomorrow,' Gardenia said slowly, 'when were you thinking we could be married?'

There was a moment of what seemed to her an awful silence, a moment when Lord Hartcourt sat absolutely still, his fingers on the stem of his wine-glass, his eyes looking down at the bubbling wine as if he had never seen it before. Then with an effort and in a voice which Gardenia knew was slightly embarrassed, he said:

'Now listen, Gardenia, we must talk about this.'

She made a little movement and her full glass of champagne crashed on to the table, some of it splashing on to her dress.

'Oh, how stupid of me!' she apologised.

'Don't worry,' Lord Hartcourt said. 'The waiter will clear it up.'

'There is some on my dress,' Gardenia said. 'I had better go to the cloakroom.'

'Yes of course, get the woman to sponge it for you,' Lord Hartcourt agreed. He rose to his feet and Gardenia moved from the table across the room. The cloakroom was situated a little to the right of the kitchen. She found her way there, and the woman came forward to help her.

'Please, *Madame*, I am not feeling well,' Gardenia said

155

in French. Her face was ashen and the woman helped her to a chair.

'Let me get you a little brandy, *Ma'm'selle*,' she suggested.

Gardenia nodded. She was past words. She felt not only faint but sick. The brandy, strong and fiery, which the woman brought her restored the colour to her cheeks and she felt a little better.

'I must go home,' she said, 'but I do not wish *Monsieur* to know. You understand? Do not tell him. He will find out in time that I have gone.'

The woman was too used to the vagrancies and peculiarities of the customers to argue or even to appear surprised.

'You can go out this way, *Ma'm'selle*,' she said. 'No one will realise you have gone, and you will find a hackney-carriage a little way down the road to the left.'

'Thank you,' Gardenia said. 'You are very kind.'

She gave the woman a five-franc note because it was all the change she had in her bag, and the cloakroom attendant was profuse in her thanks.

'I will say nothing, *Ma'm'selle*, rest assured. Only when they come to enquire why you have been so long will I tell them you have gone.'

'Thank you,' Gardenia said. She walked out into the small dirty courtyard, filled with empty wine-cases, garbage-tins and stray cats. She walked quickly and purposefully into the street on the other side.

It took her only a few moments to find the cab-rank. It was empty, but after she had waited only a few minutes an ancient carriage with an even more ancient horse arrived and she got in and directed the cabman to drive to Mabillon House.

Only when she was alone did she put her hands up to her eyes to fight back the tears. The shock had left her with a sharp pain in her breast. It was almost as though someone had stabbed her there, and she knew that that was exactly what, not Henriette, but Lord Hartcourt had done. How could she have been so foolish, so stupid, to think he meant anything else? It had never entered her head for one moment that, when he said he would take her away and look after her, he had not meant to marry her.

She supposed her folly arose from the way she had been brought up to know that she was a lady, and that in the world in which she, her mother and father lived, if a gentleman made love to a young girl it would obviously end in an offer of marriage.

She thought of Henriette and realised how pitifully inadequate she was to compete with such a gorgeous and glamorous creature. Henriette was right. It was most unlikely she could hold Lord Hartcourt's attention for any length of time, and now humiliatingly she knew where he had been about to install her. The house he had spoken of was, of course, the one occupied at the moment by Henriette.

Gardenia closed her eyes. It seemed to her that she sank down into the very depths of degradation. Then she remembered what Henriette had said about Aunt Lily. Could it be true? Was everyone tainted, dirty and evil in this city? Gardenia had an overwhelming impulse to run away, to go back to England, to pretend this whole journey had never happened, to find somewhere amongst her own people to live in decency and with self-respect.

But she had no money, she had nothing. The clothes she wore had been bought for her by her aunt—a relation who could be called a foul name by a prostitute.

Twice during the journey back to Mabillon House Gardenia felt she must faint. In the horror that possessed her and with Henriette's words, which seemed to echo and re-echo in her ears, haunting her mind she recalled her conversations with the men she had met since she came to Paris and saw they had very different meanings from how in her innocence she had interpreted them. She understood now what Bertie had been hinting at and what the Comte had tried to convey to her. She knew why men had leered at her at Mabillon House, and why those who spoke to her in the Park had stared as if they mentally undressed her.

'I must go away! I must go away!' she whispered to herself, and wondered despairingly where she could go and what she could do.

The slow and smelly old hackney-carriage drew up at Mabillon House. A footman opened the door for her to step out.

'Pay the cabman, please,' she said, and walked up the steps.

She felt stronger now, ready to face her aunt and challenge her with what she had heard. She knew it was true, but she wanted her aunt to confirm it, to make quite sure she was not making another mistake. Having been deceived once because she was so stupid, so inexperienced, and knew so little of the world, she did not want to add to this chapter of stupidity.

The Major-Domo came hurrying into the hall.

'Where is her Grace?' she asked, and even to herself her voice sounded sharp.

'Her Grace has not yet come downstairs,' the Major-Domo replied. 'The car has been ordered for one-forty-five,' He glanced at the clock. 'It is only one-forty, *Ma'm'-selle.*'

'I will go up to her,' Gardenia said, more to herself than to the Major Domo.

Even as she put her hand on the balustrade she heard a familiar voice at the door.

'I want to speak to Miss Weedon.'

The footman opened the door wider and she saw Bertie standing there.

'Gardenia, I must speak to you immediately. It is of the utmost importance,' he said.

'I am sorry ...' Gardenia began, feeling that she disliked Bertie because he too had wished to despoil her innocence and drag her down to the level of Henriette and her like.

'Don't be an idiot,' he said almost roughly. 'I told you this was important.'

He took her arm and to her surprise dragged her almost forcibly into the small drawing-room where Lord Hartcourt had taken her that very first night after she had fainted. He walked in, shut the door behind him and stood against it almost dramatically.

'What is the matter?' Gardenia asked. She was impatient with him, irritated by anything that came between her and her aunt at this particular moment.

'Listen, Gardenia, I have come here when I shouldn't,' to warn you,' he said. 'Your aunt is going to be arrested.'

Gardenia stared at him as though he had taken leave of his senses.

'What do you mean?' she asked.

'Pierre Gozlin has been with the Sûreté since midnight last night,' Bertie said. 'I'm told he has confessed that he has been selling French military secrets to the

Germans and accepting payment from Baron von Knese-bech.'

'From the Baron?' Gardenia exclaimed. 'But surely my aunt . . .'

'Your aunt is deeply involved,' Bertie said. 'I have no reason to doubt my informants who have inside knowl-edge of exactly what has happened.'

'The Baron . . . the Baron must save her!' Gardenia cried.

'The Baron has already left Paris,' Bertie told her.

'Then Aunt Lily will have to face this alone . . .'
Bertie interrupted.

'Don't you see, Gardenia, there's only one thing you can do. Get away, get out now, at once. I'm not worrying about your aunt, but you. I don't want you to get mixed up in this because you have lived in the house. The Sûreté will never believe that you weren't part of the whole damn spy-ring.'

Gardenia felt the blood drain away from her face. If Lord Hartcourt related how she had gone to his rooms, no one would believe her innocence.

'What can we do? Where can we go?'

'It doesn't matter,' Bertie said, 'but you realise that all your aunt's money will be frozen until after the trial. She will be taken to prison and I wouldn't give tuppence for her chances of being exonerated. The French are very bitter against the Germans.'

Gardenia drew in her breath.

'Then I will take her away now,' she said. 'We had best go to England.'

'I thought you would say that!' Bertie ejaculated. 'But no! That would be dangerous. They will expect you to go to England because you are English. Go to Monte Carlo, it is an independent State. You can get a ship from there.'

He drew his watch out of the pocket of his waistcoat.

'Not yet two o'clock,' he said. 'There is a train leaving the *Gare de Lyon* at two-forty-five. You can catch that.'

'But it is impossible!' Gardenia was going to say, then changed her mind. 'We . . . will do it.'

'Good girl. I thought you wouldn't fail,' Bertie said. 'And now I must go, you understand? I have perhaps risked my whole career by coming here to warn you.'

'I am grateful, deeply grateful,' Gardenia said.

'Hurry,' Bertie implored her. 'They may be here at any time. When the French start to act they act swiftly.'

He started to open the door for her to pass out. Gardenia stopped and looked at him.

'Thank you,' she said again. 'You have been very kind.'

She lifted her face and kissed him gently on the cheek, the kiss of a sister for a brother.

He smiled down at her.

'It is you I am worrying about,' he said in a low voice.

She nodded and ran across the hall and up the stairs. She was panting when she reached the second floor, not only from the speed with which she had climbed the stairs but from the fear growing within her.

She burst into her aunt's bedroom without knocking. The Duchesse was sitting in front of the mirror, putting the last finishing touches to her toilet which had just been completed by Yvonne and her two assistant lady's-maids.

'Ah, there you are, dear child,' Aunt Lily said. 'I was just going to send up to your room to see if you wished to come driving with me.'

'I want to speak to you alone, Aunt Lily,' Gardenia said breathlessly.

She glanced at the maids who started to leave the room.

'Alone?' the Duchesse echoed, raising her eyebrows. 'How charming you look, Gardenia. That gown is a masterpiece. Only *Monsieur* Worth could have created anything so exquisitely young.'

Gardenia was not listening. She was shutting the door behind Yvonne, who passed her with a disagreeable face, obviously affronted at being sent away from the room. Gardenia shut the door and locked it.

'Listen, Aunt Lily, we have to leave immediately.'

'What do you mean?' The Duchesse asked.

'Pierre Gozlin was arrested last night; he has confessed everything.'

There was no need to say any more. She knew by the stricken look on her aunt's face that the Duchesse was well aware of the consequences of a confession from Pierre Gozlin.

'We have to catch the two-forty-five,' Gardenia said.

'To Monte Carlo?' the Duchesse asked.

'Mr Cunningham thinks they will be watching the ports

and perhaps the railway stations and expecting us to go to England.'

'The Baron . . . I must tell the Baron!' the Duchesse said with a little cry.

'He already knows,' Gardenia said bitterly. 'He has left Paris and he didn't trouble to warn you.'

Her aunt put her hands up to her face with a gesture of utter despair.

'There is no time to think about anything, we have got to pack,' Gardenia said. 'I will call the maids. I will tell them we are going to England. You understand? We are going to England because you have had bad news. Yvonne is to be told to pack everything else and you will let her know where to bring it later. Do you understand, Aunt Lily?'

She walked over to her aunt and shook her by the arm. It seemed to her as though the older woman was taking in nothing.

'Yes, I understand,' Aunt Lily said in a muffled voice.

Gardenia unlocked the door and went out into the passage.

'Her Grace has had bad news,' she said to Yvonne. 'We have to leave immediately to catch the train for England. Pack as much as you can.'

Her last words were spoken over her shoulder. She was already running up the next flight of stairs to her own room.

She rang the bell for Jeanne, told her to pack her new dresses and then ran downstairs again, clutching her own passport, to find *Monsieur* Groise.

'The Duchesse has to leave for England,' she said, wondering how often she would have to tell this particular lie. 'Her Grace wants her passport and all the money that you have for the journey.'

Monsieur Groise opened the drawer of his desk.

'Her Grace lost a great deal of money the other night at the card-table,' he said. 'I was going to the bank tomorrow morning. I am afraid we have not got very much at the moment in the house.'

'Give me what you have,' Gardenia said.

He handed her what seemed to her a thick wad of notes. She wondered how long it would have to last.

She hurried upstairs again. Aunt Lily was sitting where

she had left her, but Yvonne was packing. Gardenia glanced at the clock.

'We have to leave in five minutes,' she said.

The Duchesse roused herself and gave a little despairing cry.

'My jewels,' she said. 'We can't go without my jewels.'

'No, of course not.'

Gardenia knew where the safe was in the ante-room to the Duchesse's bedroom. She lifted down the heavy leather jewel-case which stood on the shelf above the safe, then she had to go back to her aunt to get the key. It all took time and every nerve in her body was screaming hurry, hurry, hurry! She unlocked the safe and pulled it open. The heavy door swung back to reveal the specially made jewel-cases, blue velvet, pink leather, all arranged on little tin shelves.

Gardenia took them out one by one and started to place them in their right compartments in the jewel-case. There did not seem to be many.

'Is this all?' she called through the open door.

It was Yvonne who answered her, not her aunt.

'I took her Grace's emeralds and the sapphire set to Cartier's yesterday. They were to be cleaned and sent back tomorrow.'

Gardenia slammed the case shut.

'We must go,' she said to her aunt.

A little unsteadily the Duchesse got to her feet. It seemed to Gardenia as though her will-power had stopped and she could only do what she was told and would obey any order that was given her.

'Her Grace cannot travel like that,' she said to Yvonne.

The maid hurried to the wardrobe and brought back a pale cream travelling-coat made of thin gaberdine.

'Perhaps her Grace would take her sables over her arm in case it is chilly on the boat,' she suggested.

'Yes, yes, of course, that is a good idea,' Gardenia agreed.

She saw another coat there like the one Aunt Lily was wearing. 'I will take that for myself,' she said. 'It will be too big, but it doesn't matter.'

Anything, she thought, to hide their dresses, so ridiculously smart and unsuitable for travelling.

The bags were carried downstairs. It was a quarter past

two and Yvonne kept muttering about things that had been left behind.

'Shoes for the blue dress; I'm not certain I put them in.'

'Never mind,' Gardenia answered. 'You can send them on later.'

She had no idea what Jeanne had put in her own box; it was the same shabby, worn trunk she had arrived with in Paris. The trunks were on top of the car and now she helped Aunt Lily in and sat beside her.

'The *Gare du Nord*,' she said in a loud voice, and they were off, the servants standing in a little clump on the doorstep staring after them.

Gardenia had meant to change from the car into a taxi at some convenient spot; now she realised there was no time. Getting the trunks downstairs, saying goodbye had all taken time. It was five and twenty minutes past two. They would have to hurry or they would miss the train.

She picked up the speaking tube.

'I have told you the wrong station,' she said to the chauffeur. 'Drive to the *Gare de Lyon*.'

'Very good, Miss,' and she realised that he was not French but English. Aunt Lily had two chauffeurs; one called Arthur had been with her a long time. She had brought him over when she bought her first Rolls-Royce and he was the one driving now. What was even more providential, there was no footman on the box. The Major-Domo had murmured something when they were leaving about there not being time to get one into uniform and hoping her Grace would excuse it.

It was providential, Gardenia thought. Arthur could be trusted; Arthur was English.

Moving from the back seat beside her aunt she sat on the smaller seat opposite and opened the glass panel behind the chauffeur's head.

'Listen, Arthur,' she said in a low voice. 'Drive quickly, it is essential that her Grace should catch the two-forty-five. She is going to Monte Carlo, not to England. There is trouble, serious trouble, and I want your help.'

'Indeed, Miss.' It was the slow, unsurprised, unhurried voice of a good English servant.

'Yes, Arthur. Very serious trouble. There are going to be questions. The French police will be at Mabillon House, perhaps when you return. You have been with her Grace a long time. Will you help her now?'

163

'I'll do anything in my power. She's been a good mistress to me.'

'Then listen, Arthur. You've got to swear, however hard they question you, that her Grace went to the *Gare du Nord*. I want them to think she's gone to England, do you understand? At any rate until we have reached Monte Carlo.'

'I understand, Miss.' There was a pause and then the man said with a sort of apologetic note in his voice: 'Is it something to do with that German Baron, Miss?'

Servants knew everything, Gardenia thought.

'Yes, Arthur, it is.'

'I never did like him,' the chauffeur said, almost beneath his breath.

'Then keep to your story,' Gardenia admonished. 'All the servants in the house have been told her Grace has gone to England.'

'They won't get anything out of me, Miss. Don't you worry,' Arthur said stolidly.

Gardenia had almost turned away and was about to shut the connecting window when he said:

'Tell you what, Miss. I've got an idea. When I leave you here I'll drive to the *Gare du Nord*, hang round for a bit and hope one of those nosy parkers sees the car. You know what it is with policemen; they've got eyes all over their head.'

'Yes, that is a good idea,' Gardenia said. She felt somehow comforted because she had been helped by one of her own countrymen.

She moved back to sit beside her aunt.

'We are nearly there, Aunt Lily. Leave everything to me! Once I've bought the tickets just walk as quickly as you can to the train. We don't want to be seen if we can help it.'

It was nearly five and twenty minutes to three when they got out at the *Gare de Lyon*. Gardenia bought the tickets; mercifully the train was not full and the wagon-lits were not booked. Then, almost running beside the porter pushing their luggage, they hurried down the long platform. They climbed in a few seconds before the train was due to leave.

'Don't forget this, Miss.' It was Arthur's respectful voice, as he held up her aunt's dressing-case. Gardenia took it, realising as she did so it was emblazoned with a huge ducal coronet.

'Thank you, Arthur,' she said. 'You have been very helpful. I know her Grace is grateful.'

'The best of luck, Miss,' Arthur said fervently, and almost as he spoke the train began to leave. Gardenia gave him a quick wave of her hand, went into her aunt's wagon-lit and shut the door.

Her aunt was half lying on the seat with her head in her hands.

'I'm sorry, Aunt Lily,' Gardenia said. 'Is there anything I can get you?'

'Brandy,' the Duchesse muttered. 'I want some brandy.'

Gardenia rang the bell and after some time the steward brought a bottle of Courvoisier and two glasses. He set them down on the table.

'Will you be wanting dinner, *Madame?*' he enquired. 'The first service is at six o'clock.'

'We will have something to eat in here,' Gardenia said hastily. 'I will ring for you later.'

'Very good, *Ma'm'selle*. I'll make the beds up after we reach Aignon.'

He went from the compartment and Gardenia poured out the brandy and gave a glass to her aunt.

'At least we have got away,' she said. 'But we shan't be safe until we cross the frontier tomorrow morning. I wonder what time that is.'

'About seven o'clock in the morning,' her aunt said. 'I have done it so often.'

'Over sixteen hours ahead! Will it be possible for us to elude the police all that time? They could so easily send a wire and we could be taken off the train at any of the stations down the line.'

Gardenia began to wonder now if it would have been better if they had gone to Belgium or Holland, but that too would have meant going from the *Gare du Nord*. She was sure Bertie had been right when he thought the Sûreté would expect them to go north.

Aunt Lily held out her glass for more brandy. She drank the second one off as quickly as she had done the first; and now that the colour was beginning to come back to her face she looked less stricken.

'Let me take your hat off,' Gardenia said, 'and your

coat. No one will see you now and you might just as well be comfortable.'

'You are quite sure the Baron has left Paris?' her aunt asked. 'I ought to have tried to get in touch with him, to be quite certain that he knew what had happened.'

'Mr Cunningham said he had definitely gone, Gardenia said coldly.

'I was always afraid this would happen,' the Duchesse murmured, almost as though she were talking to herself rather than to her niece. 'I never trusted that Pierre Gozlin.'

'Who would?' Gardenia asked scornfully. 'He was a horrible man.'

'But Heinrich said he was clever, very clever.'

Gardenia drew in her breath.

'Aunt Lily, how could you spy against France?' she asked. 'How could you sink to do such a thing, you who are English?'

Her aunt looked at her as though she realised for the first time to whom she was talking.

'I don't admit anything,' she said almost angrily. 'The Baron knew his own business best. Pierre Gozlin was telling lies ... lies, do you hear? If he says anything against Heinrich or me, it isn't the truth.'

'Do you realise all your money will be frozen?' Gardenia asked. 'Mr Cunningham told me that, and they will take over your house, at least until after the trial. What do you own outside France?'

The Duchesse put her glass down on the table and stared at Gardenia.

'Nothing,' she said in a low voice. 'Everything I possess belonged to my husband. It is all invested in French stock, I have never bothered to change it.'

'Then what are we going to live on?' Gardenia asked in a practical voice.

For a moment the Duchesse looked worried, then she shrugged her shoulders.

'Heinrich will see to it,' she said. 'He is so clever, somehow he will contrive to get some money out to me, I'm certain of that.'

'He has gone to Germany,' Gardenia said. 'We haven't got very much with us.'

She opened her bag as she spoke and took out what

remained of the money that *Monsieur* Groise had given her. She counted it carefully.

'Five hundred and forty-nine francs,' she said. 'It seems a fortune to me but it won't last very long.'

'Is that all Groise gave you?' the Duchesse said sharply. 'That is ridiculous! He has thousands of francs, thousands in the house in case I should need it.'

'He was going to the bank tomorrow morning,' Gardenia said. 'There was a party tomorrow night, wasn't there?'

'Yes, of course—I signed the cheque today.'

For a moment the Duchesse looked frightened, then she brightened again. 'Never mind, we won't want ready cash, we will go to the Hôtel de Paris where they know me. When Heinrich sends me some money, or arranges for my own to be smuggled out of France, then we can pay, but not before.'

'How will the Baron know where you are?' Gardenia enquired.

'I will write to him,' the Duchesse said. 'I will write to him the moment we arrive in Monte Carlo. I could, of course, telegraph. We have a way of communicating with each other which his wife doesn't understand. She is a tiresome, jealous woman.'

Gardenia longed to say she was not surprised, but she thought that would be unkind. Instead, she unpacked some of the things her aunt would want that night and then did the same in her own compartment. When she returned to her aunt it was to find that the Duchesse had drunk over half of the bottle of brandy.

'There is no need to worry, child,' she said, slurring her words a little. 'I have been thinking it out. Heinrich will look after us. Dear Heinrich, how wonderful he is!'

Gardenia's lips tightened. She knew if she did not keep a tight control on herself she would find herself telling the Duchesse exactly what she thought of the Baron and how despicably she considered he had behaved.

However reprehensible it might be of her aunt to spy on the country of her adoption, it was the Baron who was at the bottom of it all and who had enticed, perhaps even threatened, her, to do all she had done. Now he had run away, saving his own skin, and he had not even made the slightest effort to save the woman who had been his accomplice.

Gardenia rang the bell and sent for some food, but when the steward came bringing some chicken and smoked-salmon sandwiches her aunt demanded another bottle of brandy. It was not only that Gardenia thought she had had enough already, it was the waste of money entailed—an expense they could ill afford.

When the simple meal was finished and the bed had been made up, Gardenia persuaded her aunt to undress.

'You will be more comfortable,' she said, 'and perhaps you will sleep a little.'

She pulled down the blind and turned out the top lights, but when she turned to go from the compartment the Duchesse stopped her.

'Stay with me,' she said. 'I can't bear to be alone.'

Obediently, Gardenia sat beside her, and then with a glass of brandy in her hand the Duchesse began to talk . . .

Eleven

As the train rattled through the darkness towards safety, the Duchesse sat in her bunk with a glass of brandy in her hand and talked and talked. She had forgotten that Gardenia was her niece, or, indeed, younger than herself. She talked as if to a contemporary, to another woman who would understand what she had felt and what she had suffered and how strange and at times entrancing her life had been. And as the hours passed Gardenia grew from girlhood into womanhood.

She was not shocked by what she heard. It was just that she began to understand for the first time so many things that had puzzled and perplexed her. She realised humbly how foolish and stupid she had been and at the same time how strange and often wonderful life with all its complexities could be.

It seemed to her as if Aunt Lily were going back into the past, mentally assessing the credit and debit of her own life for her own satisfaction.

At times Gardenia felt that if she had not been there Aunt Lily would still have talked from an inner compulsion which made it imperative for her to get everything into its right perspective, to see things as they were. In that speeding train the Duchesse was leaving behind a life that had been full and varied, and at times very satisfying, for the problematical, unknown and perhaps frightening future.

She talked of how she had come to Paris, of her first husband who had fascinated her and in whom she had seen an escape from all that had been humdrum and dreary, only to discover that he was shoddy, second-rate and a bore.

'But it didn't matter,' the Duchesse said. 'The moment I arrived in Paris I became aware of my beauty and what it could do for me! Men fell in love with me on sight, they followed me in the street, obtained introductions by hook or by crook; they wanted to acclaim me, to worship me and almost overnight as it were I became the toast of the whole city.'

She paused for a moment to fill up her glass. As the night wore on her speech became more slurred, but her brain seemed to remain clear and lucid; she neither muddled nor confused events as they happened. She spoke as though she was reading them in a book or seeing them in front of her on a stage.

'I had just been in Paris for two years when I met the Duc,' she went on. 'He, like all the other men I met, fell at my feet, told me I was the most beautiful thing he had ever seen. But where the Duc was concerned it was different; he was a connoisseur. Beauty was everything to him, his interest, his life, his love.'

The Duchesse paused and gave a little chuckle.

'People were convinced from the very beginning that I was his mistress,' she said. 'They were wrong, so wrong. All the Duc wanted to do was to look at me.'

She looked across the swaying compartment at Gardenia.

'I don't suppose for a moment anyone would believe that,' she said, 'but it is the truth. It gave the Duc the greatest thrill he had ever known in his life to see me, as the English call it, "in the altogether", posed on some glorious Eastern silk or standing like a statue on a plinth that he had specially made at the end of our big Salon.'

'Didn't you mind posing for him like that?' Gardenia asked.

The Duchesse smiled.

'I think, if I am truthful, I also was in love with my beauty. Admiration is a heady thing and, besides, as far as the Duc was concerned, it gave him pleasure and he gave me so much.'

'So he was never really your . . . husband,' Gardenia said, trying to understand.

'He gave me his name, his money and his adoration,' the Duchesse said. 'I was not interested in anything else. I suppose all those years I was what you would call a cold woman. I wanted men to admire me, I didn't want them to touch me. They tried, of course, they all tried. Although no one would believe it, I was faithful to my husband.'

She sipped the brandy before she continued.

'Of course, the women hated me. It was not only single

170

men who went after me, it was their husbands, their lovers, their sons. They loathed me and waited for their revenge. It came in time!'

'What happened?' Gardenia enquired.

'The Duc died,' the Duchesse answered, 'and then I realised how alone I was, not because I was a widow but because I was growing old. Oh, Gardenia, there is nothing more horrible, more terrifying, than to have built one's life around one's own beauty only to find it is slipping away and nothing you can do will prevent it from disappearing altogether.'

'But you are still beautiful,' Gardenia said passionately, longing to comfort her.

The Duchesse shook her head.

'I have never been clever,' she said. 'But I'm not a fool. I have watched my body coarsen and fatten, my face get old and wrinkled; and I have drunk because I hated it and that has only made things worse.'

'Oh, Aunt Lily, I am sorry!' Gardenia cried.

'The women took their revenge,' the Duchesse went on as if she had not spoken. 'They ostracised me. I had never troubled with them when I was on the top of the wave, and they were not going to have me crawling back into their society just because I no longer attracted men as I had in the past. It was then that I began to give parties. First it was because I liked gambling; it amused me to ask my old men friends to come and play two or three evenings a week. They too enjoyed gambling and gradually some of the younger ones joined in. It was all rather quiet and circumspect until I met the Baron.'

The Duchesse's voice deepened and it appeared to Gardenia as if there was a sudden light in her eyes and her raddled, weary face was transformed.

'I met him at Maxim's one Friday night,' the Duchesse said, 'and I knew the moment I saw him, the moment he spoke to me, that he was the man I had been looking for all my life.'

'You fell in love with him!' Gardenia exclaimed incredulously.

'I fell in love,' the Duchesse repeated, her voice curiously soft. 'Heinrich was the sort of man I had always dreamt about. He didn't worship me, he didn't want to sit watching me. He was a man, masterful, powerful, taking what he wanted, making me feel that nothing mattered except that I was a woman and he was a man.'

'But Aunt Lily . . .' Gardenia began, only to realise that the Duchesse was not listening to her but speaking with a note of ecstasy in her voice.

'I was happy. I can't tell you how happy I was. I knew then that I had never known what love was before. I had always despised the men who had admired me, who had made such a fuss over my beauty. In my heart I thought them poor creatures; but here was a man, rough and brutal at times—but a man.'

The Duchesse shut her eyes as if for a moment living again those hours of happiness.

'He was your lover,' Gardenia whispered, 'but . . . he was married.'

'Yes, he was married,' the Duchesse said sharply, 'but what did that matter? He needed me and I needed him. One day, Gardenia, you will understand what that means, not only to receive love but to be able to give it: that is what counts, that is what has always counted where a woman is concerned.'

'But if you were so happy,' Gardenia asked, 'why the parties? All that noise and such a lot of people coming to the house.'

The Duchesse smiled, and it was almost maternal.

'Heinrich wanted parties. He believed that Paris was gay and he had always imagined there would be noise, gambling, lots of champagne and beautiful women. That was his dream, so I gave him what he wanted. It was only too easy. There are always people ready to attend parties whoever gives them, and there are always men who want to gamble, and there are always young people who will make a noise.'

'So that is why you had them,' Gardenia said. 'I didn't understand, it didn't seem like you somehow.'

'I liked the gambling, I have always liked it,' the Duchesse said. 'It excites me. I find it hard to tear myself away from the tables and so I began to play. Heinrich liked that too!'

'Perhaps he found it useful,' Gardenia said, a note of bitterness in her voice, 'to bring people like Pierre Gozlin to your house.'

She was sorry for what she said the moment she said it.

The Duchesse's face changed: she looked suddenly haggard.

'There had been others before Pierre Gozlin,' she said. 'I knew that the Baron was using me, but I didn't care. Do you understand, Gardenia, I didn't care? I wanted him to have what he wanted. I was not French, I was English, and I always made that excuse to myself.'

'If the Germans fight the French they will also fight us,' Gardenia said. 'We have pacts, treaties.'

'The Germans are not going to fight anyone,' the Duchesse said positively. 'The Baron told me so. They only want peace. The Kaiser wants living space for his people and he wants a big navy to equal ours. Why should Britain, which is only a small island, have more ships than Germany, which is twice its size?'

Gardenia sighed. She realised only too clearly that her aunt was repeating parrotwise what the Baron had told her.

'Can Pierre Gozlin really incriminate you, Aunt Lily?' she asked. 'That is the important thing. Mr Cunningham thought he could. After all, you could always say you had no idea what the Baron was doing. They couldn't prove that you were selling secrets to the Germans as Pierre Gozlin has apparently done.'

'No, they can't prove that,' the Duchesse agreed. 'I didn't accept money—not actual money—for anything I did.'

'What do you mean by actual money?' Gardenia enquired. 'Did you accept anything else?'

The Duchesse hesitated.

'The chinchilla cape!' Gardenia exclaimed. 'Did the Baron give you that?'

'No, not the Baron,' the Duchesse said hastily. 'He would not have had money for that sort of thing.'

'Then the German Government,' Gardenia said. 'Oh, Aunt Lily, how could you have accepted such a present?'

'Heinrich wanted me to have it,' her aunt replied, simply. 'He said it would look strange, perhaps a reflection on him, if I refused their offer.'

'But Aunt Lily, you must have seen that that made you part of their plot, their scheme, or whatever it was to spy on France. You must have realised that if it was ever found out you would be convicted as a spy and nothing you could say to the contrary would be believed!'

173

'I never thought they would be found out,' the Duchesse replied, 'and Heinrich said that all we were doing was completely unimportant. In fact, he told me that because the French were so spiteful and disagreeable to the Germans, they would not even exchange the ordinary diplomatic facts which every other country except poor Germany knew.'

'And you believed that?' Gardenia asked. 'Pierre Gozlin must have told him very, very much more important things.'

'I'm afraid so,' the Duchesse replied. 'I never did like that man; he was horrible.'

The Duchesse shuddered.

'Horrible, horrible,' she said repeatedly, 'but for Heinrich's sake I would have put up with worse.'

'Do you mean,' Gardenia asked, her voice very low. 'Pierre Gozlin thought himself in love with you?'

The Duchesse gave a violent movement and her glass of brandy fell to the ground and smashed.

'Do not let's talk of it,' she said. 'I hated him, I loathed the very sight of him. Heinrich asked me to be kind to him as a favour. How could I refuse?'

Her voice was almost hysterical.

'We won't speak of it,' Gardenia said soothingly. She felt sick as she bent down to pick up the pieces of glass. Then she fetched her aunt a tumbler from the small toilet which connected the two wagon-lits.

It was the early hours of the morning, but the Duchesse still went on talking. She told Gardenia about the Russian Grand Duke who had fallen so much in love with her that he offered her a magnificent château and jewellery more magnificent than was owned by any European Queen, if only she would become his mistress. She added that he had attracted her and she had known how gay and fantastic her life would be with him. Yet her British middle-class respectability had made her force the Duc into marriage because she wanted a ring on her finger rather than diamonds around her neck.

'You had the diamonds too,' Gardenia reminded her.

'Nothing to what I could have had,' the Duchesse replied. 'Oh dear! I hate to think of all my sapphires and emeralds being left behind!'

'I don't think it matters so much as being free,' Gardenia said.

She had realised before that it was urgent that her aunt should be got out of France and now the revelations to which she had just listened made it clear that if Aunt Lily was not shot as a traitor she would be imprisoned for years, perhaps for the rest of her life.

The Duchesse seemed hardly to realise the danger in which she stood. She was talking again of the Baron, a soft caressing note in her voice which was always there when she mentioned his name.

'I will write to Heinrich as soon as we arrive in Monte Carlo. He will come to me, and perhaps we will have a little holiday together while we decide what we will do in the future.'

'Do you think he will be able to get away?' Gardenia asked.

'Heinrich can manage everything,' the Duchesse said confidently. 'But he will really be annoyed at having to leave France. He enjoyed being in Paris and, of course, that Pierre Gozlin should have broken down and confessed will be a black mark against him. Actually we don't know what that horrible Gozlin has said. He may not have incriminated anyone except me.'

'The Baron has already left Paris,' Gardenia reminded her.

'Yes, of course. I suppose they would think him guilty anyway.'

'I'm sure they would,' Gardenia answered, resisting an impulse to add a few words on what she thought about the Baron's behaviour.

It was nearly dawn when finally the Duchesse fell asleep.

The brandy bottle was empty and she looked very old and very tired as Gardenia turned out the light and went to her own bed.

She was unable to sleep but lay awake praying that they would get over the frontier, wondering what would happen if her aunt was arrested and they were taken back to Paris.

'I won't leave her whatever happens, I can't leave her!' she told herself, knowing that her mother would have wanted her to be loyal, and knowing too that it was against all her own inclinations and standards to abandon anyone in their hour of need.

The train hurried on. As the sun rose, Gardenia realised

that they must be near the sea, so she got up and dressed. She peeped into the next-door compartment, but the Duchesse was still asleep and Gardenia knew that the most dangerous part of the journey would be when they reached Nice. The train was bound to stop there for perhaps quarter of an hour before proceeding to Monte Carlo.

The conductor brought her some coffee and asked if she wished to go along the corridor for breakfast. Gardenia shook her head. She felt as though if she ate anything it would choke her, and she was quite convinced that her aunt would want nothing after all the brandy she had drunk last night.

'What time do we reach Nice?' she asked the man.

'In about half an hour, *Ma'm'selle.*'

Gardenia roused her aunt. The Duchesse groaned.

'My head is splitting open,' she said, and then opening her eyes exclaimed, 'Why are we here? Where are we going?'

'We are going to Monte Carlo,' Gardenia replied. 'Don't you remember?'

The Duchesse shut her eyes again.

'I remember,' she said. 'I pray that Heinrich is all right.'

Gardenia found the *cachet faivre*, which luckily Yvonne had remembered to pack, and with the help of two of them and another glass of brandy she managed to get the Duchesse on her feet.

The effort was worth while, for after one glance in the mirror the Duchesse realised how ghastly she looked and sat down to make up her face, mascara her eyelashes, paint her lips.

Exactly on time the train rattled in to Nice Station. Gardenia held her breath. There was the usual chatter and noise from the platform; the walking backwards and forwards up the corridor; the voices of passengers calling to porters. But no one disturbed them. A few minutes ticked by and Gardenia felt her tension relax. If Aunt Lily had been going to be taken off the train the police would have been waiting. Nevertheless, she knew how great her tension had been as finally the train began to move again, slowly steaming out of the station.

Gardenia drew up the blinds, feeling that now at least she dared look out at the sunshine, at the sea so vividly blue which made her gasp with delight. She had never imagined anything could be so beautiful. She stood at the window looking at the villas with their gardens full of bougainvillaea, at the groves of orange and lemon trees, at the people splashing in the sea, and the little boats with their white sails speeding across the water.

'I had no idea Nice could be so lovely,' she said to her aunt.

The Duchesse did not answer. She was busy putting the last touches to her face.

'I look a hag,' she said, more to herself than to Gardenia, 'but at least no one in Monte Marlo will notice anything unusual about me. You must be careful, Gardenia, not to mention to anyone why we have left Paris.'

'I am not likely to do that,' Gardenia answered. 'I am not proud of it.'

'No, of course not,' her aunt said, 'but we don't want people to think there's anything unusual in my coming to Monte Carlo so late in the season. I shall just say I have been ill ... no, people will know I have been well ... I shall say you have been ill: that will be our story.'

Gardenia longed to ask if it really mattered, but she knew it did matter to her aunt and she thought perhaps it was best for the Duchesse to try to behave as though things were quite normal. Sooner or later, Gardenia thought with a little shudder, if there was a trial, people were bound to know what had happened. Then she thought that perhaps, as State security was concerned, it might be all hushed up. Pierre Gozlin would never be heard of again, but the Duchesse could never go back to France.

'Aunt Lily,' she asked suddenly, 'are you sure, as you said last night, that you have no money outside France, no securities or property in England?'

'Alas!' the Duchesse answered. 'Everything I possess was my husband's, and naturally as he was French we invested in France.'

'Then what are we going to live on?' Gardenia asked.

Just for a moment the Duchesse looked stricken.

'The Baron will arrange everything,' she said. 'We must just trust him, Gardenia. After all, if it comes to that, the German Government owes me a lot of money. I have never taken much from them all these years, only the chinchilla cape, my sables and a diamond ring. They must be in my debt.'

Gardenia said nothing. She had an uncomfortable feeling that once the Duchesse was no further use to the German Government they would not worry about her unduly. She was not going to say so to her aunt—things were difficult and depressing enough without her adding to them.

They crossed the frontier and there was just a perfunctory inspection. The train halted, French officials walked down the corridor, glanced at their passports and proceeded to the next compartment. Gardenia felt an overwhelming sense of relief. It was all over in a few seconds and then the train came puffing into the station of the tiny municipality and they were safe!

It was only a few minutes before a large and extremely comfortable car transported them to the Hôtel de Paris. The Manager was waiting in the hall and there was no disguising his delight at seeing the Duchesse.

'This is a tremendous surprise, *Madame*,' he said. 'But something must have gone wrong; we didn't receive a letter making your reservations.'

'You didn't get a telegram from me, *Monsieur* Bloc?' the Duchesse enquired.

'No, we have heard nothing,' he replied.

'Really! I shall discharge my secretary as soon as I return to Paris!' the Duchesse exclaimed. 'I told him to wire you just as we were leaving. We came on an impulse because my niece has been feeling so unwell. I think she must have picked up one of these new-fangled germs of which we hear so much. Anyway I said to her, "Gardenia, we will go to Monte Carlo. The sea, air and the sunshine will put you right in no time!" '

'I promise your Grace it will do that,' *Monsieur* Bloc agreed. 'By very good fortune, and because, of course, it is a little late in the season, your Grace's favourite suite is available.'

'Aunt Lily, we don't want a suite,' Gardenia whispered, feeling that the expense was more than they dare incur.

The Duchesse brushed her aside.

'That will be delightful,' she smiled. 'You know I like that particular view and being able to have my breakfast on the balcony.'

'Let me take you up, your Grace,' *Monsieur* Bloc suggested, 'and if everything is not to your satisfaction you have only to mention it, you know that.'

The Duchesse was all graciousness, and soon they were

178

ensconced in an enormous suite overlooking the sea. The bedroom, sitting-room and smaller room for Gardenia were all expensively luxurious.

The Duchesse tipped the baggage-men and rang for the waiter.

'I am exhausted, Gardenia,' she said, sinking down in one of the satin-covered chairs. 'I think a bottle of champagne is what we need.'

'Oh, Aunt Lily, do listen!' Gardenia begged. 'We have got a few hundred francs left of what *Monsieur* Groise gave us, nothing else, nothing at all. These rooms must be exorbitantly expensive, we can't afford them.'

'Don't worry, dear child,' the Duchesse said confidently. 'I am writing to the Baron today, but if it makes you happier I will send him a telegram. Give me a telegram form from the desk and bring me that little black book in my dressing-case. It will have the Baron's home address in it, and also the code that we use when we write to each other.'

'Is it safe?' Gardenia asked.

'Of course,' the Duchesse replied impatiently. 'The Baron thinks of everything. His wife is jealous; he suspects that she might open his letters, and she would certainly read his telegrams, so we have our own ways of communicating with each other.' The Duchesse gave a little laugh. 'She has never suspected, the stupid woman.'

The Duchesse wrote out the telegram, and because Gardenia was so anxious it should go off at once she took it downstairs to the *concierge*, rather than entrust it to a page-boy.

The *concierge* promised to send it immediately.

When Gardenia came back to the suite she found that the Duchesse was undressing.

'You will have to help me, dear, I am afraid,' she said, 'I am so lost without Yvonne. I want a bath; then we will go down and have some lunch.'

'Don't you think you ought to go to bed?' Gardenia enquired.

'Yes, dear,' the Duchesse agreed, 'but we will have lunch first, and this evening we will go to the Casino. I know you will be shocked, but I am really looking forward to it. An unexpected holiday is always exciting and there is nothing that will cheer me up more than having a little gamble.'

179

'But, Aunt Lily, you can't afford it!' Gardenia cried.

'Nonsense,' the Duchesse said. 'How much did you say we had left?'

Gardenia fetched the money from her handbag and counted it out. She counted it twice.

'It's not as much as I thought,' she said. 'The tickets were very expensive and then I had to pay for the brandy on the train; that came to quite a lot. I am afraid, Aunt Lily, I hardly know how to tell you, there is only eighty-two francs here.'

'Nonsense,' the Duchesse said crisply. 'There must be more!'

'There isn't,' Gardenia said.

The Duchesse thought for a moment, then she rose and went to her jewel-case.

'Take this bracelet,' she said, 'and go to the jeweller opposite the hotel. Ask for *Monsieur* Jacques. Tell him that you have come from me. Say I have arrived in Monte Carlo unexpectedly without having had time to arrange letters of credit. Tell him it was because of illness. He won't ask any questions, he is very discreet. And say that I want to borrow money on the bracelet. Tell him I want five thousand francs, he will give it to you.'

Gardenia longed to refuse, to say it was something she couldn't possibly do, it sounded so embarrassing! But she felt she had to look after Aunt Lily, and anyway they couldn't possibly manage with the money they had. Five thousand francs would keep them going for a long time, she thought.

She put the bracelet in a safe place and unpacked her aunt's luggage. She found that in the hurry Yvonne had forgotten quite a lot of things, but she was determined not to mention them in case her aunt should want to purchase replacements.

It took such a long time getting the Duchesse dressed after her bath, finding her a gown, hat, gloves, bag, and shoes, that she was quite impatient when she learned that Gardenia wished to change too.

'We shall have to have a lady's-maid,' she declared. 'I will tell *Monsieur* Bloc to engage me one. I can't think why you bothered to unpack: you could have rung for the chambermaid, she would have done it.'

'I know,' Gardenia said, 'but I thought she might think it strange the way things were jumbled into the trunks.

After all, you have been here before and she wouldn't have expected Yvonne to pack without layers of tissue-paper.'

'What a sensible girl you are!' the Duchesse exclaimed. 'I am so glad you are with me, Gardenia. This would have been far harder to bear without you.'

'You really feel that?' Gardenia asked, glad that her aunt should want her.

'Of course I do,' the Duchesse said affectionately. 'This is all a terrible shock to me, Gardenia, but I think you understand I have got to keep up a brave front. I must not let the world know anything has happened. The Baron would not like that—he always says that appearances are very important.'

'Well, he would be proud of you,' Gardenia said. 'I thought last night you were going to collapse.'

'I am made of sterner stuff than that,' the Duchesse said.

She poured out what remained of the champagne and drank it.

'Hurry, Gardenia! While you are changing I will go downstairs and find out who is staying here. Even though it is the end of the season there are sure to be some of my friends left. Then we will have lunch in the dining-room which was done up last year in King Edward's honour. You will see how magnificent it is. Hurry, child, hurry!'

It seemed to Gardenia that she was hurrying for the rest of the day. After lunch the Duchesse insisted on going for a drive before she went to rest, and then Gardenia helped her to undress and into bed.

As soon as that was finished there was the visit to the jeweller an ordeal which was not as frightening as Gardenia had expected. *Monsieur* Jacques was all smiles and willingness to help once he heard the Duchesse's name.

'Five thousand francs?' he said. 'Well, I will be honest with you, *Ma'm'selle*: for anyone else we would not advance such a large sum, not even on a bracelet of this value. For the Duchesse that is different. She is a very valued customer and I am sure it is only a question of a few days before her affairs are in order.'

'We came away in such a hurry,' Gardenia explained, 'the banks were closed.'

'I quite understand,' the jeweller said.

He put the new notes into an envelope and handed

them to Gardenia with a bow, and thankful that things had not been worse she hurried back to the hotel.

The Duchesse was asleep and for the first time Gardenia was able to go to her own room and realise how utterly weary she was. She slipped into the bed and it seemed to her as though her eyes had hardly closed when there was a knock on the door and the chambermaid told her the Duchesse required her presence.

Aunt Lily was sitting up in bed.

'Did you get the money?' she asked eagerly.

Gardenia gave her the envelope.

'Five thousand francs. Well, that is something at any rate.'

'It rather depends how much we are paying for these rooms,' Gardenia said hesitantly.

'Don't fuss, Gardenia,' the Duchesse admonished her. 'You are becoming a bore about money. Everything will be all right as soon as the Baron gets my wire. If he can't come immediately he will understand the plight I am in and will send me some money.'

Gardenia only hoped her aunt was not being over-confident.

'I suppose you realise the time,' the Duchesse said. 'It is seven o'clock. You must get dressed, Gardenia. Wear your best dress tonight: first impressions are always important. People are very smart in the Casino. I will wear the black sequin. I saw Yvonne had packed that. I hope she remembered the ospreys which I always wear in my hair.'

The ospreys had been forgotten but there was a bird of paradise which was equally becoming, and Gardenia was forced to admit that her aunt looked magnificent when finally she was dressed, glittering with black sequins and with her enormous diamond necklace encircling her neck.

'I was a fool to let *Monsieur* Jacques have my bracelet,' the Duchesse frowned. 'I am certain he would have given me the money without it. Never mind, I have a smaller one I can wear over my gloves. Bracelets are always a nuisance with kid gloves anyway.'

Gardenia dressed in a hurry, wearing an exquisite gown of pale green chiffon, embroidered with tiny patterns of sparkling spring flowers. She had no jewellery, just a bunch of rosebuds to wear at her breast, but her reflection told her that she looked very young and very lovely.

As she looked at herself in the huge mahogany frame mirror, almost for the first time her own unhappiness swept over her like a flood tide. She had been concentrating so fiercely on all that concerned her aunt. She had been so desperately tired after sitting up all night. It was only now, as she saw herself in her elegant sparkling gown from Worth's, that she remembered that it was not of the least consequence how she looked because Lord Hartcourt would not be there to see her. Nor would she ever again hear his voice or feel the strength of his fingers on hers.

The ache which had been in her heart all the time almost like a wound was still there; she knew, though afraid of her own feelings she had not consciously recalled him to her mind, the misery and heartbreak that had been with her every moment. She might have tried to hate him, but she knew she still loved him.

Now, because of all her aunt had said the night before, she realised the gulf that separated them. For the first time she understood what the woman at the dinner party had meant when she said that her aunt was 'the Queen of *demi* Paris.' She understood at last the sharp division that lay between society and the *demi-monde*. The only link between the two was the men who could have a foot in both worlds; but, as far as women were concerned, the 'ladies' lived behind a high fence of respectability over which there could be no trespassers.

Now, because of this new adultness which had come upon her during the long train journey, Gardenia could see how stupid and obtuse she had been for not understanding before what people so obviously had been trying to say to her. She realised that never for one moment had it entered Lord Hartcourt's mind that she was not in the same category as her aunt, that she was not part and parcel of the *déclassées* and gaudy women who frequented Mabillon House because 'decent' women would not cross the threshold.

She realised how things must have deteriorated since the Baron had let in the riff-raff. At first Aunt Lily must have known quite a lot of nice people. They might, as the Duchesse had said, have been ready to take their revenge, but they would not have completely ostracised her. Then once the parties had started—parties which had not only amused the Baron but which he had found so useful for his nefarious espionage schemes—there was no hope. Lily

Mabillon—Duchesse or no Duchesse—was classed with the *demi-monde* and only men could visit Mabillon House.

There was in fact every excuse for Lord Hartcourt; and yet Gardenia could still feel the terrible shock and the faintness that had crept over her when Henriette had ranted at him and she had realised what he was suggesting before his mistress came to the table.

With an effort that was heroic she put the thought of Lord Hartcourt from her. Later she could have time to cry about what she had lost and to know that her whole life would be empty and void because for a few moments she had loved a man and thought he loved her. Now, as things were, she must concentrate on looking after Aunt Lily, praying that the Baron would come up to expectations and that somehow in some miraculous manner Aunt Lily's future would be assured.

All eyes were on the two women as they went into the *Salle Privée* at the Casino, and there was no doubting the sincerity of the greeting Aunt Lily received from quite a number of men, old and young, standing round the tables.

'By Jove, this will liven things up!' one middle-aged man exclaimed, and Aunt Lily rewarded him with a little pat on his cheek before she introduced him to Gardenia.

Almost too swiftly, before Gardenia realised what was happening, Aunt Lily had gravitated towards a table where they were playing *Chemin-de-Fer*. She sat down and to Gardenia's horror drew the crisp franc notes which had come from *Monsieur* Jacques from her handbag.

'Aunt Lily!' she whispered in anguish.

The Duchesse brushed her aside.

'Don't worry me, child,' she said lightly. 'I hate being talked to when I am gambling. Go and find a charming young man to give you a drink. Which reminds me, I need some champagne.'

One of the attendants hurried forward to put a small table beside her and bring to it a bottle of champagne in an ice-bucket.

Gardenia turned away. She felt she could not bear to watch. She went to one of the other tables, staring with unseeing eyes at the people playing roulette, but almost as if she were mesmerised she returned to her aunt's side.

With a little beat of her heart she saw that the Duchesse was winning: the pile of chips in front of her was growing.

But as the evening progressed it decreased rapidly. It got lower and lower and ended in nothing.

The Duchesse drew some more money from her bag, and Gardenia saw with dismay they were the last remaining notes which *Monsieur* Groise had given her in Paris. She longed to speak but knew there was nothing she could say.

Aunt Lily was laughing gaily in an unconcerned manner with the men on either side of her. She sent for another bottle of champagne.

Gardenia clenched her fingers together and prayed. If this money went they had nothing. Surely Aunt Lily must realise that.

A tremor ran through the people playing at the table. It was almost a physical thing, Gardenia could feel it.

'*Banco,*' It was the Duchesse who spoke.

Gardenia didn't understand the game but she could see it was a duel between a dark middle-aged Greek and her aunt. Everyone was straining forward, but at the same time they were very quiet.

Gardenia realised the silence was due to the fact that while the great pile of money rested in front of the Greek, her aunt had staked nothing. Everyone was waiting. Gardenia saw her aunt open her handbag and knew before the white-gloved fingers went inside that there was nothing there. Then with a gesture, magnificent as it was unexpected, the Duchesse reached up, unfastened the huge diamond necklace from her neck and threw it on the table.

'Twenty thousand francs!' she said.

A little gasp went round the onlookers.

The Greek bowed.

'As you wish, *Madame.*'

He slid the cards out of the shoe. Two for the Duchesse, two for himself. The Duchesse held hers close to her face so that they could not be seen. The Greek looked at her to enquire if she wanted a card. She shook her head. The Greek turned his cards up.

'*Cinq à la banque!*' the croupier called.

The Greek drew a card.

'*Neuf à la banque,*' the croupier said without a vestige of emotion in his voice.

The Duchesse rose a little unsteadily to her feet and threw down her cards.

The Duchesse had lost.

She turned and walked blindly from the table. Gardenia followed her. There was nothing she could say or do. Aunt Lily had lost. They were both of them lost!

Twelve

Gardenia spent the night in tears. After she had got the Duchesse upstairs to their suite at the hotel, her aunt had collapsed completely. Gardenia had to undress her and get her into bed. Owing to the champagne she had drunk and the shock of realising that she had lost at cards, the Duchesse was now past coherence or conversation.

Gardenia therefore did her work in silence, then went into her own room and shut the door. Only when she was undressed and had pulled back the curtains to look out over the sea had the tears come coursing down her face, and she cried with the abandonment of a small child.

She told herself that she was crying over the hopeless position in which her aunt was now placed, over her fear for their future and over the disastrous circumstances which were accountable for this whole impossible situation. But in her heart she knew this was not true. She was crying because she was lonely and afraid, and because her whole body ached and yearned for the love she had known for such a very brief moment—a love which seemed now to have been snatched away from her as soon as she reached her arms out towards it.

Even in the depths of her despair she could recapture that moment, wonderful and beautiful, when she had loved and thought herself loved in return, and the whole world had seemed golden and glorious because she had believed Lord Hartcourt's affection for her was as deep and absolute as hers for him.

'Fool! Fool!' she cried, despising herself for her own stupidity and lack of sophistication; but even self-accusation did not assuage the aching emptiness which was a physical pain whenever she thought of it.

She cried for hours; then she pulled herself together and knew there was no one now to help her aunt except herself and she had got to make plans and insist that the Duchesse carried them out.

If Gardenia had grown from childhood to womanhood

in the train, listening to her aunt's confidences, now she grew from a frail dependent relative into something harder and more resolute.

She turned from the window, for the romantic beauty of the sea was too beautiful to look at for long, and instead walked up and down the soft carpet of her bedroom.

Something had to be done and it must be done quickly! She added up in her mind what their assets were: the few remaining diamonds that her aunt had in her jewel-case—several brooches, a pair of ear-rings, one or two rings. They would all fetch something, though nothing like their true value. Gardenia knew shrewdly that by now the whole of Monte Carlo would be talking of her aunt's gesture in flinging her diamond necklace on the table, and they would know with the perception of wolves smelling blood that something was wrong with the Duchesse's finances: if it were not so she would have obtained the money to continue gambling in a less spectacular way.

Gardenia knew the Manager tomorrow would be making enquiries. Tomorrow rumour might bring a whisper of what had occurred in Paris, and then they would be asked to leave.

She thought of all the things that her aunt had left behind—the magnificent pictures on the walls at Mabillon House, the furniture, the Sèvres vases, the collection of gold and jewelled snuff-boxes in the little drawing-room, the gilt and diamond dressing-table set in her aunt's bedroom. All worth thousands and thousands of francs, but now confiscated by the French Government without any likelihood of her ever seeing them again.

Almost involuntarily, Gardenia's thoughts went to the chinchilla cape, and though she was aware of its value, she was glad it had been left behind. It was a symbol of treachery. While the Duchesse might take such things lightly, she knew she would never have been able to look at the cape again without feeling sick and ashamed.

All that remained then, besides the Duchesse's jewellery, were her clothes and the sables which she had worn in the train. Gardenia didn't know much about such things, but she was quite certain that second-hand clothes would fetch very little. Actresses and the lower order of prostitutes would not be prepared to pay much even for Worth models, and who else was likely to demean herself by wearing the Duchesse's cast-offs? Poorer women would find chiffon and laces, brocades and diamanté, embroidered evening gowns, about as much use as a carpet-sweeper in the desert. What then were they to do?

Gardenia, covering her face with her hands, heard Lord Hartcourt's voice telling her he would look after her and protect her. If only he could be here now, she thought, and hated herself for her own weakness.

As soon as it was light she dressed, and leaving the hotel went to the shipping office. A policeman directed her to where it was situated and she had a long wait until the door was opened by a middle-aged, unshaven clerk.

He was polite to Gardenia until he realised she was asking for the cheapest accommodation on a ship to England. Then he became almost unpleasantly familiar and ended up by inviting her to have supper with him that evening. Despite this impertinence, Gardenia managed to extract the information that the *l'Hirondelle,* a small and ancient cargo-vessel, was sailing the next day. It took six passengers and, while Gardenia's heart sank at the thought of the discomforts the Duchesse would have to endure, she knew it would be madness to book on one of the more expensive ships which would use up almost entirely what slender funds they had left.

She booked a double cabin and told the clerk she would bring the money later in the morning.

'I will trust you,' he said with a sidelong glance, 'so long as you tell me at the same time where we can meet tonight.'

'I will have to find out and let you know,' Gardenia replied.

There was no point in antagonising him, and he had already told her that if they did not catch this particular ship it meant a wait of three or four days.

It wasn't only that they couldn't afford to remain in Monte Carlo that length of time, it was also that Gardenia could not trust her aunt to be in close proximity to the Casino without playing at the tables.

She hurried back to the hotel to find the Duchesse was still asleep. Gardenia sat in the expensive sitting-room, longing for something to eat, but knowing that even to ring the bell was to spend money which they could not afford.

The hours crept by and it was noon before her aunt

finally awoke. She was in her usual state of suffering from a bad headache and looked old and sallow.

Gardenia fetched the inevitable *cachet faivre,* but when the Duchesse demanded brandy she shook her head.

'We can't afford it, Aunt Lily,' she said.

The Duchesse started to expostulate, then the memory of what had happened last night came back to her.

'My . . . necklace,' she stammered, 'my . . . diamond . . . necklace.'

Her hand went to her throat as if by some miracle she expected to find it still round her neck.

'How could I have done it? Oh, Gardenia, how could I have done it?' she moaned.

'I am afraid you lost everything, Aunt Lily,' Gardenia said gently. 'We have nothing left, nothing.'

'My jewels, they are still there,' the Duchesse said, a note of hope in her voice.

'There are not many left,' Gardenia told her. 'Aunt Lily, listen to me. We must go to England. We can't stay here, you can't afford it. I doubt if we'll even be able to pay the hotel bill as it is.'

Aunt Lily started to protest, then sank back into her pillows.

'Heinrich will have received my telegram last night, or, at the very latest, this morning,' she said at length.

'He may not be in Germany,' Gardenia said. 'Or even if he is there is no reason to think he is at home in Prussia.'

'No, of course not,' the Duchesse agreed. 'We may have to wait a day or two. The telegram will be sent on. He should be here by the end of the week.'

'Aunt Lily, we can't risk it,' Gardenia urged. 'We can't stay here running up an enormous debt. Think what this suite is costing you.'

She paused to let that sink in and added:

'In England we could live very simply and I can get work of some sort. You will be able to look up old friends. Surely you must have friends in England?'

'I am not going to England or anywhere else until I have seen the Baron,' the Duchesse declared with surprising force. 'He will write to me, I know it. Don't be so despondent, Gardenia. Don't you understand, he loves me? He will come to me as soon as he realises where I am.'

Gardenia gave a little sigh. She wished she could share her aunt's optimism. Knowing the Baron, she had a feeling he would wriggle out of his responsibilities somehow and, even if he did help her aunt financially, she was quite certain it would not be with any large sums of money, not enough to keep her in the life to which she had been accustomed.

'We had much better go to England,' she said softly. 'The Baron can visit you there just as easily as he can visit you here. In fact, it is nearer! There is a ship leaving tomorrow morning: Aunt Lily, I thought if we were on it we should at least prevent ourselves running up any bigger bills than we have already!'

The Duchesse looked at her.

'What you are really saying is you don't trust me near the Casino,' she said. 'Perhaps you are right. I think I go a little mad when I start to play. I am always utterly and completely convinced that I shall win the next time. Oh my necklace, my beautiful necklace!'

Gardenia felt there was nothing she could say. She was determined, all the same, that she would try to persuade her aunt to come away.

'Let us get dressed and go out to find something to eat,' she coaxed. 'There must be a cheap place somewhere in the town. We can't possibly afford to eat here. I saw the bill yesterday when you signed it. The price of our luncheon and dinner would keep us for a week in England.'

'I don't want anything to eat,' the Duchesse said sulkily.

'I think you will feel better, even if you only have some coffee,' Gardenia said.

'Then ring the bell ...' the Duchesse began, only to check the words as she saw Gardenia's face. 'All right,' she conceded, 'we will walk up the town and look for some sordid little café. I'm sure I've never had to do such a thing before!'

Gardenia said nothing. She knew the Duchesse was suffering.

She helped her to dress, putting on one of the elegant and expensive Worth gowns and knowing when they were both ready that they looked like millionairesses rather than two poverty-stricken women with only a few diamonds between them and starvation.

'Bring my diamond brooch,' the Duchesse said. 'We will see what one of the jewellers in the main street will give us for it.' She hesitated, then added: 'I think it unwise to return to *Monsieur* Jacques, don't you?'

'I thought of that,' Gardenia said. 'The one thing we must not do is to let the hotel or anyone else realise the true state of our affairs.'

'Even though they have known me a long time, I have a feeling you are right,' the Duchesse agreed. 'There is no sentiment in Monte Carlo when it comes to money. They have had too many debts, too many bankruptcies, too many suicides. I have heard them talking and there has never been a word of friendliness or understanding for those who have been foolish enough to chuck their money away on the tables.'

'That is what I thought,' Gardenia said. 'Come on, Aunt Lily, perhaps we will both feel better when we have had something to eat.'

The Duchesse used her usual cosmetic which hid the lines of unhappiness, misery and disappointment on her face, and as they reached the hall of the hotel Gardenia was amazed how the older woman managed to pull herself together to smile at the attendants who bade them good morning, to nod to the Manager who bowed as she passed through the swing-door and down the steps into the sunshine.

'They are nothing but jackals,' she whispered to Gardenia. 'If they knew the truth they would be at us, picking the very flesh from our bones.'

'I know,' Gardenia said unhappily. It was difficult to feel that she was not acting in a very bad play.

She strolled with her aunt through the gardens with their bright colourful beds of flowers and trickling silvery streams. The leaves of the palm trees were rustling overhead in the faint breeze from the sea. It was very warm and the Duchesse was panting a little by the time they reached the main shopping street.

They found a small café and ate a frugal meal of coffee and fresh croissants. The Duchesse looked longingly at the bottles behind the bar, but with what Gardenia saw was a tremendous effort she did not ask for a drink.

'I must have some friends here who will give us dinner,' she said. 'There is no one of any interest at the Hôtel de Paris, but there may be someone at the Splendide or the Alexander. I will get the *concierge* to telephone; I will tell him I am trying to arrange a dinner party. He will quite understand.'

'I still think we ought to leave tomorrow,' Gardenia said.

She saw her aunt's lips tighten and added:

'The ship doesn't sail until the afternoon. Shall we make a pact that if you haven't heard from the Baron by the morning you will telegraph again telling him that we have gone to England?'

Her aunt drew on her gloves.

'I will think about it,' she said coldly. 'Suppose he came and I had left? Suppose your friends in Paris, Lord Hartcourt and Mr Cunningham, have reported what they know to England, what will happen then?'

Gardenia gave a little start.

'I had not thought of that,' she said.

'England and France are hand in glove against the Germans,' her aunt said sharply. 'I should imagine all diplomatic secrets are exchanged. So you see, Gardenia, it is not such a clever idea as you think to go to England.'

'Then where can we go?' Gardenia asked despairingly.

'I think for the present it is best to remain here,' her aunt replied.

'But, Aunt Lily, you must see that we can't afford to stay at the Hôtel de Paris. That suite alone is costing us every day more than we would spend in a fortnight or even a month in England. We must be sensible.'

'Dear child, you are very like your mother,' the Duchesse said almost condescendingly. 'She always worried herself over trifles. Something will turn up, it always does. Now come, we will go back to the hotel and get the *concierge* to ring round and see who is staying here. I used to know an old man who had a villa just over the Italian border. I wonder if he is still alive.'

The Duchesse called for the *addition*, tipped an exorbitant amount which left the waiter almost incoherent with gratitude, and swept from the restaurant, leaving behind her a trail of expensive perfume.

Gardenia followed her miserably.

'What about the jeweller?' she asked.

'I tell you what we'll do,' the Duchesse replied. 'You go back to the hotel and then you can slip out again and go to the jewellers on your own. I think, dear, it would be rather indiscreet for me to take my jewels in person. I feel sure you will understand.'

Gardenia understood all too clearly: the Duchesse was

evading what she felt was an uncomfortable and unpleasant action. But there was no point in arguing, and when her aunt hailed a hackney-carriage to drive them back to the hotel she did not even protest.

'I really couldn't walk any further,' the Duchesse explained. 'It was very inconsiderate of you, Gardenia, to drag me up that hill so fast. My doctors always said I must be careful of my heart. Besides, it is much too hot for walking.'

'The carriage has got to be paid for,' Gardenia said in a small voice.

'They will do that at the hotel,' her aunt replied. 'It will go on the bill.'

They drove in silence. Gardenia wished she could enjoy the sunlight and flowers and the glimpse of the sea sparkling an azure blue beneath the great rock on which stood the Palace of the Princess of Monaco, but it was difficult to think of anything except that they themselves were plunging down a steep hill into a bottomless pit.

The carriage drew up at the Hôtel de Paris. The Duchesse prepared to alight and at that moment through the swing-doors came a man accompanied by a very beautiful woman, her hat a mass of ospreys fluttering in the breeze.

Gardenia recognised the Baron first; then as the Duchesse reached the pavement she looked up and saw him too.

She gave a little cry of sheer unbridled pleasure.

'Heinrich!'

It seemed as though it was difficult for her to say the word, her whole face had lit up and both her hands went out impulsively towards him.

The Baron stood looking down at them. He was wearing his uniform and he placed his high peaked cap on his balding head. His hand went to his eye-glass, steadying it in his eye.

'Heinrich!' the Duchesse cried again.

The Baron turned deliberately and gave his arm to the woman beside him.

'Let me help you down these steps, my dear Contessa,' he said.

He moved slowly and deliberately, passing the Duchesse without looking at her and escorting the woman with the ospreys across the road towards the Casino.

The Duchesse stood staring after him, her face ashen-white. For a moment Gardenia thought she might fall and her hand went out to hold her aunt's arm. Then faltering-ly, a little unsteadily, as if she had received a blow between the eyes, the Duchesse walked up the steps and into the Hôtel de Paris.

She didn't speak until, reaching their own suite, she sank down on the sofa.

'He cut me,' she whispered. 'Did you see, Gardenia, he cut me?'

'The swine! The beast! How dare he do such a thing!' Gardenia stormed.

'He looked at me as though he hated me,' the Duchesse sobbed; and now the tears were running down her face, the mascara with which she had blackened her eyes running with them, making her look very old and raddled, a woman who could have no further attraction for a man.

'It was a filthy thing to do!' Gardenia cried.

'Why should he hate me? Why?' the Duchesse asked. 'I love him. I did everything he asked of me. I refused him nothing.

'He was using you, Aunt Lily, surely you can see that now?' Gardenia said. 'He was not worth your love. You were just useful to him.'

The Duchesse took off her hat very slowly and laid it down beside her on the sofa.

'I used sometimes to think he asked too ... much of me,' she whispered. 'Those men he brought to ... the house ... but he made it sound so unimportant beside ... the love we had for each other.'

The Duchesse's voice, broken and almost incoherent, was so pitiful that Gardenia could only kneel down beside the sofa and put her arms round her.

'Don't, Aunt Lily!' she said. 'Don't torture yourself. He isn't worth it. Forget him. We will go away. We'll go to England.'

'Where we know no one,' the Duchesse replied. 'I gave up everything for Heinrich, all my friends. He hated them, abused them; he said it was because he was jealous of them, but I think he wanted to separate me from anyone who was respectable and decent. Oh, Gardenia, how could he desert me now?'

Her tears seemed almost to choke her, and now the

Duchesse cried until she was exhausted, her breath coming fitfully between her lips.

'Come and lie down', Gardenia urged.

She helped her aunt into the bedroom and on to the bed. She covered her with the eiderdown and drew down the blinds to keep out the afternoon sun.

'Try and sleep, Aunt Lily,' she begged.

'I can't, I can't,' the Duchesse said. 'I can only think of Heinrich and the way he looked at me. Do you think he meant it, Gardenia? Do you think that perhaps there was some reason for him not wishing to speak to me at that moment? That he will come back later and explain everything?'

'You know, Aunt Lily, there is very little likelihood of that,' Gardenia said quietly.

'How could he? How could he have done it?' the Duchesse wailed, the tears flowing all over again.

Gardenia remembered that in her aunt's dressing-case there was a little bottle of sleeping-pills. She found them and went to the bathroom for a glass of water. When she came back the Duchesse said:

'I have just remembered that the Baron owes me money, not a great sum, but he sold one of my pictures in Germany. He told me that one of his Generals was particularly anxious to have a Renoir like the one which the Duc had bought some years ago. I said he could have it for ten thousand francs. It was not as much as it is worth.'

'Ten thousand francs!' Gardenia said.

'It would be useful now,' the Duchesse muttered through her tears.

'Of course it would,' Gardenia answered. 'Drink this, Aunt Lily, and you will feel better. We will talk about it and decide what to do.'

She gave the Duchesse the sleeping-tablet and went from the room, closing the door. She had no intention of allowing the Duchesse to subject herself to any more humiliations from the Baron. But she was determined that he should pay back at least what he owed. She glanced at the clock. They had been late having lunch and now it was nearly three-thirty. She picked up the telephone and spoke to the *concierge*.

'Is Baron von Knesebech staying in the hotel?' she asked.

'No, *Ma'm'selle,*' the concierge replied. 'Herr Baron was here for lunch, but we have not the honour of accommodating him. He is at the Splendide.'

'Thank you,' Gardenia said.

She sat down on her bed and started to make her plans. The Baron had gone to the Casino. He would stay there until perhaps four-thirty, then he would return to his hotel. The Duchesse's conversation in the train had enlightened her as to what the French meant by *cinq à sept*. At five o'clock the Baron would doubtless be visiting or being visited by the attractive Contessa with the ospreys.

Gardenia waited until it was twenty past four. Then she tidied herself, picked up her gloves and went downstairs. She walked out of the Hôtel de Paris and across the gardens in front of the Casino. She knew where the Splendide was, because she had seen the name emblazoned over the gates as she and her aunt had walked under the palm trees before lunch.

Just outside the gates she sat down for a moment on one of the benches by a trickling stream with its artificial rocks and goldfish lurking beneath the water-lilies. From her bag she drew out a veil which belonged to her aunt and which was spotted with tiny black velvet spots. It was not a great disguise, but she was ashamed, even though she was unknown and of no interest to anyone, to be calling on a man as despicable and unscrupulous as the Baron.

She may have appeared brave as she walked into the Splendide, but her heart was thumping as she went up to the *concierge*. 'I wish to see Baron von Knesebech.'

She expected him to lift the telephone and to ask her name. She had her answer ready, but to her surprise the man merely said:

'Herr Baron is expecting you, *Madame*. Room 365 on the third floor, if you please.'

The porter opened the lift door and Gardenia stepped into it.

The *concierge* had confused her, she thought perhaps, with the Contessa. At any rate it saved her from any further lies. The page-boy led her down the corridor. The key was on the outside of the door of Room 365. The page-boy knocked and opened the door.

'*Merci,*' Gardenia said.

She found herself in an *entresol* confronted by three doors. The one directly opposite was half open and she saw it led into the sitting-room. As there was no one to announce her she went in.

The room was empty; the connecting door that she guessed led into the bedroom was open and she could hear the sound of running water as though someone was washing. The Baron must be titivating himself up for the woman he was expecting, Gardenia thought. He would get a surprise when he saw who had arrived.

Gardenia looked round the room. It was the usual luxurious hotel sitting-room. The Baron's tunic emblazoned with his medals was hanging over the back of a chair. It was a writing-chair in front of a desk which stood by the open window.

Casually Gardenia looked at it, not really taking in what she saw, thinking rather of what she would say when the Baron emerged from the bathroom and found her standing there. Something captured her attention. A telegraph form. She wondered if it was the one which had been sent by her aunt, and then she saw that beside it there was a small open book. Without realising what she was doing, she stepped forward and looked closer. Then as she looked at the book she knew what it was—a book such as she herself had searched for once before! But while the one she had been looking for would have been in English, this was in German.

She picked it up. The sound of running water still came from the room beyond. Gardenia turned and walked slowly and without haste from the sitting-room. She opened the outside door and shut it quietly behind her. She moved away down the corridor and knew that she had her revenge on the Baron—a revenge so drastic and so overwhelming that for the moment even she could hardly contemplate the magnitude of it.

She walked down the stairs, not wishing the liftman to remember her or perhaps wonder why she had come from the Baron's apartment so quickly.

The hall downstairs was full of people. She moved amongst them, she hoped without being noticed, and was out of the front door and on to the drive in a matter of seconds. Only when she reached the road and started to wend her way through the traffic towards the Hôtel de Paris did she realise what this meant. She could, if she wished, blackmail the Baron for any amount of money or she could send the book to the British, and even as she thought of the latter course she knew to which member of the British Foreign Office she would wish to give it.

Gardenia reached the Hôtel de Paris. Now because she was so excited she felt as though the lift carrying her up to her aunt's suite was slow, and when she stepped out of it she ran down the corridor.

She had the keys of both her aunt's bedroom and the sitting-room in her handbag. She opened the door of the bedroom and went in. It was very quiet in there. As the room seemed somehow hot and over-scented, Gardenia crossed to the window and drew up the blind.

'Aunt Lily,' she cried excitedly. 'I have something to tell you!'

Her aunt was asleep, lying back against the pillows. Gardenia felt that perhaps it was unfair to wake her up, but she knew she had to show her the little grey book.

'Aunt Lily!' she called again, then stopped.

There was something different from how she had left the room. The bottle of sleeping-tablets was not where she had left them. She had put them on the dressing-table after she had taken one out and given it to her aunt. Now the bottle was lying on top of the eiderdown. It was empty and the top had fallen on to the floor. Gardenia's heart gave a frightened leap. The bottle had been full. She had thought when she opened it that at least they would not have to buy any sleeping-tablets for a long time!

She picked it up and her hands were trembling. There was no need for her to touch her aunt. She knew that she was no longer breathing. The Duchesse had taken the easiest way out. She was dead.

Gardenia stood looking down at her.

'Poor Aunt Lily,' she said aloud, and yet she knew she did not really pity her.

It might be wrong, indeed it might be wicked, to take one's own life; but with her beauty, her money, her love gone, there had been nothing left for the Duchesse but misery. She would have hated being poor, she would have hated not arousing the admiration of men whoever they might be. In her own way and by her own standards she had done the sensible thing, and Gardenia, while she could feel the pathos of it, knew that she could not cry.

Very softly she crossed the room and pulled down the blind again. In a little while she knew she would have to telephone for the Manager, she would have to ask him to come to the sitting-room, she would have to tell what had happened. But just for a moment she wanted her aunt to be at peace, to know nothing perhaps but utter forgetfulness, the wiping away of all misery and the peace of death.

'I must pray,' Gardenia thought to herself. She pulled off her veil and hat and knelt down quite simply beside her aunt's bed. None of the prayers she had learnt as a child or which she had used in her girlhood somehow seemed fitting. So in her own words she prayed that God would understand.

She rose from her knees a little comforted. It was only now she realised how alone she was. Her aunt had gone and there was nothing for her to do but to go back to England and find work which would at least keep her from starvation.

She stood looking down at the Duchesse: the lines had gone from her face; she looked younger and really beautiful as she lay there.

Gardenia felt the tears coming to her eyes and told herself she must not give way, there was so much for her to do, so much to plan. She saw that the little grey book which she had stolen from the Baron was lying on the eiderdown and she picked it up. Nothing of the Baron's should be beside her aunt now. He had murdered her as surely as if he fired a pistol at her, and she only hoped that when her aunt's death was announced he would realise what he had done.

Almost angrily, because she hated even the thought of him, Gardenia pulled open the door into the sitting room. The room was full of sunlight and for a moment, after the darkness of her aunt's room, it was difficult for her to see. Then she perceived there was a man in the room, a man standing looking out through the open window towards the sea.

For a moment Gardenia thought it must be the Baron, and then something in the shape of the head and the set of the shoulders made a sudden flame flicker through her and she quivered as though she had suddenly come to life.

'Gardenia!'

He turned from the window and came quickly towards her.

'Lord H ... Hartcourt!' she stammered his name, her voice hardly above a whisper.

'The train was late,' he said, 'and they told me you were out. I was waiting until you returned.'

'You came to see me?'

Her eyes were searching his face. She thought it must be imagination or the sunlight, but he was looking at her with an expression which made her heart pound in her breast.

He took her right hand in his and touched her cold fingers with his lips.

'My darling,' he said. 'I came to ask you if you will honour me by becoming my wife.'

'Oh no, no.' She could hear herself crying out the words. Then her hand was free and she walked blindly away from him to hold on to the sofa.

'You have not forgiven me,' Lord Hartcourt said. 'I don't blame you. I could kill myself for being so stupid, for hurting you as I did, for humiliating you, for my own stupidity.'

'No,' Gardenia said. 'It wasn't that. I didn't understand.'

'I saw it all afterwards,' Lord Hartcourt said in a low voice. 'I was so blind, so stupid. I must have seemed to you an insufferable cad. Forgive me, Gardenia. If you will marry me I will be the happiest man in the world.'

'No, stop!' Gardenia pleaded. 'Please stop. I have got something to say to you and I want to say it first. You must listen to me.'

'But of course, my darling,' he answered. 'I'll listen to anything you want me to.'

Gardenia dropped the little grey book down on the soft cushions of the sofa. It had suddenly ceased to be of any importance. It was only much later she was to learn what a blow she had struck at German pride and diplomacy.

'I want to tell you,' she said in a voice which trembled, 'that I realised after I had left Paris how blind, stupid and childish I have been. You see I had been brought up very simply. I didn't understand that a woman like my aunt could be a Duchesse and yet belong not to society but to the *demi-monde*. It was only when I knew and when she explained to me what her life had been that I understood exactly what you and Mr Cunningham expected of . . . me.'

Lord Hartcourt would have spoken, but she put her hand up to stop him.

'Of course that was what you thought,' Gardenia insisted. 'It was only that I didn't understand. So everything you said and did bewildered me, and when you kissed me,' her voice faltered for a moment before she continued steadily, '... and I knew that I ... loved you, I thought of course that meant we would be ... married and be together for ever.'

'That is what it should have meant,' Lord Hartcourt said, his voice deep with emotion.

'But I didn't understand,' Gardenia continued, 'until that day in the restaurant, and when I asked you if you meant to marry me and you said no, I thought the end of my world had come. I was ashamed and humiliated and, I suppose, in a way disgusted.'

'My darling, forgive me,' Lord Hartcourt murmured.

'No, let me finish, please,' Gardenia said. 'But I have been thinking about it afterwards. I understand now what Aunt Lily has made of her life and what in a kind of way, because I am her niece, she has made of mine. So I ... thought that if I ever saw you again ... and if when you ... saw me you still ... wanted me, I would ... come to you ... and live with you ... because I love you and ... because I understand now it is better to have a little happiness in life than ... none at all.'

There was a pause, then Lord Hartcourt with a sort of strangled exclamation went down on one knee and taking the hem of Gardenia's dress in his hands raised it to his lips.

'That is what I think of you,' he said hoarsely, 'my stupid, ridiculous, wonderful little love. I am not worthy to kiss the hem of your dress. No Gardenia! Do you really think that I only want you in that way? I thought I did! I was stupid, conceited, arrogant and stuck-up and altogether a fool because I didn't understand that I had been offered the most wonderful and perfect thing any man could ask for in life. The true and real love of someone who was innocent, trusting and unspoiled by the world.'

He rose to his feet. He was very close to her and Gardenia held her breath.

'I love you,' he said softly. 'I love you and I want you and only you to be my wife. I have known a lot of women but I have never, and this is the truth, Gardenia, asked one of them to marry me, and I don't want you on any other terms, I want you as my wife, as the mother of my children, as the woman I love with all my heart and worship because she is pure and perfect.'

Gardenia was trembling but it was with happiness that was almost too great to be borne.

'Oh, Vane,' she said unsteadily, 'I love you so terribly.'

He swept her into his arms, his lips found hers and she knew then that nothing in the whole world mattered to either of them except this wild, glorious, passionate and overwhelming love which seemed to consume them both like a flame, leaping higher and higher.

'I love you,' Lord Hartcourt said, not once but a dozen times and then again, 'I love you, oh Gardenia, I love you.'

Time stood still and it might have been a century later that Gardenia drew herself from his arms.

'There is something I have got to tell you,' she said.

'Let me just go on looking at you,' Lord Hartcourt said. 'I don't think there has ever been anyone so beautiful in the whole world.'

He would have kissed her again, but she put up her hand and laid it against his lips.

'Please, Vane, you must listen to me,' she said. 'Aunt Lily is dead. She had taken all her sleeping-tablets. I think in a way her whole world had come to an end.'

Lord Hartcourt nodded.

'That is the truth,' he said. 'That was one of the things I was going to tell you. The warrant is out for her arrest, she could never under any circumstances go back to France.'

'But, you see, all her money is there,' Gardenia explained.

'I was afraid of that,' Lord Hartcourt said, 'and even if she had got to England things might have been difficult. Bertie told me that he had advised you to go to Monte Carlo and it was the best thing he could possibly have done.'

'He was very kind,' Gardenia said. 'Without him we would never have got away.'

'Had I known about it too I would have come with you,' Lord Hartcourt said. 'As it was, I waited for one thing only, Gardenia, and that was to give in my resignation.'

'You've resigned!' she exclaimed.

'Yes,' Lord Hartcourt smiled. 'I am going to live in

England with my wife. My estates need attention, I shall have plenty to occupy me. Besides, I want to be with you.'

'Are you sure, quite sure?' Gardenia asked, a little tremulously, 'that I am the right wife for you? What would people say and think?'

'I wouldn't care what they say or what they think,' Lord Hartcourt said. 'But they are going to have nothing to say, not because it worries me, but because in the future it might worry you. I am going to take you back to England at once, Gardenia. The fact that your aunt's dead is going to make things easier, as it happens, and there will be no scandal about that because if there is one thing the authorities in Monte Carlo hate it is a suicide. They will announce the Duchesse has died of a heart attack. We can leave everything in their hands.'

'You mean that I am to go away at once?' Gardenia asked.

'At once,' Lord Hartcourt said. 'I am not going to have you making any more decisions. I am going to look after you, Gardenia, as I ought to have done from the very beginning. I am going to take you back to England to my mother. She is a very understanding person, but there will be no need for her to know too much. She lives in a world of innocence where people like the Duchesse and the *demi-monde* of Paris have never encroached.'

Gardenia gave a little sigh.

'It sounds safe and very wonderful,' she said.

'You are quite certain you want to marry me?' Lord Hartcourt asked softly.

'I know only that I want to be with you now and for always,' Gardenia said simply.

'Oh, my darling, that is exactly the right answer,' he said softly. 'I love you.'

ON SALE WHEREVER PAPERBACKS ARE SOLD
—or use this coupon to order directly from the publisher.

BARBARA CARTLAND

V 2705	**Again This Rapture** $1.25 (#36)	
V2823	**Audacious Adventures** $1.25 (#41)	
V3162	**Blue Heather** $1.25 (#54)	
V2795	**Enchanted Moment** $1.25 (#40)	
V3048	**The Enchanted Waltz** (#26) $1.25	
V2409	**Golden Gondola** $1.25 (#20)	
V3239	**A Halo For The Devil** $1.25 (#55)	
V2844	**The Hidden Heart** $1.25 (#10)	
V 2636	**The Innocent Heiress** $1.25 (#15)	
V2490	**An Innocent In Paris** $1.25 (#24)	
V3240	**The Irresistible Buck** $1.25 (#57)	
V2635	**Kiss Of The Devil** $1.25 (#32)	
V2593	**A Kiss Of Silk** $1.25 (#30)	
V3174	**A Light To The Heart** $1.25 (#56)	

Send to: PYRAMID PUBLICATIONS,
Dept. M.O., 9 Garden Street, Moonachie, N.J. 07074

NAME

ADDRESS

CITY

STATE   ZIP

I enclose $_____ _____, which includes the total price of all books ordered plus 25¢ per book postage and handling if the total is less than $5.00. If my total order is $5.00 or more, I understand that Pyramid will pay all postage and handling.

Please note: A book you have ordered might not be available at this time. To expedite your order—and provide all of the "good reading" you want—we suggest that you allow us to make reasonable substitutions of books in the same category, and at the same price—only if necessary!

☐ Yes, you may substitute if necessary. ☐ No substitutions, please. No COD's or stamps. Please allow three to four weeks for delivery. Prices subject to change.   P-15

ON SALE WHEREVER PAPERBACKS ARE SOLD
—or use this coupon to order directly from the publisher.

BARBARA CARTLAND

V2734	Open Wings $1.25 (#37)	
V3242	Out Of Reach $1.25 (#60)	
V2690	The Pretty Horse-Breakers $1.25 (#35)	
V3243	The Price Is Love $1.25 (#61)	
V2650	Reluctant Bride $1.25 (#34)	
V3020	Secret Fear £ (#23) $1.25	
V2429	Stars In My Heart $1.25 (#21)	
V2887	Stolen Halo $1.25 (#44)	
V2689	Sweet Adventure $1.25 (#17)	
V3189	Sweet Enchantress $1.25 (#58)	
V2920	Sweet Punishment $1.25 (#45)	
V2577	The Unknown Heart $1.25 (#29)	
V2996	Wings on My Heart $1.25 (#47)	
V2504	Wings of Love $1.25 (#25)	
V2749	We Danced All Night $1.25 (Autobiography)	

Send to: PYRAMID PUBLICATIONS,
Dept. M.O., 9 Garden Street, Moonachie, N.J. 07074

NAME _____

ADDRESS _____

CITY _____

STATE _____ ZIP _____

I enclose $_____, which includes the total price of all books ordered plus 25¢ per book postage and handling if the total is less than $5.00. If my total order is $5.00 or more, I understand that Pyramid will pay all postage and handling.

Please note: A book you have ordered might not be available at this time. To expedite your order—and provide all of the "good reading" you want—we suggest that you allow us to make reasonable substitutions of books in the same category, and at the same price—only if necessary!

☐ Yes, you may substitute if necessary. ☐ No substitutions, please. No COD's or stamps. Please allow three to four weeks for delivery.
Prices subject to change   P-17